Other Books by this Author:

Out of the Storm

The Bridge Club Series

Deception Bridge
Broken Contracts
Premonition Bridge

The Whispering Art Series

Watercolor Whispers
Whispered Warnings
Waiting for the Whisper

Waiting for THE WHISPER

GLORIA BOSTIC

Year of the Book
135 Glen Avenue
Glen Rock, PA 17327

Print ISBN: 978-1-64649-169-8
eBook ISBN: 978-1-64649-170-4

Library of Congress Control Number: 2021908414

Dedication

To my husband

Thank you, Lee, for your continuing love, support,
and encouragement. I love sharing life with you.

To my sons

Mike, John, and Eddie
You bring more joy to my life than you will ever know.
I thank God for the gift of each of you.

To my grandchildren

Mike, Jr., Elise, Emily, and Grace
Grandchildren are the delicious icing on a mother's cake.
Thank you for adding so much sweetness to my life.

To my sister and my BFFs

Darleen Muhly, Michele Harper and Bev Stiffler Smith
Dar, I'm so glad to have a sister who is also a best friend.
Michele and Bev, I'm so glad to have two friends
who I love like sisters. I love you all!

Acknowledgments

I have only reached the end of this final book of The Whispering Art Series with the support of my editor and publisher, Demi Stevens. I had an idea, and I wrote words... lots and lots and lots of words, but it was only with her help that I was able to shape those words into the book you now hold. Thank you, Demi, for all your suggestions and feedback and for catching repeated words, missing words or punctuation, and all those other little things I can easily miss even on the fourth or fifth reading.

More than anything else, though, your love, friendship, and assurances kept me moving forward from the first messy draft to the final, beautifully formatted book. Thank you, my friend!

Chapter One

Small town Pennsylvania life was exactly what Mia Reed had remembered and expected it to be—well, except for a serial killer and a marriage proposal—and her work at the Reed Mental Health Center in Madison had settled into a normal routine... or so she thought.

"I'll be with you in a minute, Samantha," Mia said to her next client. She motioned to the attractive man sitting next to her. "Detective Bishop, would you come this way, please?"

Mia guided the detective into her office, closed the door behind her, and walked into her fiancé's arms. "What are you doing here, Ron?" She snuggled into the warmth of his embrace. "I have two more clients to see before I'm done."

"Ah, but I'm not here to see you."

"What? Now I'm hurt," Mia teased, pulling far enough away to look up into those captivating blue eyes she loved so much.

"I'm here to interview Dr. Block about the assault and theft last night."

"Oh, yes. Of course. I didn't think he'd even be in today." She thought the staff psychiatrist would've been too shaken after what he'd been through. Her grandfather's practice, the Reed Mental Health Center, had seemed like the safest place in the world... until now. "Why didn't you talk to him last night?"

Ron explained that his partner had been the one on the scene. "But Jason said the doctor was pretty rattled. I'm here to follow up, and as much as I'd rather stay here with you, I believe you have a client of your own to see."

Mia reluctantly withdrew her hands from around his neck, but Ron pulled her in to steal one more kiss before heading back to the waiting room. Alone again, with only the lingering scent of her fiancé's aftershave, she looked at the beautiful marquis-cut one-carat diamond on the third finger of her left hand. Mia still found it hard to believe the man she'd fallen in love with all those months ago had never mentioned the huge untouched inheritance that had been collecting interest since the murder of his parents fifteen years earlier.

Right now, though, it was time to meet with Samantha Collins, and since this particular client had paranoid tendencies, it wasn't a good idea to keep her waiting.

"Who was that man?" Samantha asked as soon as the door closed behind her. She flipped her long blonde hair back and took her usual seat next to Mia's desk, preferring not to have her back to the door. Then she looked at her phone for the second time since entering Mia's office.

"Is something wrong? Were you expecting an important call?" Mia asked, ignoring her client's question about Ron.

"What? Oh no. I was just checking the time. Was that guy another client?" Samantha Collins was not one to be ignored. "I've seen him before. Was he talking about me?"

"No, not at all." Though Mia was tempted to tell Samantha how ridiculous that sounded, she bit her tongue. "That was Detective Bishop. He's here on official business, but I happen to know him personally and needed to speak with him for a moment." Noticing her client once again glanced at her phone, Mia added, "I believe we began your session a few minutes late, and I apologize, but we'll make up the time at the end. So how was your week?"

"It was okay, I guess, but that neighbor I was telling you about, he's still watching me. I'm sure of it. I think he was peeking from behind his curtain when I got home last night." Samantha's foot was bouncing rapidly, and Mia could see the rise in her anxiety level.

"I know this feeling of being watched is upsetting to you. Have you been taking your meds?"

"Yes! Well, maybe not every day. I get so sleepy, you know?"

"I understand." Mia watched as her client's foot bounced faster, and she knew the paranoia would only get worse without medication. "Have you told Dr. Block about the side effects?"

"Yes, but he said it's something I have to get used to. That my body has to adjust to it or something."

"Well, in the meantime, have you been practicing your relaxation exercises?"

"Sort of... but I've been so busy. I don't always remember."

"I understand, but how's that working? Do you feel better when you practice your relaxation or when you don't?" Mia wondered if the attractive woman had even practiced enough to know the difference.

"I guess when I do it, but I get distracted sometimes."

"Okay, sure. I know we have lots of distractions around us. So, let's talk about what you might be able to do to lessen them." Mia spoke to her client about setting up her environment by turning off the TV, turning off the ringer on her phone, closing the curtains, and possibly using earbuds to listen to the relaxation exercise Mia had recorded for her.

"Now, what about your drawing? Have you played around with that anymore?" Mia had witnessed the positive effect art therapy had for Samantha and encouraged her to pursue the hobby at home as well as behind the easel during their sessions.

"I did!" Samantha suddenly became more animated. She smiled for the first time since coming into the office and leaned forward in her seat. "I got a sketchpad and a book on drawing animals. I think I can learn to draw after all."

"That's great, Sam. I'm sure you can." Mia had seen her client's actual potential. "But remember, how good the drawing turns out isn't as important as how you feel while you're doing it. How about if we use the rest of our session for your art?"

Once actively involved in creating, Samantha's shoulders relaxed, her foot stopped bouncing, and her brow smoothed. When Mia told her how impressed she was with the relaxing scene of a lake surrounded by weeping willows, Samantha beamed. But when told their time was about up, she quickly checked her phone again.

"Yes, we ran over a little bit, but I wanted you to have time to finish your drawing." Mia knew her client would have been upset if she didn't have her full session length. Better to go over a little than for Sam to believe she'd been cheated out of even one minute. Saying goodbye to Samantha, Mia couldn't help thinking a woman that gorgeous was bound to turn heads. *It's no wonder she thinks people are looking at her... they probably are.*

Mia now had no time to write detailed notes before bringing her last client back, nor did she have much time to change gears to meet the next person's needs, but fortunately she was seeing her favorite lady to end the day which made it easier to be totally present.

Miss Edna, as Mia addressed the silver-haired ninety-three-year-old Edna Schmidt, had first sought counseling to deal with the grief of losing her husband several years earlier. After a sixty-five-year marriage, the anguish was understandable, but her depression had not lifted in the three years since she'd been widowed.

Edna lived in the same senior community as Mia's "Aunt Bonnie"—who was actually a friend of the family—and who had finally persuaded her to seek counseling. Mia was soon enchanted by the lovely lady and her kind heart, and she was reminded of a special Alzheimer's patient she'd had back in Pittsburgh. But Edna didn't suffer from any noticeable form of dementia. She was always well dressed with impeccable makeup and her blue eyes were sharp, as was her mind.

Losing her husband had been compounded by giving up their big old family home of sixty years—it was too much for Edna to handle on her own—and then losing her ability to drive. There were simply too many losses. Her children lived out of state and worried about her being alone even in a senior living community, and they had each tried to convince her she should come live with one of them or go to a nursing home. Edna, however, was not ready to give up her independence. She was a sweet but feisty lady, who simply suffered from the depression all the losses in her life had forced upon her. Fortunately, she was improving, and Mia always felt good when she got her weekly hug at the end of their sessions.

Today was no different. And she got a second hug from Aunt Bonnie who was waiting to pick up her friend and neighbor.

Normally at the end of the day Mia was anxious to head home, take a walk, have dinner, and relax with her artwork. She had claimed the large walk-out basement as her studio in the house she shared with her sister, Julie, while her sister got the biggest bedroom with a sitting area she used to do her writing.

Knowing this was Julie's night to fix dinner and seeing that the rain hadn't let up, Mia had no need to hurry home, so she wrote up her client notes and decided to hang out a while longer to see if she could find out more about the previous night's attack on Dr. Block.

"What are you doing still here?" Sarah Reed asked, sticking her head in the door. "I thought you were done almost an hour ago." When Mia explained why she was hanging around, her mother came the rest of the way into her office and took a seat. "What did you want to know? I might be able to fill you in."

"A lot of things. Like do they have any idea who did it?"

"No... Douglas said all he knew was that it was a male—young, he thought—and that he didn't hear him come in. He said he was reading over someone's file, heard a noise, and that quick, whoever it was knocked him out cold. I can't believe he wouldn't go to the hospital to get checked out." Sarah shook her head. "Unbelievable, isn't it?"

"Yes, and scary," Mia added. "But why? I mean, the guy just hit him on the head and left? Do they think it was a patient? Maybe somebody didn't like something he said, or what?" The idea that a patient could turn on their therapist was hard for Mia to imagine since the bond she had with her clients was so positive, but then,

Dr. Douglas Block wasn't known for his gentle, warm and friendly bedside manner.

"I don't know, hon. Your fiancé might be able to tell you more. I saw him leaving here earlier." Sarah checked the time. "Okay, I'm heading home. Your dad's in charge of dinner tonight so between him and Destiny, I'm guessing it's going to be pizza or subs. You know your little sister's power of persuasion." Sarah walked around the desk and kissed her daughter on the forehead. "Will you and Ron be coming to dinner on Sunday?"

"Absolutely. See you then." Mia hoped it was true. Ron said he would be free, but what if he got another case? She was beginning to think the only ones who could be sure her detective boyfriend would show up were the murder victims. Or what if he got another clue in the cold case he'd become totally obsessed by since reuniting with his sister? Not that Mia blamed him for wanting to find his parents' killers, but she sometimes found it difficult sitting on the back burner.

Shaking off her doubts, Mia focused on the work before her, and it wasn't until she had completed her newest client's treatment plan that she noticed the time and the deafening quiet beyond her door. Grabbing her coat, shoulder bag, and umbrella, Mia strode to the doorway but hesitated and scanned the hall before heading toward the waiting room. Never before had she felt uneasy leaving her office in the evening, but then no one had ever been assaulted there until last night.

The rain had slowed to a fine mist, but Mia pulled her coat tightly around her, dashed to her Civic, and locked the door before finally letting out her breath. *This is ridiculous,* she thought. *Or is it?*

Chapter Two

None of this makes sense. Detective Ronald Bishop had gone over his partner's notes trying to put two and two together, but why would someone break into the Reed Mental Health Center, go straight to a psychiatrist's office, assault him, and leave? What was the motive? It had to be a grudge. Dr. Douglas Block was a shrink so he saw lots of people who were messed up. Why would the actions of one patient have to make sense? *Mia wouldn't like me calling this a guy a shrink though.*

Ron was engaged to marry Mia Reed, the art therapist on staff at the center. Of course, she was a shrink too, but he didn't think of her that way. Ron viewed her as more of a miracle. A miracle he was lucky enough to have found, and who he planned to keep in his life. Thinking about her made him smile. It always did.

"Detective Bishop?" The voice startled Ron from his reverie, and he quickly got to his feet to follow the psychiatrist.

"Yes. And you're Dr. Block?"

The man who led Ron through the waiting room door and down the hall to his office looked to be in his late fifties or early sixties, with a full head of gray hair, and walked with shoulders slightly hunched. He gestured for Ron to have a seat next to the desk then settled into his big brown leather chair.

"I appreciate your thoroughness, Detective, but I'm not sure what more I can tell you. I told Det. Evans everything I knew last night." The doctor gently rocked back and forth in his chair tapping his pen on the notepad in his lap. Ron noted the serious bags under his eyes.

"Of course," Ron said, "and I appreciate you taking the time to let me go over it with you again. We do try to be thorough, and sometimes victims of such violent incidents remember more details after they've had time to recover." It was Ron's turn to tap his pen on the small notepad he pulled from his pocket. "So, you said you didn't hear the assailant come into your office? You didn't hear the door open or see the person come in?"

"No, the door must have been slightly ajar so it didn't make any noise when he came in."

"You said you didn't see the person until right before you were struck on the head, but you did say 'he.' So, you're sure the assailant was a male?"

"Yes. Like I told the other detective, he was very quiet, but I suddenly felt his presence and glanced up before he hit me."

"So, you did get a glimpse of this person. Do you remember anything about his appearance? Anything at all?"

"No, I'm sorry. It all happened so fast." The doctor rubbed the deep lines in his forehead. "I, um, I think he was tall, but then he was standing over me, so I can't be certain."

"Okay, that's all right. Did you happen to notice the color of his hair?"

"Dark. I think it was dark brown maybe."

"Can you remember anything else, Doctor?"

"I really can't. I'd like to be more helpful, but like I told the other detective, I must have been knocked out, and when I recovered, he was gone. I checked the building as soon as I got my bearings, but the place was empty. That's when I called 9-1-1."

"I'm sorry for what you've been through, and we're going to do everything we can to find your assailant. By the way, did you go to the hospital and get checked out?"

"No, Detective. I'm fine."

"But a blow like that... you could have a concussion."

"You forget, I'm a doctor. I know all the signs and symptoms of a concussion." He began tapping his pen again. "And when I got home, my wife kept an eye on me. She takes excellent care of me." The doctor snickered. "Apparently she forgets I'm a doctor too."

"Sounds like a good woman," Ron said, trying to make up for his embarrassment at forgetting the psychiatrist was a medical doctor. He thanked Dr. Block for his time and asked him to let them know if he remembered anything else at all before heading back to the waiting room. Since it was mid-hour, there were no clients waiting, so he took the opportunity to ask the receptionist a few questions. But like everyone else Ron had interviewed—except Dr. Block—she had already left before the alleged assault. So, there wasn't a whole lot to go on. Ron only knew they were looking for a male suspect who *might* be tall and *might* have dark hair. *Thanks a lot!*

A check of the time told him Mia would still be with her client, so with no legitimate excuse for hanging around, he headed back to the station to compare notes with his partner, Det. Jason Evans.

When he arrived, however, it was their middle-aged captain who met him in the hall.

"Hey Bishop, I have another case you might want to take a look at," he said. Webb and Jason Evans had been partners for years until their former boss retired and Webb was promoted to captain. That left Jason in need of a new partner, and with perfect timing, Ron Bishop had chosen to move away from Pittsburgh—and closer to the woman who had stolen his heart—just in time to fill the position.

Ron followed Webb into his office, aware of the difference between this rather small, cold space and the warm, luxurious office he'd visited a short time earlier, but before he could take a seat or hear about this new case, his phone vibrated. "Sorry Captain, but I'd better take this. It might be the victim I just interviewed. Maybe he remembered something."

With a nod of approval from Webb, Ron took the call. It was in fact, Dr. Block, and when asked if he remembered something from the previous night, Ron learned that wasn't the reason for the call.

"No, Detective, but I discovered something else you should probably know."

"Yeah? What's that?"

"I think while I was unconscious, I was robbed."

"All right. Sorry to hear that," Ron said pulling out his notepad. "What was taken?"

"Not much... some of the meds I have here, samples, but I'm afraid he also took my prescription pads."

When Ron had finished writing down all the information he could get from the victim, he ended the call. Turning back to his captain he shook his head. "This isn't good."

"What's that?"

"Apparently the guy that attacked this psychiatrist took a bunch of drugs *and* prescription pads. Sounds like we've got a druggie with plenty of ammunition."

Chapter Three

Mia pulled into the garage, turned off the windshield wipers and engine, and headed into the house wondering if she'd have time for a quick walk before dinner. The delightful odor that greeted her in the kitchen changed her mind. When she peeked in the crockpot, the aroma of the beef stew her sister had prepared told her she'd rather eat than walk in the rain.

"Hey Jules, I'm home! When do we eat?" she called to her sister. "Hello Simmie, I love you too." Mia's Persian cat, Simeon, returned her greeting with one of his rare meows that spoke more to his hunger than an actual 'I'm glad to see you.' He then walked over to his empty bowl and gave her a look. "I know, I know. I'm hungry too. Where's that sister of mine?"

"Here I am," Julie said bounding down the stairs. "We can eat whenever you're ready."

"I am so ready!"

"You wanna grab the salad out of the fridge?" Julie said as she ladled out stew for each of them.

"This is nice, and do I smell fresh baked bread?"

"Yep, now aren't you glad I got that bread maker?"

Mia had to admit she'd thought it was another splurge for something they'd never use, but the loaf of warm bread Julie was setting on the table changed her mind.

"This is the perfect meal for a rainy, raw autumn day. I think Simmie and Willie are hungry too, but they'll have to wait." Mia put the salad on the table which was already set for the two of them.

Julie looked over at her own cat, William Shakespeare—Willie for short. "Yeah, I guess I could have fed them, but I wanted to finish my edits. I've got a deadline that's creeping up on me."

A second meow from her normally quiet feline, along with his stare and one slow blink, melted Mia's resolve, and within a few more minutes both the sisters and their cats were feasting.

"So how are the wedding plans coming along?" Julie asked.

"Slow. All we really know right now is the ceremony will be at our church and the reception either in the fellowship hall or back at Mom and Dad's."

"I know it's a big house, but are you sure there's enough room?"

"Yeah, absolutely. But if not, we can always use the church. Anyway, we plan to keep it small. Well, pretty small... just our families and a few close friends and coworkers—and Ron only has his sister and her family. Oh, and of course I'm inviting Betsy and her parents."

Though five years apart in age, Mia and Betsy Walters had a special bond, created when they were children. Traumatized by her parents' separation and her mother's alcoholism, Betsy had come to live with Mia's grandparents when she was five, and Mia had instantly become very protective of her. Even after Susan Walters—now sober for twelve years—had recovered and was reunited with her daughter, Mia and Betsy continued to have a special connection. Everyone agreed, it must have been that connection which provided seven-year-old Betsy with the dream that was instrumental in rescuing Mia when she'd been kidnapped a few years later.

"Do you think Betsy is too old to be a junior bridesmaid?" Mia asked.

"Hmm, I don't know that there's an age limit, but she's not a little kid anymore."

"Then do you think she'd be insulted if I asked her?"

"Maybe. How 'bout asking her to be a bridesmaid instead? Especially since Destiny's going to be a junior bridesmaid, right?"

Mia agreed that might be a better idea.

"So, you've got Morgan, Destiny and possibly Betsy as bridesmaids, and yours truly as maid of honor. Who did Ron get to be his best man?"

"He thought it might be nice to ask his sister's husband, Kevin. And to keep things balanced, I thought maybe Cody and Bobby could be in the wedding party. But now he'll need one more. What do you think?"

By the time they'd finished dinner and cleaned up the kitchen, Mia was ready for a short walk followed by time in her studio. She wondered if there would be any inspiration today, hoping for a clue to who attacked Dr. Block, but when she finally sat before her easel, Mia felt nothing. There was no familiar itch, and all she had for her efforts was a lovely seascape.

"Well, Simmie," she said to her silver-furred friend who almost always kept her company as she worked, "I don't know about you, but I think this looks like a lovely spot to honeymoon." Mia sat back in her chair and let her imagination take her into the image.

It was only when her cell phone sounded that she came back to the reality of being home in the art studio of her little cottage.

"Hello there," she said. "I think I've found the answer to where we should go for our honeymoon."

"Yeah? Where's that?" Ron asked.

"Maui."

The silence at the other end of the phone made Mia wonder if she had made a mistake, but when she was about to ask if he'd heard her or didn't like the idea, Ron uttered the one-word answer, "Perfect."

"Are you sure? I mean if that's too much, there are lots of other possibilities—"

"Mia, didn't you hear me? I said that's perfect. I can't think of any place better. They say it's paradise. Although, anywhere I am with you as my bride will be a paradise."

Mia wished he was with her now instead of on the phone. She wanted to put her arms around him and get lost in his kisses... and more. She wasn't sure how she was going to get through the next few months.

"Tell you what. Why don't I stop by the travel agency and pick up some literature on Hawaii? Then we can look at it together after dinner tomorrow night. And I'm curious. Why Maui? Or do you think maybe Oahu? Wakiki?"

"Absolutely. Grab brochures on all of them. I don't really know why I said Maui. I've never been to any of the islands." Then, changing the subject, Mia asked, "Have you found out who broke into the center last night? Or are you any closer to finding out?"

"Not really. Your Dr. Block couldn't give us much of a description, but apparently there wasn't actually a break-in."

"Really? What are you suggesting?"

"My guess is the assailant was already in the building. The doctor said he's sure the front door was locked, and we couldn't find any sign of a break-in. No broken windows or anything."

"So, are you saying someone hid in the building until everyone left?" Mia rubbed the goosebumps on her arms. "Like maybe one of our clients did this?"

"That's a definite possibility we're looking at. It's a bit sticky with all the confidentiality you people have, but I'm hoping we can get some answers tomorrow." Ron told Mia about the stolen drug samples and prescription pads. "We don't have much of a description on this guy. All we've got is a male... maybe tall, slender, and with dark hair. Not much help there. It would be a whole lot easier if you'd just draw us a picture of the culprit," he teased.

"I would if I could, my dear. Maybe I'll get an itch." Mia knew Ron would understand what she meant. There were times when she would get an itch or tingling in her right hand—the one that held the pencil, charcoal, or paint brush—and it would persist until she answered its call. The images that emerged from those itches were unique. They were not of her making.

Of course, it was her God-given talent that allowed such creations to spring forth, but they were never a conscious choice.

Nor were they anything she could have conceived or possibly known. Mia sometimes wondered if her gift of artistic ability was for the sole purpose of creating these extraordinary images.

Mia first met her detective while he was working on a case involving one of her patients back in Pittsburgh, but what really drew them closer together was when her itch produced the image of a blonde-haired, blue-eyed woman totally unfamiliar to Mia. When Ron saw it, he immediately recognized his twin sister who had been missing for fifteen years.

But these singular pictures had never come at Mia's bidding. She had never asked God for help in creating one. Until now.

Chapter Four

Ron did a double-take when he saw his sister sitting in the waiting room of the RMH Center Friday morning. Robin Bishop had been missing so long he had nearly given up hope of ever seeing her again. He still couldn't believe they'd found each other. Yet here she was. She may have changed her name and her hair—now short-cropped and red—because of all she'd been through, but it was his sister... his twin... alive and right in front of his eyes.

When their eyes met, Ron noticed a peculiar look cross her face. Embarrassment? But she had already confided that she was seeking therapy, and she certainly had no reason to be ashamed of that. Deciding not to risk embarrassing her further, he gave her a wink and a smile, and proceeded to the receptionist window.

Before he could reach it, Robin put down the magazine she'd been paging through and called to him.

"Can you give me a call later? There's something I wanted to discuss with you."

Ron promised to call on his break, then had another idea. "How about lunch? Do you have time when you're done here?"

Robin happily agreed, and they shared a quick embrace which made a middle-aged woman titter and Ann, the receptionist, look inquisitive.

"She's my sister," he told Ann. Better not to have people at the center think he was two-timing Mia. "Could you let Dr. Block know I'm here, please?"

A little over an hour later Ron sat across from his sister munching tortilla chips at the Chili's in Madison. Although she and her husband owned their own diner in the neighboring town of Sweet Glen, Robin preferred to eat elsewhere, especially when she had something personal to discuss. Rachel Long, her new legal name, seemed to have it all together, and most of the people working for her and her husband, Kevin, had no idea of the trauma she'd suffered as a young girl.

If walking into her living room at the age of fifteen, finding both her parents murdered, then being taken by the two men who had killed them, and being told her brother was also dead had not all been horrific enough, the murderers had then kept her prisoner in their basement and abused her for six years.

"My therapist says it's PTSD," Robin said. "And it all makes sense. But it doesn't make the flashbacks any less scary."

Every time his sister talked about what she'd been through, Ron's heart hurt and he felt the anger burning inside. To think that the men who did this were never identified, that they'd never paid for the murder of his parents or for what they'd done to his sister, made him sick with rage. "I hate that they did this to you," was all he said.

"It seems like so long ago now—a lifetime in some ways—and yet it still haunts me." Ron saw the anguish on her face. "But the worst thing is, they're still out there, Ronnie. I mean they could be hurting other people... and even if they're not, God knows they shouldn't get away with what they've done."

Ron reached across the table and put his hand on hers. "I made you a promise, Robin, and I intend to keep it. We're going to find them and make them pay."

"But, that's not all." Robin closed her eyes and with her palms together, thumbs under her chin, she blew out a big breath. "I thought I saw one of them."

"What?" Ron's eyes went wide. "Where? Where did you see him?"

"Well, that's just it. I'm not absolutely certain. I mean I was in Walmart, but I turned away so quickly and hurried out of that aisle. Then when I peeked again, he was gone."

"But you're fairly certain it was him?"

"Yes. No. I mean, I'm not sure." Robin squeezed her lips together, took another deep breath, and said, "It's just that I thought I saw him before—more than once—and then he wasn't there. Sarah, my therapist, said it could all be part of the PTSD."

"All right, let's do this. How 'bout you work with our forensic artist and see if we can come up with a picture so we know who we're looking for?"

"Couldn't your girlfriend do it? Oh, I mean you fiancée?" Robin asked smiling.

"Yeah, she probably could, but that's not actually her specialty. Our forensic person is trained to take what you're saying and get a good likeness down on paper. They're pretty amazing at what they do."

Before leaving the restaurant, Ron called and made the arrangements so Robin could meet with the forensic artist first thing Monday morning.

"Now, how else can I help you?" Ron wanted to take away all his sister's fear and remove the tortured look from her eyes.

"Not a thing," Robin said. "Wait, actually you could do something for me."

"Anything... what is it?"

"Join us for Sunday dinner so you can get to know Kevin and little Ronnie better."

Having only recently discovered he had a nephew, Ron was delighted at the idea of spending time with the little guy, but Sunday would be a problem. "Oh man, I'm supposed to have dinner with Mia and her family Sunday." As Robin's smile faded, he quickly tried to put it back. "Why don't you join us?"

"At Mia's house?"

"Well, no. At her Mom and Dad's. You met them that night you came over after they helped paint my apartment."

"Yes, I remember them, but now that Mia's mother is my therapist..." Robin shook her head as she was putting her fajita together. "I don't know. I'm afraid it would be weird. I mean that might be uncomfortable for both of us."

Ron had forgotten Reed Mental Health was indeed full of Reeds. Dr. Andrew Reed founded the practice, his daughter-in-law, Sarah, joined some years later, and now his granddaughter, Mia, had moved back to the area and become an art therapist there. Three of the eight full- and part-time staff members were Reeds.

Ron could understand his sister's hesitation—sort of—but he still hadn't put the smile back on her face. "You know what? We have dinner with Mia's family all the time. Why don't I have dinner with *my* family this time?"

"Really? Are you sure?" There it was. The smile he'd been looking for. "And Mia too, of course." Now all he had to do was break the news to his fiancée.

Chapter Five

"But I already told Mom we'd be there," Mia said into the phone. She didn't appreciate Ron changing their plans without first consulting her. Though he was apologetic, it didn't change the fact that she'd have to tell her mother they wouldn't be coming to dinner this week after all, and she knew Sarah would be disappointed.

Besides, she looked forward to seeing her family every Sunday. "Well, maybe you ought to go to your sister's, and I'll still go to my parents'." There was silence on the other end of the line. "I mean that would give you more time to get to know your new brother-in-law and nephew."

After another long pause Ron answered, "Sure, I guess we could do that, but I was kind of hoping you'd want to get to know my side of the family too."

Ugh. Mortified by her lack of sensitivity for even suggesting it, Mia rubbed her head. "You're right. I'm sorry. Of course, I want to get to know them. Let's do it."

Mia heard relief and joy in Ron's voice when he answered, and could almost see the twinkle she knew must be in his heavenly blue eyes. Recognizing she'd made the right choice, Mia made a mental note that she must learn to share him now.

"So, I'll see you at six. Don't be late. I'm cooking."

"Uh-oh," Ron said before chuckling. "Yeah, I'd better not be late, or I might get burnt offerings."

Mia knew he would never miss an opportunity to tease her about the time she'd tried to prepare his favorite dish for his birthday and burned it so badly they wound up having dinner at the Sweet Glen Diner. "Careful, buddy boy, or you might be asking Simmie to share some of his dinner."

She smiled at the way he laughed in earnest at that.

"Oops, not another word, and I promise not to be late."

Ron was true to his word showing up on their doorstep ten minutes early.

"Hey, there's my favorite detective," Julie said letting him in.

"Whoa! This one's mine, sis. You need to find your own." Mia greeted him with a big hug and smooch.

"Yeah, they're pretty disgusting, aren't they, Willie?" Julie's cat was a lot more vocal than Mia's Simmie, and he was currently expressing his hunger more than his disdain for the performance of the humans. "All right, Willie my boy. Let's get you some food." Julie opened a can for the two felines. "You guys better quit sucking face before we wind up with blackened meat that ain't supposed to be blackened."

"All right, you two," Mia said when Ron's laughter joined Julie's. "One meal. I burned one meal! You guys act like I'm hopeless." She shook her head and rolled her eyes, then quickly went to the stove to make sure they wouldn't wind up at the diner again.

Julie had been doing most of the cooking since the sisters moved in together, and the arrangement was perfect because Julie worked mostly from home as a freelance writer while working on her first novel. But Mia usually only saw clients until two or three o'clock on Fridays so she enjoyed making Friday night's supper. Tonight, she had prepared baked pork chops—one of Ron's favorites she'd learned—Green Beans Almondine, Mexican corn, and whipped potatoes. A man's meal in her mind, fit for her man. And this time nothing burned, and everything was delicious.

When she brought out dessert, Ron groaned. "Now where am I supposed to put that?"

"Well, if you're too full—"

"Whoa, get back here!" he called when Mia turned to return it to the kitchen. "There's always room for Jell-O and whatever that thing is in your hands."

"This *thing* is a Pumpkin Mousse Trifle," Mia said ceremoniously setting it in the center of their table.

"Yep, it's that time of year. Pumpkin everything," Julie said, "but she's getting pretty fancy isn't she, Ron?"

"Yeah, it looks almost too good to eat... almost! Full or not, I can't wait to dig in, and I can't believe you did all this." He looked up at Mia and rubbed his hands together in anticipation.

"It was no big deal. I used a store-bought pound cake and that's half the battle."

"They say the way to a man's heart is through his stomach, or something like that, and obviously Mia is after yours," Julie said.

"Well, I'd never turn down a meal like this, but I think Mia knows she already has my heart."

Mia and Ron exchanged a message that needed no words, and Mia struggled to pull her attention from those hypnotic blue eyes.

"Okay, dish me up some of that stuff," Julie said breaking the spell, "so I can take it upstairs with me and leave you two lovebirds alone."

Mia felt the heat in her cheeks and quickly did as her sister asked. "Sorry, sis. We don't mean to chase you off."

"Sure you do, but not to worry." Julie took her dessert and headed for the stairs. "I've got a date to see a late movie and I need to get ready soon."

"What? Who's the lucky guy?" Mia and Ron both gave Julie their full attention.

"Don't worry. It's not another serial killer." She laughed nervously, but they all remembered the last date she had which could have ended with her lying dead at the bottom of a ravine if Mia's gift hadn't helped them find and rescue her in time. Mia sickened at the memory of cracking the killer's skull with the huge rock that had been laid before her, but if she hadn't followed the whispered warning, her sister would have been the fiend's fourth victim.

"Sorry, bad joke," Julie said.

"So, tell us about your date. What's the guy's name?" Ron was obviously anxious to put the memory behind them.

"You know him, Mia, and I think you've met him too, Ron. It's our veterinarian, Dr. Curtain. *Drake.*" Julie smiled, and Mia noticed a slight rosiness in her cheeks that hadn't been there a moment earlier.

Mia smiled. "Nice!" She noticed the curious look on her fiancé's face. She wondered if he remembered the very good-looking Dr. Drake Curtain. She also wondered if he might be a wee bit jealous.

Chapter Six

Robin inspected the dining room and was satisfied with what she saw. The table looked perfect with her beautiful autumn centerpiece and candles and their best china and flatware. She hadn't purchased the expensive china herself, but it had finally been unpacked for her to use. It was something Kevin's first wife had gotten—mostly as wedding presents—that he had packed away after the tragic death of her and their child.

It wasn't exactly what Robin would have picked herself, but it did have a floral edge pattern in cornflower blue, her favorite color. She had to laugh when she realized the color of the scoop-necked top she was wearing matched the color of her dishes... and her eyes.

"He's sound asleep already." Kevin's voice interrupted her reverie. "I thought he might hang on until they got here, but he played himself out."

"I'm sure he'll wake up soon enough to have plenty of time to spend with his Uncle Ron. His naps are getting shorter lately. I'm afraid it won't be long before he gives them up altogether." Robin lit the two candles in her centerpiece of red, orange, and gold hues.

"Rachel, are you shaking?" Kevin had tried calling his wife by the name she was given at birth, but she would always be Rachel to him, and she'd told him he didn't need to change that. Since she had legally changed her name years ago, she was indeed, in her mind as well as his, Rachel Cooper Long.

On the other hand, to her brother she would always be Robin.

"I guess I'm a little nervous. I want everything to be perfect," she said scanning the table and the rest of her surroundings.

"It is. You've got the place so clean, we could literally eat off the floor." Kevin wrapped his arms around his wife. "Stop worrying. Besides, your brother isn't coming to judge you on your table setting skills."

Robin knew he was right about Ron, but what about Mia?

Moments later she opened the door to greet her brother and his fiancée. After getting a big hug from Ron, she had an awkward embrace with Mia. It wasn't that Mia was awkward since she was the one who initiated it. On the other hand, it had been many years since Robin had been close enough to another female to share an embrace, and she hoped Mia didn't feel her discomfiture or mistake it for something else.

"I'm so glad you came, Mia. It's going to be wonderful finally having a sister."

"Where's my namesake?" Ron asked.

Seeing his disappointment, Robin assured him the little guy would be up from his nap soon enough.

"So, when is the big day? Have you finally settled on the date?" Kevin asked.

"Yes, we have. I know it may be corny, but since it falls on a Saturday this year, we decided to get married on Valentine's Day."

"That's perfect!" Robin said. She turned to her brother. "And is this husband of mine going to need a tux?"

"Definitely," Ron answered with a crooked smile. "It's going to be a small but fancy wedding."

"Not really," Mia interrupted. "I mean not all that formal. But Mom and Dad said it's not every day that they get to give their daughter a wedding, and they are insisting on making it special for us, and... oh, I'm sorry Robin, I mean Rachel."

Robin realized her sudden thoughts about her own parents must have shown in her demeanor. She could see the mixture of confusion and pity on Mia's face. "What? No, don't be silly... and you can call me Robin or Rachel. It doesn't matter really. I, I—"

Kevin came to her rescue, putting his arm around her and pulling her in for a hug. "This lovely lady has prepared us a wonderful dinner," he said kissing her on the cheek. "And I for one am getting hungry. How about you guys?"

Robin smiled gratefully at him and led everyone to the table.

"Can I help you with anything?" Mia asked looking relieved.

"No, I've got this. You all go ahead and sit down and tell Kevin what kind of wine you'd like."

Back in the kitchen, Robin leaned on the counter for a moment to slow the pounding of her heart. Hearing Mia talk about her parents planning the wedding nearly sent her into a full panic attack. Her own parents hadn't been there to plan her wedding. She'd had no family in attendance because they'd been viciously murdered.

As she took several slow deep breaths, she worked to push back the thoughts of the murderous fiends who had robbed her of that and so much more and who could still be a threat today... to her new life and all the happiness she had finally created for herself.

"Are you all right, sweet cheeks?" Kevin put his arms around her waist and whispered, "It's okay... you're going to be okay."

Robin was glad she had finally confided in her husband. He had been nothing but supportive since she told him about being held prisoner and abused all those years by the men who had killed her parents.

"I know. Thanks, hon. We'd better get this food on the table."

Back in the dining room, Robin asked, "Have you picked out your dress yet?"

"I actually went to Dora's Bridal Shop and got one off the rack. It just needs alterations and I think it will be perfect."

Robin saw how animated Mia became when she talked about the wedding, and she also noticed how Ron watched her with a twinkle in his eyes.

The mood was light and fun throughout dinner with discussions of weddings and children, and became even more delightful when, in the middle of enjoying their lemon chiffon pie, little Ronnie came running out of his bedroom carrying his favorite stuffed panda bear and rubbing his eyes. He went straight to his mother's lap and hid his face while he continued to wake up.

"What did I tell you, Daddy?" Robin asked Kevin. "Our punkin-head's naps are getting shorter all the time." She ruffled the child's hair. After about ten minutes shy waking-up time, Ronnie became the center of attention and decided to run back and forth to his toy box and show his uncle each of his toy trucks, one at a time. By the end of the afternoon, he seemed totally at ease with Unca Won and Aunt Mee, and Robin could see they were both delighted with their new names.

It was nearly four o'clock when Robin noticed Mia discreetly checking her phone for the second time. She also saw her exchange several glances with Ron before he picked up his nephew and gave him a squeeze.

"Well little guy, Unca Won and Aunt Mee have to be going now."

"No... no go," Ronnie said.

"Yeah, gotta go. But we'll come see you again real soon, okay?"

Ronnie hopped off his uncle's lap and ran back to his mother, burying his face in her lap.

"Are you sure you wouldn't like another cup of coffee or piece of lemon pie?" Robin asked hating to see them go.

Ron and Mia exchanged another look before he said, "No, I couldn't possibly eat another thing."

"We're supposed to stop in and see my family before we head home," Mia said, "but this has been so nice, and your dinner was absolutely wonderful. I especially loved the pie."

"Thank you, and I'd be happy to give you the recipe if you'd like."

Mia said she'd love that, and Robin got their jackets out of the closet. "I think you'll need these. It looks like it's getting pretty breezy out there, and since we turned the clocks back, sunset is so much earlier."

Robin hated that it would soon be dark before she left the diner on the days she worked the evening shift. "I hope we can do this again soon."

"Absolutely," Ron and Mia answered in unison. Then exchanging a meaningful look with his fiancée, Ron added, "but it wouldn't have to be such a big fancy Sunday dinner."

"Right," Mia chimed in. "We could do a Saturday brunch or Friday night supper..."

"Sure, whatever," Robin said quickly. "Whatever works for you. Just so I get to spend time with my brother... with you both. We've lost so much time." She felt the heat rising in her cheeks and the lump in her throat.

Ron threw his arms around his sister and said softly, "Count on it!"

Still in his mother's arms, the toddler squirmed to escape the hug and ran to his father.

"Hey, how would you like to come with us to my family's Sunday dinner next week?" Mia asked. "I know they'd love to have you, and we're all going to be family soon."

Robin said she wasn't sure how that would work out with the little one's afternoon nap, but Mia assured her they could find a place for him to sleep, so the Longs thanked her and said they appreciated the invitation. But Robin had an uncomfortable feeling that this Sunday dinner may have caused a bit of discomfort for her brother and his girl.

After waving goodbye as they pulled out of the driveway, Robin closed the door behind her and hurried to the kitchen to get her little boy, who was now crying for his supper, something to eat.

"What's wrong, Rache? You look a little down. I thought it was a great visit."

"Oh, it was for sure. I just have a feeling Mia doesn't like me."

"What are you talking about?"

"I think she's jealous."

Chapter Seven

"I'm afraid your sister doesn't like me very much," Mia said as they pulled out of the driveway and headed toward Madison and her parents' home.

Ron's head snapped around to face her long enough that Mia reminded him to watch the road. "Why in the hell would you say that?" he asked.

"Hey, you don't need to swear. It was a feeling I got when we were leaving, that's all."

"Well, I think you're being ridiculous. I was there, and I didn't hear her say anything or do anything to make you feel that way. I think you're imagining things, and I don't know why."

"It was just a feeling... and I don't appreciate being called ridiculous!"

"Seriously?"

They rode in silence for the rest of the short drive to Craig and Sarah's house where they could tell from the cars in the big circular driveway, most of the family was still hanging out. They were greeted with hugs all around, and Mia instantly brightened, but when she looked at Ron, although he had put a smile on his face, she sensed a heaviness between them. *Why did I have to say anything?*

"Mom," she said to Sarah, "How would you feel about having Ron's sister and her family join us for Sunday dinner next week?"

"Oh, that would be great. We've met Rachel, but we haven't had a chance to meet her husband, and he's going to be your best man, right Ron?"

"Yeah." Ron plopped into the easy chair by the window. "It wouldn't be just the two of them though. My nephew, Ronnie, is three years old."

"Even better," Mia's youngest sister, Destiny, chimed in. "I love little ones that age."

"And Ronnie is so cute," Mia added, checking for a reaction from Ron.

Everyone agreed they couldn't wait to have the Longs join them for dinner, so Mia relaxed a little seeing Ron's pleasure at the family's reaction. But he still hadn't looked at her.

When Sarah asked about wedding plans, Craig announced he was going for a stroll to walk off some of the big dinner they'd had.

"Mind if I join you?" Ron asked. Grabbing his jacket, he followed his future father-in-law out the front door.

"What's wrong?" Julie asked.

"What do you mean?" Mia wasn't sure she even knew what was going on with Ron.

"I'm getting a bad vibe, sis. Did you guys have a lover's spat?"

"No, don't be silly," Mia answered way too quickly. Looking around the room she saw all eyes were now focused on her. "I mean not really. I just got a funny feeling that his sister might not like me, and when I mentioned it, he got all bent out of shape."

"Why wouldn't she like you?" Sarah asked. "You're perfect!"

"All right, Mom, let's not get carried away." Julie winked then looked at her sister and laughed. "But you're okay."

Mia appreciated her stepmom's reaction, but she wasn't feeling anywhere near perfection at the moment.

When Sarah asked what made her think Rachel didn't like her, she had trouble explaining. Searching her mind to try to understand it herself, she finally said, "Remember what I told you about how her parents were murdered, and she thought Ron had been killed too?" Everyone in the room nodded sympathetically. "Well, when she asked about the wedding today, I mentioned that you and Dad wanted to make sure my wedding was special, and she got this weird look on her face." Mia bit her lower lip. "I think I upset her because she doesn't have her parents... but that's not my fault. And besides, I lost my mother too. She's not the only one who's had losses."

Julie's jaw dropped and Sarah simply shook her head. "But you have me," Sarah said.

"I'm sorry. I know that. I just..."

"It's okay, Mia. I know what you're saying." Sarah leaned forward in her chair. "But you can't really compare losing your mother in an accident—even though it was horrific—to the way Ron's sister lost both of her parents... and her brother for all those years."

"I know, I know. And I didn't mean to upset her."

"Well, sweetie, I think you could be projecting a little bit. She may have been upset thinking about not having her parents any longer, but I doubt she blames you or was angry with you for mentioning that you do."

"There you go. Listen to your psychologist Momma. She knows what she's talking about." Julie looked from her sister to her mother and back again. "C'mon, Mia, let's get you a piece of Mom's pie."

Mia followed her sister into the kitchen where Julie surprised her with a big hug. "What was that for?"

"Because I love my sister, and because you looked like you needed one."

"I'm fine, really. Oh yum! It's her deep-dish apple pie," Mia said when Julie cut her a large slice. "This is a good day for pie. Robin had lemon chiffon for dessert, and that was delicious, too."

"Bet Mom's apple pie is better!" Destiny said having quietly followed them into the kitchen to grab another piece for herself.

"Of course, it is, Squirrel. And especially in autumn when apples are so good. But I did ask Robin for her recipe when I saw how much Ron enjoyed his sister's pie."

"So, you and Ron are going to be fine, right? I mean you wouldn't dare mess this up. We've already picked out my gorgeous Maid of Honor dress, and I love it! So, this wedding must happen."

Mia was sure her sister was trying to make her feel better, but the idea of the wedding not happening hadn't even crossed her mind. That was ludicrous.

"All right, you two. Leave some of that pie for the rest of us."

The sisters all jumped. They hadn't heard their father and Ron come in.

"Julie, can I see you and Destiny for a minute?" Craig asked.

Left alone in the kitchen, Mia and Ron stood awkwardly for a minute before saying, "I'm sorry," almost simultaneously. They sealed their mutual forgiveness with an embrace that ended in a kiss, removing any doubt there would be a wedding.

Carrying their apple pie back to the family room, they settled into the loveseat which had obviously been vacated for them, and Mia didn't miss the conspiratorial smile that passed between Julie and their father. Craig may have been Mia's father and only Julie's stepfather, but they were as close as if they were blood. And though Julie had kept her biological father's name, Winters, she had added Reed when Craig officially adopted her.

Now Mia watched the two of them and wondered why their bond sometimes seemed even closer than hers was with her dad. *What is it about Julie that makes everyone love her more?*

Well, not everyone. Mia knew there was one person in the room who found her the most important person in the world and loved her more than anyone else. Then she felt the vibration of the cell phone Ron had shoved in his pocket.

"Oh, I'd better take this," he said getting up to leave the room. "It's Robin."

Chapter Eight

"What's wrong?" Ron said into the phone. He had stepped out onto the back patio to take the call.

"I hate to bother you, but I can't stop thinking I did something to upset your girlfriend."

"Don't be silly. You didn't do anything wrong, and I'm sure I'd know if you did. Besides, how could anybody be upset after that feast you prepared for us? You've gotten to be as good a cook as Mom was." As soon as he said it, Ron got choked up and worried that his words probably had the same effect on Robin.

"That's one of the nicest compliments you could give me. I've spent quite a few years in the restaurant business now, and I've picked up a few things here and there. But getting back to why I called, are you sure I haven't done anything wrong? I... I got the uneasy feeling that maybe Mia didn't like me."

"You women," Ron said then snickered. "You're not going to believe this, but Mia said she's afraid you don't like her."

"Oh no. What did I do to make her think that?"

Ron paced back and forth across the patio and wondered if he should have said anything. "Listen kiddo, you didn't say or do anything wrong. And neither did she as far as I could tell. Besides, you're my sister, and she's going to be my wife. You have to like each other. It's a given." He liked the sound of relief and the little laugh he heard on the other end of the line.

"You're right, of course. I can't wait to have a sister and to get to know her better, but she's so smart and talented, and I never even finished high school."

"That's not your fault. And you're plenty smart. You don't need a piece of paper to prove that." Ron hated to hear the insecurities his sister had because she'd been deprived of an advanced education. "I have an idea. Why don't you and Mia get together some time—just the two of you—so you can get to know each other better?"

"I'd like that, but I don't know if she'd have time. She's so busy with work and all..."

"Don't be silly. I'm sure she could find time, and I bet she'd love it. Why don't you give her a call sometime? Oh, and she already said something to Sarah and Craig, her parents, about you guys coming for dinner next Sunday, and they loved the idea."

"But what about Ronnie?"

Ron laughed again. "I think they were more excited about seeing him than any of us, especially Mia's little sister, Destiny."

There was a long pause and Ron was about to end the call and get out of the cold and back to his fiancée when Robin said, "There's something else."

"What's that?" he asked looking through the slider and noticing how Mia was watching him.

"It's about Buddy," she said.

Ron was suddenly on high alert at the mention of one of her kidnapper's names. "Okay, what about him?" he asked going down the steps out of sight into the yard.

"I didn't want to say anything earlier and spoil our visit, but I saw him again."

"What? Are you sure?"

"No... no, I'm not absolutely positive. I mean, there have been other times when I thought I saw him, and it turned out it was just someone who looked like him... or there was no one there at all when I looked again..." Robin's voice faded off with the final words. Ron wasn't sure how to respond, but before he could, his sister said, "But this time, I could swear it was him." After six years as his prisoner, she assured him she could never forget that face... no matter how hard she tried.

"All right. Where did you see him?"

"I was driving through Madison, and he was walking down the street. He was by himself. I didn't see Charlie anywhere."

Ron pulled his hand through his hair. "Okay, when you meet with our forensic artist tomorrow morning, as soon as you're finished, we'll talk more. Robin, we're going to get these guys. I promise."

After ending the call, Ron stood transfixed, imagining the terror his sister must be feeling. The sound of the slider startled him, and he looked up to see Mia holding his coat and watching him with a wrinkled brow.

"Sorry," he said.

"You must be freezing. What did she want? Was it about me?"

"No, Mia. Well yeah, partly." He saw the crease between her brows deepen as he accepted and slipped into his jacket.

"So, I did say something that offended her—"

"No!" Ron interrupted curtly. When he saw Mia's reaction he quickly went to her side. "Listen, she was upset because she thought you didn't like her." Ron could see that didn't help when her mouth fell open and her eyes got glassy. "But you didn't do anything wrong, I swear. Robin is just insecure. She thinks you're so smart and talented, and she didn't even get a high school diploma."

"But that's not important, and besides, it's not her fault!"

"Of course not. And that's what I told her." Ron closed the little distance between them and took Mia's hands. "I suggested the two of you ought to get together for lunch or something and get to know each other better."

"Really?"

"Yeah, why? Don't you like the idea?"

"No, it's fine. You might have asked me first before putting it out there though."

Ron heaved a sigh. "The two women in my life are driving me crazy." He groaned and put his hands on his cheeks. That evoked a giggle from Mia. *Thank goodness. Women!*

"Did she want anything else?" Mia gave him a hug that said everything was okay.

"No. I wish."

"Why? What is it?"

Ron told her about Robin's anxiety because she thought she saw one of the men who had held her captive for six years. "She thinks he's here in Madison."

"Oh no, that's horrible. Did she call the police?"

"Um, yeah. She called me," Ron said wondering if his fiancée was having a brain freeze.

Mia laughed. "Oh yeah, I guess she did. What are you going to do?"

"First thing in the morning, she'll be working with our forensic artist to get images of both these bastards—sorry—and then we're going to find them. We have to find them."

"You will, Ron. I know you will." Mia stroked his cheek, kissed him, then whispered in his ear, "Now, can we please go back inside and spend some time with my family before we freeze?"

Chapter Nine

Ron had told Robin the artist would be able to come up with a sketch of their suspects, not only how they looked as she described them from years ago, but also how they would appear today.

Robin was fascinated by the process but cringed when she saw the final result. She found herself staring at the images of two men she'd hoped never to see again. Through the use of technology, they looked a little older, especially Charlie—feeble and sickly and like not much of a threat at all. Looking at the sketch, she could almost hear his hacking cough.

And now, as the artist presented Robin with the finished sketch of Buddy, her breathing quickened and she felt her heart racing. "Yes, that's him." She fought the urge to jump up and run away. She might have done exactly that if her brother hadn't chosen that moment to join them.

"Are you all right, sis?" Ron asked.

"Yes, I think so," she said in spite of the uncontrollable shaking. He must have known better and wrapped her in a safe, warm embrace. But then she felt him stiffen.

"Is that them?" he asked. Robin could only nod.

It suddenly struck her that he was seeing their parents' murderers for the first time, and she hadn't thought about how that might affect him. Looking up into his face, she saw a mix of emotions that seemed to reflect so much of what she felt.

His eyes were squinted, and he gritted his teeth. Then squeezing his lips together, he loosened his hold on her and picked up the two drawings. After studying them for several seconds, he turned to Robin. "Are these pretty accurate?"

"Yes, Ronnie, that looks like them." She heard herself revert to the name she'd called him as a child. Maybe because at the moment she felt like a child... a frightened child. "Now what?" she asked.

"Now we get an APB out on them. Especially this scum," he said waving the picture of Buddy. Although Robin hadn't shared all the gruesome details, she'd told him enough to let him know Buddy was crueler to her than his father had been. The old man used her, but he didn't intentionally inflict the kind of pain on her that his sadistic son did.

"Look, I've got to take care of this, but if you want to hang out here for a while—"

"No, I really should get back to the diner."

"Are you sure you're okay to drive?"

"Yes, of course," she said grabbing her purse off the back of the chair she'd been sitting in while giving her descriptions. She was still shaken, but all she wanted now was to get out of the police station and back to an environment where she felt safe... most of the time.

On the drive back to the diner, Robin tried to take her mind off of the ugly memories stirred up by working with the forensic artist, so she decided to take Ron's advice and call Mia. Maybe it was time for them to get to know each other better. She envied the younger woman's talent. Robin had tried to teach herself to draw while she sat in that barren basement hoping the men upstairs would leave her alone. It was the only thing she had to do besides read and reread the few books Charlie, the older one, would get for her. So, she drew pictures of birds flying free and dreamed of somehow finding her own way to freedom.

Robin was proud of the improvement in her skills and had continued to draw after she escaped and even after she got married, but once Ronnie came along, there wasn't much time for hobbies. Between helping to run the diner, taking care of her home, and being a mommy, her days were filled. Yet now, when she thought of Mia, she thought of drawing.

Robin pulled into the back of the Sweet Glen Diner's parking lot and turned off the engine, but before going inside, she made a quick call.

"Hi Mia, I was wondering if maybe you'd like to get together and have lunch or something one day." When Mia didn't answer right away, Robin wished she hadn't called. Why would she think someone like Mia would have time for her?

"That would be great, Rachel," Mia said at last. "I was trying to think when would be a good time that would work for both of us. I don't know how flexible your schedule is."

Mia told her she was able to arrange her own schedule, so they tossed around several possibilities and settled on breakfast at the diner before Mia went to work Wednesday.

Ending the call, Robin was relieved that her future sister-in-law seemed so willing to meet for breakfast, but that feeling didn't last long before her anxiety level went up. *What in the world will we talk about?*

Once inside the diner her fretting about breakfast with Mia Reed was quickly put out of her mind as she dealt with a bit of chaos. The young man Connie had hired to bus tables hadn't shown up, and the newest waitress was as slow as a sloth. Robin wasn't sure she was going to work out. Meanwhile the other three waitresses were hustling to try to keep up with taking orders, bringing customers their meals, and cleaning up after the ones who left.

Robin immediately grabbed an apron from the kitchen and bussed two of the tables herself.

"Thank God you're here," Connie whispered, passing her in a rush. As manager, Connie usually acted as hostess, but whenever they were short-handed, she picked up the slack.

The next hour sped by until the lunch rush thinned out, and when she was sure everything was under control, Robin hung up her apron and called Kevin to let him know she was on her way home.

Back outside, she pulled her jacket tightly around her, noticing how much the wind had picked up. Leaves were blowing everywhere, and she hoped they wouldn't all be stripped from the trees before they reached the peak of autumn color which should be mere days away.

She hopped in her vehicle and backed out of her parking place behind the building, but as she rounded the corner of the diner and headed for the parking lot exit, she saw him.

It was Buddy.

Chapter Ten

Mia finished her Greek yogurt with blueberries and wheat thins at her desk and looked over her next client's file. It was Adam Grant, one of Mia's first clients at the Reed Mental Health Center, and she'd been pleased with the progress he was making. The young man suffered with PTSD and was a recovering alcoholic who had seen his former therapist fall to her death before Mia moved back to the area and came to work at RMH.

Initially the police had thought the woman's death to be a suicide, but Adam was convinced from the very start that she would not have done that. He knew she would not take her own life because he knew her beliefs. She had once told him suicide was the killer of hope.

Before long, as two other women appeared to have jumped to their deaths, the police finally realized Adam Grant was right. Nancy Owens was murdered along with them. And had it not been for Mia's intervention, her own sister Julie would have been the serial killer's fourth victim.

Adam's progress had been slow, but he was definitely growing stronger and more confident. Yet when she led him into the office and he took a seat in his usual spot, Mia noticed he was extremely agitated.

"How's it going, Adam? Is something wrong?"

He had been staring at the floor, and when he raised his head and his eyes met hers, her suspicion was confirmed. His expression looked tormented.

"It's that cop."

"What cop? What happened, Adam? Are you in some kind of trouble?"

"I didn't do anything!" he nearly yelled.

"Okay, take a breath. I believe you," she said in her most soothing voice. "Can you tell me what's going on?"

Dropping his head into his hands, Adam said, "It's crazy. I didn't do anything, and I'm not even sure what they're accusing me of."

"Who?"

"The police! They were questioning me about where I went after my appointment with you last week." He looked Mia in the eyes and said, "I went home. And then they wanted to know if anybody could vouch for that. I live alone, man... no, nobody could vouch for me, but I just went home." Adam took a deep breath and blew the air out slowly. "When I leave here, I'm usually pretty well spent, you know? And so I go home and put on some Rock and chill for a while."

Mia began putting two and two together thinking about when she had last seen Adam and realizing that was the day Dr. Block was assaulted.

"And they wouldn't even tell me what it was all about. What do they think I did? Do you know?"

"I might," Mia said wondering how much she should tell him. She didn't want to interfere with the case or say anything Ron wouldn't want her to say, but she was certain Adam had nothing to do with it, and she could see he was agonized. She saw the expectant look on his face and knew she had to say something. "There was an incident here at the center that day, but I'm not at liberty to say anything more."

"Do you think—"

"No, Adam. I don't believe you had anything to do with it. I'm sure you didn't. I imagine the police are questioning everyone who was here that day." Mia hoped that was the case and that they didn't actually think her client was responsible for the attack. She also hoped their suspicions wouldn't be too much for Adam to handle. "Are you going to be okay?"

"Yeah, I guess."

"You've come so far. Don't let their questioning get to you. If you know you're innocent, that's all you need to get through it."

"If?" he said looking at his therapist like a deer caught in the headlights. "You don't believe me?"

"No, I mean yes! I do believe you," Mia said hastily to repair any damage her poorly chosen words may have caused. She couldn't risk losing his trust. "Adam, listen to me. What I'm saying is since *you know* you're telling the truth, you need to hold onto that. I need you to take care of you."

"Okay, yeah, I know that, and I'm still clean and sober and I'm not going to drink today."

Mia knew that was how an alcoholic had to do it—one day at a time—and Adam was making that choice today. She spent most of the rest of his session reaffirming his successes in recent months and talking about how working third shift was going for him, but all the while thoughts of Ron or his partner, Jason, questioning Adam were bouncing around in her head. By the time she walked her client out at the end of his session, she was becoming rather agitated herself.

Mia checked the little clock on her desk to see if she had time to call Ron, but with only eight minutes before her next client, she decided to wait. She might need more than a few minutes for what she wanted to say to him.

Anyway, for now, in all fairness to dear Miss Edna, she had to get ready for her next session, and she was glad it was one of her favorite clients and a relatively easy hour. With her sweet, elderly lady it would be more like a fifty-minute visit with a dear friend than work.

However, when Miss Edna got settled on the end of the forest green leather couch and turned to face her therapist who always sat on the other end for their chats, Mia didn't see the usual pleasant smile. The elderly lady still hadn't spoken and looked demoralized to the point that Mia was almost certain something was wrong. Something had happened. This day was turning into a real challenge.

"Miss Edna, what's wrong? You don't seem quite yourself this afternoon."

"I'm sorry, dear. I just feel awful." Edna opened her purse and got a tissue to wipe her eyes which had quickly filled with tears. "It's my neighbor. I saw the ambulance come right before lunch, and... I'm sorry... when someone like that passes away..." Miss Edna's tears flowed, and she couldn't go on, but Mia needed a moment to think anyway. *Her neighbor*, she thought, *which neighbor?* Edna Schmidt lived next door to Aunt Bonnie. Mia's grandmother, Bonnie's lifelong friend, would be devastated if... "I know he was getting up there in years, just like me," Edna said, "but he was the picture of health, and then, with no warning, he's gone."

Mia moved closer and put her hand on Edna's arm. "I'm so sorry." Knowing it was a man, she felt some semblance of relief, but she still wanted to ask for the person's identity. She hoped it wasn't Aunt Bonnie's husband. She finally asked softly, "Which neighbor was it, Miss Edna?"

"It was that nice Joe Marconi, my best friend's husband." Edna suddenly stopped and looked up at her therapist. "Oh dear." Her chin quivered and the tears began again. "I'm so sorry. I didn't think... I mean I forgot, I forgot Bonnie's your aunt. Oh my, it's your uncle, and you didn't know, and I... I'm so sorry, dear."

"It's all right," Mia said losing the battle to fight back her own tears. She quickly wiped them away and took the tissue Edna was now offering her. "Joe isn't... wasn't actually my uncle. Well, Aunt Bonnie isn't actually my aunt either," she said.

"Oh yes, I know dear. But I don't think she could love you more if she were. She's so proud of you... and your sister and brothers too." Mia knew that was true and Bonnie felt like her real aunt, but she hadn't developed as close a relationship with Bonnie's second husband. Several years after Uncle Frank died, Aunt Bonnie had married Joe Marconi, and Mia knew he treated her like a queen. *Now she's lost two husbands.* Mia's heart broke for Bonnie Dixon Marconi, and Mia knew her Grandma Val would want to be with her to comfort her. They had been best friends for as long as she could remember.

I need to call and let her know what happened.

"How did you get here, Miss Edna?" Mia asked suddenly remembering it was Aunt Bonnie who usually transported her.

"Oh, another of our nice neighbors, Anna Fisher, came over when she saw the ambulance, and when I said I'd have to cancel my appointment she offered to bring me. Most everybody in the community is so kind, you know."

"Yes, I do. I'm glad to know you have so many good people around you."

It was about ten minutes later that Miss Edna mentioned again how a very nice neighbor, Anna Fisher was kind enough to bring her to the appointment that day. Mia didn't think too much of her repeating this information—it was certainly easy to forget you've said something when so upset—but Mia became concerned when, at the end of the session, Edna got to her feet and said a third time, "You know, I have a nice neighbor, Anna Fisher. She brought me today."

Mia thought of her Alzheimer's patient back in Pittsburgh and hoped she wasn't seeing the beginnings of dementia in Miss Edna.

A quick check of the time told Mia she'd better hurry if she wanted to contact Grandma Val before getting her next client, but when Valerie Reed answered, Mia could tell she already knew. She sounded like she had a terrible cold, obviously because she'd been crying with her friend.

"Yes, I'm with Bonnie now, hon. But I appreciate you taking the time to call."

"Okay. Please give her my love, and tell her if there's anything at all I can do—"

"Of course."

Another check of the time, and Mia hurried out to the waiting room. She knew if she kept Samantha Collins waiting, it would trigger the woman's paranoia. She would have to call Ron later. *Could this day get any worse?*

When Mia's long day finally ended, she made the call that had been on her mind ever since her session with Adam Grant. She didn't get the answer she was looking for. Ron must have been in the middle of something because it went straight to voicemail. After the briefest hesitation, she decided to leave him a message.

"Hey Ron, I had a very disturbed client on my hands today. I'm not sure what you or Jason said to him, but he was definitely upset." She paused before adding, "And I'm sure Adam didn't do it. Call me." Mia slid the phone in the side pocket of her backpack handbag, and decided the only cure for the way she was feeling was to go home and down to her retreat. It was time to put all else out of her mind and paint.

That's when she felt the itch.

Chapter Eleven

Ron saw he had missed a call from Mia and hurried to check the message. He listened to it twice and shook his head.

"Something wrong?" his partner Jason asked.

"Huh? Oh, no, it was just Mia."

"Trouble in paradise?"

"Nah, nothing like that." Ron looked over the short list of RMH clients they'd interviewed. "Did you talk to Adam Grant?"

"No, name doesn't ring a bell." Jason checked the same list and said, "I questioned these three." He put checks by each of their names.

Ron groaned. "I was afraid of that. I probably should have made sure I didn't talk to any of Mia's clients, but they were pretty close-lipped about details. All I knew was they were patients at the center the day of the assault. So, I guess I'm in the doghouse."

"Good luck, buddy."

"Yeah, thanks," Ron said hitting Mia's number. It went straight to voicemail so he left a message for her to call him back and dropped the phone on his desk.

It started to vibrate almost immediately. *That was quick.* He took a breath and braced himself for an angry girlfriend.

"I saw him today." Robin's voice was trembling.

"Which one?" he asked, immediately switching gears.

"The younger one, Buddy. And Ron... he saw me. I was in the car, pulling out of the diner parking lot, and he looked right at me."

"Are you okay? Where are you now?"

"At home. I don't know for sure if he recognized me, but he did kind of a double-take and I took off. I was afraid to look back. And I didn't see the old white pickup, but I don't know if he's still driving that." Robin rattled off the details of her detouring drive before finally heading home when she was sure no one was following her.

"Listen. You stay where you are. I'll head over to the diner myself and show them the sketches of who we're looking for. Have you told anyone there what's going on?"

"No. I didn't want anyone to know, but I guess I should."

"Don't worry about it. No one at the diner needs to know why we're looking for these two. But I'll make sure to let the staff know they're considered dangerous. I don't want anyone tipping these guys off."

Ron was as good as his word. Without thinking about Mia or her concerns, he rushed to the Sweet Glen Diner and shared the sketches, leaving one tacked up in the kitchen out of sight of the local diners.

He wasn't there long before heading back to his car. When he got outside, he heard the squeal of tires as Kevin Long came to a stop, and waved him down.

"Is he here?" Kevin shouted.

"No, and nobody remembers seeing him inside. He must have changed his mind about going in when he saw Rob—I mean Rachel."

"You can call her Robin. I know who you mean... but what's this guy look like? She said you have a picture."

Ron could tell Robin's husband was distraught and knew he needed to calm down, but Ron understood the rage he must be feeling. He knew how the thought of those men hurting his sister stirred a seething fury in him and thought it must be the same—maybe worse—for her husband.

"Why don't you get in?" he said motioning to his vehicle. "I've got copies of the sketches."

Kevin hopped in the passenger side and took the picture Ron handed him. He stared at the image and Ron saw him squeezing his lips together, shaking his head in a futile attempt to gain control over the intense anger that threatened to erupt.

"We're going to get them, Kevin. I promised Robin, and I'm promising you." He knew Kevin heard him by the nod of his head as he continued to stare at the images.

"Which one of these bastards is Buddy? This one, huh?" he said showing Ron the sketch of the younger man.

Ron nodded.

"That sonofabitch! I'd like to—"

"I know. Believe me, I know. But the best thing you can do right now is be with your wife. She needs you."

"You don't think... I mean, do you think they'll go there to the house?"

"No, I'm not saying that. Although we can't be sure, but I just meant she needs your support."

"Yeah," Kevin said, already halfway out of the car. "Thanks, Ron. And hey, get this guy!"

Ron gave him a thumbs up and watched as Kevin sped out of the lot and down the road in the direction of home. *That guy's gonna get a ticket if he's not careful. But I'm not gonna be the one to give it to him.*

He made a quick call to fill in his partner on the latest and let him know there had been a sighting of the younger suspect.

"Do we have a make and model of the vehicle or maybe even a license number?"

"Nope. None of the above. The witness—who happens to also be the victim, my sister—saw him in the parking lot of her diner, but he was on foot. Truth be told, she kind of freaked and took off."

"Can't say I blame her from what you told me."

"How 'bout I pick you up in about ten minutes and we cruise around and see if we can find this piece of shit?"

Chapter Twelve

Mia stared at the image her itch had created. *Why?* She was looking at a very good likeness of Dr. Block sitting at his desk just like she'd seen him so often.

"Well Simmie, this is no help at all. I was hoping for a clue. Something to help us figure out who hit this guy in the head last week," she said showing the finished drawing to her cat. Simeon didn't answer. He simply thumped his tail. "Oh really? You don't care for the good doctor?" Mia giggled. "You're not alone. He is a bit quirky."

She held the picture at arm's length and studied it for a minute, then drew it closer and inspected every detail. Certain there had to be a reason she'd been called to draw it, Mia wondered, "Maybe it needs other eyes to see it... Shall we show it to Ron and see what he thinks, Fuzzy Butt? And speaking of Ron, why hasn't he called?"

Mia looked around for her phone.

"Oh crap!"

In her haste to get to her studio and scratch the familiar itch, she realized she'd left her bag up on the kitchen counter where she dropped it when she got home, and her phone was in it.

She jogged up the steps with the Persian who excitedly darted past her to see what was going on now.

"Nuts!"

"What's wrong?' asked Julie who was standing in the kitchen tearing lettuce for their dinner salad.

"I left a message for Ron to call me, then I went and left my phone up here and missed his call."

"Oh no, you missed a call from your beau!" Julie laughed. "So call him back."

"Brilliant idea, Jules. Now why didn't I think of that?" Mia stuck out her tongue, making her sister laugh harder. "Smells good in here. What's for dinner?" she asked hitting call back. No answer.

Julie took the lid off the pot full of chicken corn soup and ladled some into each of the red and black bowls sitting by the stove. "It's really, really hot. It should be good to eat by the time we finish our salad." She cut some crusty bread and brought that and the salads to the table. "So how was your day?"

"Oh my God, I forgot to tell you about Joe."

"It's all right. Grandma called Mom and she called me this afternoon." They sat in silence for several minutes before she added, "Death sucks."

"Yeah. It really does. Poor Aunt Bonnie. And she's been through it twice. It doesn't seem fair."

Julie nodded glumly, then seconds later smiled. "Okay, enough sadness for now. It's not good for digestion. New subject, please."

"Don't look at me. I can't think of any real bright spots to my day at the moment."

Julie put down her fork. "Okay, then let me tell you my news."

Mia looked up at her sister who was beaming.

"I got an agent!" Julie squealed.

"What? Oh wow!" Mia knew her sister had been sending out query letters, and she knew how important this was to her. "That's fabulous!"

Julie prattled on with excitement all through dinner, and Mia was truly happy for her, but by the time they carried their dishes to the dishwasher and loaded it, she had really heard enough and was ready to move on.

"Jules, can I show you something?"

"Sure, what?"

"Be right back." Mia dashed down to her studio and quickly returned with her latest creation. "What do you see?"

Julie frowned then answered, "Is that the psychiatrist at the center? What's his name… Dr. Block?"

"Yes."

"Oh—kay… so what? I mean why did you draw him of all people?"

"I told you about him getting attacked, right?"

"Oh, yeah." Julie cupped her chin. "I still don't get it."

"Don't feel bad. Neither do I." She answered her sister's puzzled look. "I didn't plan it."

"Ooooh, one of those, huh?"

"Yeah, but I can't figure it out. What's it supposed to mean?" Mia carried her tea into the living room and curled up on one corner of the sofa while Julie settled on the other end with her coffee.

"Well, this isn't the first time you've drawn something and didn't know what it was all about until later. Like when you drew that picture of a woman you'd never seen and it was Robin. You didn't know anything about her being a missing person."

Mia nodded, but she wasn't satisfied. She wanted to find the clue that must be hidden in this picture. She wanted to prove Adam Grant had nothing to do with it. She shot a quick text to her fiancé asking him to call or stop by. She needed to see him.

No response.

What the heck? She checked the time. Ron should be home by now… unless he was in the middle of a case. But still, *how long does it take to send me a quick text?* Mia wasn't used to being ignored, especially by Ron, and she didn't like it.

"Do you want to watch a movie?" Julie had flipped the TV on and was checking Netflix.

"Sure. See if you can find a rom-com. Something light." This day had given her quite enough drama.

Chapter Thirteen

After over an hour driving around Sweet Glen and Madison, Detectives Bishop and Evans were about ready to call it a night. The two towns had built up so much over the years. Unless you looked for the little sign, you wouldn't know you were leaving one and entering the other. The Long's diner was just across the line in the smaller town, and they lived a little farther out. Ron had circled back to ride by both places several times but didn't see any sign of disturbance.

The detectives were aware that catching sight of this guy on the street was a real long shot. Even so, Ron had been hopeful. Now his hopes were fading.

He was ready to give up when he had a thought. "You know, there's that little dive next to the motel on Glenwood Blvd. just outside of town," Ron said. "You up for checkin' one more before we call it quits?"

"Why not? It's worth a shot." Jason Evans seemed almost as anxious to get this guy as Ron. He had a sister who had been attacked by a perv years before, and also carried a passion for putting guys like that away ever since. "What about the other guy? Did Robin ever see him around here?"

Ron shook his head. "No, just this one."

They entered the Wildhorse Tavern and waded through the stale smoke searching the few faces sitting at the bar—no sign of Buddy—and went straight to the bartender.

"What'll you have?" the guy behind the bar asked lazily.

"Just some information." Ron showed him ID, and the guy looked around nervously. Apparently, any attention from the cops couldn't be good. "Hey, don't worry. We're not here to cause you trouble. All we want to know is if you've seen this guy," he said showing the sketch he'd brought along.

"Hey, Mel," the bartender called to the fellow sitting two barstools down. "Isn't this the guy that was in here a while ago?"

The other man set his beer down and took a look. He squinted at it. "Might be."

One of the only other people in the place left the video game he was playing long enough to peer over Mel's shoulder. "Yeah, that's him. Real asshole. Bumped into me on his way out, then gave *me* a dirty look. That's the guy. What'd he do?"

"How long ago did he leave?" Jason asked ignoring the question.

"I'm not sure. It's been a while though."

That's a big help. "Did you happen to see what he was driving?"

"No, man. I wasn't gonna follow him outside. He mighta thought I was lookin' for a fight, and he was a big sonofabitch."

Ron shook his head. Though he was disappointed, at least he knew they were close.

The bartender's voice stopped the detectives as they headed for the door. "Maybe check next door. A lot of guys there walk over and hang out here to drink a few beers. They're usually lonely."

Taking his advice, the detectives made another quick stop, and the desk clerk recognized the guy in the sketch immediately. "Yeah, he was here."

"Is he here now?"

"You just missed him. Left a few hours ago. Ya might wanna check over at the bar. He tossed a duffle in his truck and headed that way after he checked out."

"What was he driving? What kind of truck?" Ron asked.

"Looked like a real beater. Probably about a 2005 or '06 Chevy pickup. Red, needed body work. That's all I can tell you."

"Do you have the license number?" Seeing the clerk's blank look, Ron added, "Don't you take the make, model and license number when they check in?"

The clerk seemed amused. "We don't bother with all that. People pay cash, we give 'em a key."

Once they were convinced there was no more information to be gained at the bar or the motel, Bishop and Evans cruised the area once more, this time looking for a beat-up, red pickup. They radioed the information in to get all local police and state troopers on the lookout. Copies of the sketch had already been sent out to every cop and first responder in the county. Now all they had to do was find that face in that vehicle. That's all.

"This guy is either long gone or he's stashed the truck, Ron, but we've got everyone on the lookout for him. I think we need to call it a night."

Ron nodded, did a quick U-turn and headed back to the station. He checked his phone. *Shit!*

"I've seen that look before," Jason grinned. "Now what did you do?"

"Looks like I might be in trouble with the little lady. She sent a couple messages." He dropped the phone on the console. "I meant to get back to her sooner, but we've been kind of busy, right?"

"Hey, I'm not the one you have to convince," Jason said putting his hands up.

"Yeah. I know. I'd better give her a call, but I've got something else to take care of first."

Ron knew Mia might be a little irritated, but he was more concerned about his sister at the moment. Mia would have to wait.

There was a certain amount of paperwork that Ron wanted to get done before heading to his next stop, but as soon as he finished the bare minimum, he texted his girl with a quick apology and a question.

Leaving the station now. Have to stop in and see Robin.
Do you want me to stop by after?

The reply was short.

Tired. Going to bed early. Don't bother.

Shit! But I've got to check on Robin.

Twenty minutes later, Ron was ready to knock on Robin's front door when it occurred to him someone banging the door at this hour might panic her. He decided to warn her first and took out his phone.

I'm at your front door.

Seconds later a text came back.

What?

Oh shit! He'd been in such a hurry to send the text, he'd sent it to the wrong person.

Sorry, sweetheart. Meant to text Robin. Love you.

He hated to leave it at that, but it was getting late. He pulled up the correct recipient and was about to type his message when the porch light came on. Kevin Long opened the door.

"How did you know it was me?"

Kevin pointed to the newly installed camera mounted above the door. That gave Ron a certain amount of reassurance. His sister was in good hands.

Ron told his sister and brother-in-law what they'd learned. Told them to keep an eye out for an old red pickup. Told them to be careful and call him if they saw the truck or the murderous fiend who drove it.

Back in his vehicle, Ron rubbed his head which was beginning to throb, then headed home. *It'll be okay. Mia will understand... I hope.*

CHAPTER FOURTEEN

"It's going to be okay, Rache."

Robin wanted to believe her husband, but Buddy was actually here. Here in their town. Was it a coincidence? She knew she didn't look anything like the skinny girl with the stringy blonde hair who had escaped from him and his father all those years ago. She had a new name, along with short, red, well-coifed hair, and she was a woman... not a scared little girl. She couldn't let him get the best of her.

"You're trembling," Kevin said and held her closer. "I'm not going to let anything happen to you, sweet cheeks. I promise."

"I know, Kev. But when I heard Ron's car pull in... I thought— "

"I know, I know."

No, you don't! Robin wanted to scream the words out loud. He had no idea of the hell she'd endured. He couldn't possibly understand her fear and revulsion. But she also knew he cared. He hadn't left her side since he got back from talking to Ron earlier in the day.

"Your brother told me to take care of you," he said. "And that's exactly what I'm going to do."

Even when it was time to put Ronnie to bed and she went in to read him his bedtime story, Kevin was right there. Little Ronnie loved being sandwiched between his parents in his big boy bed.

She appreciated how much Kevin wanted to be there for her and reassure her. But she was also beginning to need some space. Some time to think.

"I'm going to take a bath." Robin gently released herself from his arms and turned toward the steps to the bathroom. When Kevin took a step in the same direction she added, "And don't you dare follow me." She smiled to signal she was all right... even though she wondered if she'd ever be all right again.

Kevin took a step back, put his hands up in defense and said, "I'm just going to the kitchen to get a beer, I promise."

"Do you have to?" The words had come out before she even thought about it, and she wished she could call them back. "No, I'm sorry. Go ahead."

"I think maybe I'll have a root beer," he said softly with a wink that showed he understood and didn't mind.

Robin lit the lavender candle in the bathroom, filled the tub with luscious bubbles, and lowered herself in the hot water up to her chin. Trying to put Buddy out of her mind, she breathed in the relaxing scent, but couldn't help remembering those horrific days when all she had was a sink to cleanse herself.

Her less than peaceful thoughts were interrupted by a gentle knock on the door. Out of a kindness she wasn't really feeling, she told Kevin to come in. Her husband appeared carrying one of their fine china tea cups.

"I thought you might like a cup of chamomile."

Robin's heart was instantly warmed by the tea, but even more by her husband's thoughtfulness. It felt good to be loved.

***

The next morning Robin arrived at RMH at ten o'clock sharp for her appointment with Sarah. It took no time at all for her therapist to notice her extreme level of agitation. Though she tried to breathe evenly and held her folded hands tightly in her lap, she couldn't stop shaking.

"What's been going on since our last session?"

Robin told Sarah the events of the previous day, up to and including her reaction to Kevin insinuating he knew how she felt. As the words tumbled out, she could feel herself losing control.

When the tears finally began to flow, Sarah was ready with the tissues, but she hadn't yet said a word. She sat across from her client so quietly that Robin began to wonder why she was here. Did this woman even care? Yet when she finally looked up and made eye contact, she saw the answer to her question. In those eyes she saw understanding and compassion.

And when Sarah finally spoke, her voice was as soothing as a mother's caress. "That sounds like an overwhelming kind of day, Robin, but you got through it, didn't you?"

Robin felt the words of encouragement. They lifted her up while they calmed her down.

"You're stronger than you think you are."

Robin nodded and sniffed. "If you say so, but I'm scared."

"Being scared doesn't mean you're weak." Sarah leaned back in her chair. "With all you've been through and knowing this man is around here somewhere, I'd be more worried about you if you weren't scared. Let's talk about what you can do to take control."

By the end of their fifty-minute session, Robin was feeling more in control. Still cautious, she scanned the parking lot before heading to her car. Though she refused to live in fear, she wasn't going to be reckless.

Chapter Fifteen

Mia parked near the entrance of the Sweet Glen Diner and checked the time. She hadn't wanted to be late meeting Robin for breakfast, so instead arrived ten minutes early. She was debating whether to wait in the car or go inside to warm up with a cup of tea when she saw her future sister-in-law wave to her through the front window.

Robin greeted her warmly and led her to a booth near the back. "Tea, right?"

Mia nodded as she slid into the booth and slipped her arms out of her coat, pulling it back over her shoulders.

"Do you think it's too cold in here?" Robin asked with concern.

"Not at all, but it certainly is brisk outside this morning. This was a great idea, Robin. So, how are you?"

Robin laughed nervously. "Okay, I guess. Did Ron tell you about Buddy being here in Madison?"

Of course he had, and now Mia thought it had been foolish of her to ask the poor woman how she was doing. When she explained that Ron had told her about all the events of the last few days and apologized for being insensitive, Robin assured her she didn't take it that way at all.

"I appreciate you asking... really. Do you know what you'd like to eat?" she said pointing to the menu. "The blueberry pancakes are delicious."

After placing their order, they turned the conversation to the wedding and plans for the future.

Robin asked where they'd be living, and Mia felt the smile thoughts of her future with Ron always brought. "We plan to start looking for a place after Thanksgiving. I know that only gives us a little over two months before the wedding, but we can always stay at his apartment if we haven't found anything by then."

“You’re not moving out of the area, are you?”

Mia rushed to assure her they had no such plans. “With both of us working in Madison, we hope to find something right here in Sweet Glen.”

“Oh, that’s wonderful! I’m so glad.” Robin thanked their waitress for the food placed in front of them, and they both dug in to pancakes covered in whipped cream.

“You weren’t kidding,” Mia said. “This is so good, especially on a weekday morning. What a treat.”

The conversation wandered through different topics, eventually hitting on Mia’s work at RMH. “I think it’s amazing that you can use art to help people the way you do, and you’re so talented.” Robin glanced at the painting of the diner Mia had gifted her which now hung on the wall near the register. “I wish I had your talent.”

“Have you ever tried drawing or painting?”

Mia listened with fascination when Robin shyly explained how she had spent countless hours drawing while being held captive and that it had been the only escape from her terrible reality.

“I’d love to see something you’ve done.” Mia was sincere in her desire.

“If you promise not to laugh...” Robin pointed to the wall right above where they sat, and Mia saw a lovely picture of an eagle soaring in an azure sky. She saw no reason to laugh. It was actually quite good. “I put it way back here because I know it can’t compare to anything a real artist does.”

“Stop it! Robin, this is enchanting.” Her future sister-in-law looked like she was about to object, but Mia didn’t allow it. “I’m not kidding. It’s hard to believe you’re self-taught. You have natural talent.”

The time flew by as the two women grew more comfortable with each other, and when Mia left the diner, she finally believed she and Robin would become good friends.

***

Mia shuddered at the result of her latest creation. When she got home from work, she'd grabbed a quick dinner—Julie's critique group was meeting a day early so she had already eaten—and curled up on the couch with Simmie and a copy of *Rebecca*. As much as she wanted to read the book Julie had recommended and couldn't believe Mia had never read, Mia couldn't focus. Following a vaguely familiar urge, she gave up and headed down to her studio to relax at the easel. There had been no itch, no sense of urgency, simply a bit of an inclination. She had never expected to paint the alarming scene she was now staring at.

Mia recognized it as the north side of her favorite lake, but it was not the serene image she would have predicted. The water was dark with a beautiful reflection of moonlight, but through the darkness, near the bottom right of the panorama, there was a body.

It was somewhat blurred—not clear enough to make out any features—but she could tell it was a man, and from the pose, Mia didn't believe he was sleeping. This was a dead body.

"Ron, I think somebody, a man, is hurt... or dead... at the lake," she said into the phone.

"What? Why are you at the lake? Where did you see him?"

"No, Ron, I'm not at the lake. I didn't see him there. I drew him."

Ron had learned not to ignore Mia's drawings. Twenty minutes later he was at her door picking up Mia and the picture, and ten minutes after that they were at the spot where Mia was sure they would find the body.

Ron and Jason, who met them there, searched the area but found nothing.

"I don't understand." Mia could only shake her head in disbelief. "He, I mean it, the body, it should be there." She looked at her colored pencil drawing and back at the scene. Then she looked at the questioning expression on Det. Jason Evans's face. But when she looked at Ron, she was relieved to see him still looking around and scratching his head. He didn't give up easily and she knew he had complete faith in her.

He called for a complete search party including a cadaver dog, but to no avail. The dog, who was known to do an excellent job, found nothing. There was no dead body.

Although Ron, and even Jason, said they didn't blame her for the wild goose chase, Mia was humiliated and confused. *Why did I draw that?*

Lying in bed hours later she wanted to pray, but she was at a loss. Never before had her impulse to draw something—something that seemed to come from her higher power—resulted in such a mystifying ending. *Now I can't even trust my gift.*

Chapter Sixteen

"What do you think, Julie?" Mia slid the paper across the table for her sister to examine. "Which one looks better to you?"

"You're hilarious," Julie said when she finished laughing. The page simply had three signatures.

1. *Mia Nicole Bishop*
2. *Mia Reed Bishop*
3. *Mia Nicole Reed Bishop*

"C'mon Jules, help me out here. This is an important decision." Mia retrieved the piece of paper. "I'm going to have to live with this name for the rest of my life."

"Okay, you'll always be Mia Nicole, but for your actual signature I personally don't think you want all four names. You'll get writer's cramp just signing checks. I'd go with the second one."

"Yeah?"

"Yeah, I like Mia Reed Bishop, and nobody pays much attention to middle names anyway. It suits you. Hey, what's Ron's middle name anyway?"

"Orion. He said his mother loved that constellation in the winter sky, and she liked the idea of his initials spelling ROB." When Julie stopped giggling, Mia added, "His sister's given name was Robin Oriana Bishop... so also ROB. I looked it up, and Oriana means sunrise." Mia smiled thinking it was a beautiful choice.

"Oh, I like that. That's so pretty." Julie carried her supper dishes into the kitchen and called over her shoulder, "What time is lover boy supposed to get here?"

"Not 'til eight. Apparently, he and Jason are working on a case and were going to order dinner in. He said something about having to run an errand after." Carrying her own dishes to put in the dishwasher, Mia added, "But what about professionally?"

"What about what, professionally?"

"My name. I mean, at work with my clients. Should I stay *Mia Reed* at the center, or do you think my clients will be comfortable with me changing my name?"

"Good grief, woman, you need to chill. Don't they call you Mia anyway? So, what are they going to care if your last name is different?"

Julie was right, of course. It wasn't that important, but Mia chose to think about the details of her future rather than dwell on her bewilderment of the previous night or the sadness of her Uncle Joe's funeral earlier in the day. She was choosing to think happy thoughts.

"Of course, you're right. I'm being silly. Mia Reed Bishop it is." Mia loved the sound of it and could hardly wait for February fourteenth to walk down the aisle and take the name of the man she loved.

She also could hardly wait for Ron to arrive that night. It seemed like she had barely spent any time with him since the weekend.

"I think Ron and I will hang out in the den tonight, so we don't bore you to death with our wedding planning." They had converted the small room off Mia's art studio into a cozy den for when either of them wanted complete privacy. It had no windows, but Mia painted a gorgeous outdoor scene, resembling the southern end of their very own nearby lake, that gave the feel of looking out. There was a small TV, seldom used, and everything was decorated in shades of autumn, a real contrast to the beachie colors they'd used upstairs.

"Actually, I'm planning to be up in my bedroom, so you won't bother me."

"But it feels like we're always chasing you upstairs. That's not fair."

"You're not chasing me, honestly." Julie grabbed a water out of the fridge. "I have a Skype call scheduled with my agent at seven-thirty, a synopsis I want to finish, and that new book by my author friend in Pittsburgh I'm dying to start reading tonight."

Mia knew Julie didn't mind spending time in her huge second-floor master bedroom. It was big enough for her computer desk as well as the little sitting area where she'd put the comfy pink chair she'd brought from her old apartment over the coffeeshop.

"Okay, if you're sure." Mia checked the time. "Ron probably won't be here for at least half an hour, but it's almost time for your call."

"Oh shoot, I'd better get set up."

Julie hurried upstairs and Mia spent the next half hour alternating between doodling and pacing back and forth to the window. One of her doodles reminded her of the sketch she'd done the night before but without a dead body. She quickly crumpled up the paper and tossed it in the trash before checking for her fiancé again.

When she finally saw Ron pull in, her spirits lifted. She put all thoughts of that drawing aside and rushed to meet him at the door.

Ron drew her close with one arm, and after the long, passionate kiss Mia had been waiting for, she looked into her favorite blue eyes. "So, what was this mysterious errand you had to run?"

"First I have a question for you. Do you think the center and your clients can manage without you for a two-week honeymoon instead of the one week we'd planned?"

They had talked about a week in Hawaii, but two weeks sounded pretty good to Mia. "Hmm, well since I have an in with the owner, I think I might be able to swing it. Are you thinking two whole weeks in paradise?"

"I'm not thinking about it. I've arranged it." Ron pulled an envelope from behind his back and held it up.

Grinning from ear to ear, Mia seized the envelope, hurried to the table with Ron right behind her, and pulled out the contents.

He had been thorough, and it was all there. Two round-trip tickets, hotel reservations, and even several side trips. "What? The Hilton Hawaiian Village? Seriously?" Mia threw her arms around her fiancé and kissed him in a way that showed her appreciation.

"Yes, my dear, since neither of us has ever been to Hawaii, I thought it would be great to start there. Oahu's Waikiki beach is all my parents talked about from their own honeymoon, and since you mentioned Maui, two weeks gives us some time for island hopping."

"This is going to be amazing." Mia could barely contain her excitement. "I don't know how I can stand to wait nearly three more months. Oh, and look." Mia opened the wedding plan notebook she'd started almost immediately after Ron's proposal. "I thought we could check these catering places out Saturday."

"Sounds good. I'm all yours."

Mia was about to show him the pictures of various flowers she thought would be perfect for a February wedding, when his cell phone vibrated. The call didn't take long, and Mia could tell from the deepening crease between his brows that it wasn't good news.

"I'm sorry, sweetheart. You're not going to believe this, but some guys were screwing around down by the north end of the lake and found a body." Getting to his feet, Ron scrolled through his phone to the picture Mia had drawn the night before. He dropped the phone back in his pocket, the look on his face evidence of his bewilderment. "I've got to go."

Mia stood stunned, watching him go out the front door. It was moments later when she wondered if she should have gone with him, but Ron had the picture. She wondered if the body would be as she'd seen it, and fought back a feeling of nausea.

"Don't mind me. I'm just grabbing another water." Julie bounded down the steps. "Where's your beau?"

"He had to go." Mia fell into the easy chair by the front window.

"Already? How come?"

"He got a call about a homicide."

Mia looked up at her sister who blanched. Ever since she had nearly become a victim of a serial killer, the word homicide had a different impact. Julie sat across from her. “Any details?”

“No, but the body was found somewhere by the lake.” They sat in somber silence until Mia’s phone binged. She checked the image Ron had texted, gasped, and turned the phone for Julie to see.

“Holy macaroni, sis. That looks just like what you drew.”

Mia nodded. Her mind was spinning. Nothing quite like this had ever happened before.

“All right, this is downright spooky.” Julie moved to sit on the arm of her sister’s chair. “Are you okay? You look a little pale.”

“Am I okay? I don’t know. I don’t understand. What good is it to draw something like this? It doesn’t make sense. I mean how does this help anything?”

Mia looked at her phone when it binged again. It was another text from Ron.

> Sorry I had to rush off. Don’t think this one’s a homicide. Looks like an overdose.

Chapter Seventeen

Since Robin's recent therapy session with Sarah Reed, memories she'd tried so hard to forget were now as vivid as if they'd happened yesterday. She could feel that basement's dark gray walls and the sense of hopelessness closing in on her. She found herself reliving the constant torment she'd endured for six long years at the hands of the two men who had killed her parents. Now, all these years later, she knew they'd lied about killing her brother, but not her parents. She could still see their bodies... their blood.

She shook off that haunting memory and tried to focus on what she needed to remember, but no matter how hard she tried, Robin couldn't remember the name of the town where she'd been held captive. She finally gave up, realizing she may never have actually seen or heard it. It's not like she got out much. The only time she saw the outside of that house was when Charlie decided to put her to work cooking, cleaning, and—after the first year—getting groceries... with Buddy as her armed chaperone.

She was thrilled to actually get outside every couple of weeks, even if it was only to the store, and for a long time she hoped someone would see she needed help... would recognize her and call the police.

But that never happened, and eventually Robin knew her only hope was to find her own way out.

Now, more than ten years after her daring escape, she was finally ready to take the next step. Although she had managed to break away physically, they still had a hold on her. She was still afraid. Still looking over her shoulder... especially since she had spotted Buddy right here in the town where she lived with her husband and young son.

Robin could never be sure that changing her name and color and style of her hair would be enough to keep them from finding her. It was time to remove the fear by locating them and putting an end to their miserable existence. And now she had a detective to help her get it done.

So, when Robin's therapist, Sarah, had suggested using hypnosis to help her remember details of her captivity, although she'd resisted at first, she finally agreed. During her session Tuesday she hadn't remembered too many details, but each day since, memories kept flooding in... especially at night when all the busyness of the day was done, three-year-old Ronnie was asleep in his bed, and she and Kevin had their quiet time together before their own bedtime.

This time, however, it was the middle of the day on Friday afternoon when Robin pulled into the little grocery store parking lot a few miles from home. She enjoyed getting away from the big chain stores and picking up some special items at Doc's Deli and groceries, and she liked supporting local small businesses.

Robin grabbed her list and hopped out of the car, but when she looked in the direction of Doc's, she saw something else. Right before her eyes, as real as if she'd stepped back in time, was a different place. She saw the large, scripted name over the front door—Dottie's.

Falling back against her car, Robin struggled to catch her breath. When she looked up again, she was staring at Doc's, but she didn't go in. She got back in the car, took her phone out of her purse, and called her brother.

"I remember the name of the little store near their house, Ron. It was Dottie's." She tried to control the shakiness of her voice.

"Are you okay?"

"Yes, I think so. It was just so weird the way I remembered. I actually saw it, Ron. Is that going to help?"

"Absolutely. Now that we know it's a small town in the eastern part of Ohio, it's a long shot, but the name of the store could be just the detail that will help us find it. If we do locate that store, do you think you could find the house from there?"

Robin thought of that house—that prison—and began to hyperventilate.

"Robin, are you there?"

"Yes, yes. Give me a minute." She closed her eyes and tried to slow her breathing.

"Where are you? Do you want me to meet you?"

"No, I'm all right. Or at least I will be. To answer your question about finding the house, I'm not sure, but I think I could find it."

"Maybe I'm asking too much."

"No! It's not too much. It's something I have to do. Ron, it's not only what they did to me. They killed Mom and Dad." Her voice caught on the last word. She had loved her daddy more than anyone in the world. He was such a good man. Such a perfect dad. And they took him away. "Ronnie, you were right. They have to pay."

Ron promised to call her later so they could make a plan. In the meantime, Robin went into Doc's. She still needed to get the rest of her ingredients for a fresh salad for dinner and a box of mac and cheese. Little Ronnie wouldn't want any part of the stir-fry shrimp she was making for Kevin and herself, and she didn't mind occasionally making something special for him. The toddler loved his mac and cheese, and that along with some grape tomatoes would suit him fine.

Once inside the store, Robin grabbed her produce and what she needed for her little boy then headed for the registers. On her way she passed a uniformed police officer, triggering another memory of a policeman who didn't take notice of the scruffy looking waif she'd been back at Dottie's. This time the officer smiled and nodded in her direction. He had a good smile, and Robin couldn't help wondering if he would have seen her. If he would have come to her rescue.

But none of that mattered anymore. Robin/Rachel Long didn't need to be rescued. She refused to ever be a victim again. *I am a survivor.*

Chapter Eighteen

Finding Dottie's Grocery had turned out to be a lot easier than Ron imagined. He found Dot's Market in Kettering, Dottie's Detour in Atwater, and Dottie's Corner Store in the little town of Easterberg, about an hour west of the Pennsylvania border. Bingo! A quick call to Robin confirmed his hunch. She remembered that below the big letters spelling out "Dottie's" were the two smaller words, "Corner Store."

He feared getting his sister's hopes up, but he was certain they were going to find the store, find the house, and find the scum he'd dreamed of locking away since the night they'd invaded his home and destroyed his life.

And now he felt almost guilty believing they'd destroyed his life. The loss he'd felt couldn't begin to compare to what Robin had been through. Thinking about her ordeal made his hatred grow into a rage that threatened to consume him.

He decided to stop by her house when he left the station to see for himself that his sister was all right. Kevin answered the door, and Ron heard the familiar sound of little feet running across the floor.

"Unca Wonnie," his nephew squealed.

"Hey, little buddy," he said swinging the toddler up into his arms. Robin stood on the other side of the room with a strange look on her face. "What's wrong, sis?"

"Nothing... it's just, we don't call him Buddy."

Holy shit! "Hey, I'm sorry. I didn't think—"

"No, it's not your fault." Ron saw Robin struggling to control her emotions, putting a crooked smile on her face. He also noticed Ronnie had suddenly gotten very quiet and was looking at his momma.

"Down," he said wiggling to get free, and as soon as his little feet met the floor he went running to his mother and wrapped his tiny arms around her neck.

"Looks like this guy knows when his mother needs comforting," Ron said sheepishly. The child may have no idea why the name Buddy upset his mother, but he felt her hurt.

"Yeah, it's pretty remarkable." Kevin took his jacket and nodded toward his little boy. "He seems to have a sixth sense. It's like he wants to take care of her... so do I."

"But I don't want my little boy to worry about his momma. Mommy's fine, Ronnie," she said giving him a little squeeze. "Why don't you go get your new fire engine to show Unca Wonnie?"

The toddler didn't have to be asked twice. He took off for the playroom like a shot.

"Can you join us for dinner? We're having shrimp stir-fry and there's plenty. Ronnie's having macaroni and cheese because he doesn't like shrimp... or stir-fry. Maybe he'd be willing to share."

"Thanks, but no. I'm heading over to pick Mia up for dinner when I leave here. I just stopped by to see how you're doing and to ask if you're up for a road trip to Ohio tomorrow."

He saw his sister stiffen, but she agreed.

It was Kevin who didn't seem so sure. He was by her side in an instant circling her with his arm. "Are you sure you're ready for this, sweet cheeks?"

Robin nodded.

"I'm going with you," he said looking at Ron.

And Ron was about to agree, but Robin wouldn't hear of it.

"No!" she said. "I've got this."

Ron was sure Kevin would object, and he couldn't blame him, but Ronnie charged in with his fire truck and Robin gave them both a good reason for Kevin to stay home. "I need you to stay here with Ronnie. It's going to be a long day, and I really don't want to leave him with a sitter that many hours."

Kevin grudgingly agreed and Ron assured him he would take good care of his wife.

"I appreciate you two fighting over who's going to protect me, but I'm not that fragile, honestly. I don't need anyone to 'take care' of me."

Ron heard her and appreciated her courage and resolve, so he tried to hide his look of uncertainty, yet seeing her raised eyebrows he realized she saw it. "Sorry, sis, but I am your older brother after all."

He was relieved to hear her laugh at his old tease and delighted by the way his three-year-old nephew giggled with her. Seconds later the toddler's contagious laughter had them all joining in.

Ron hated to tear himself away, but he didn't want to disappoint Mia by being late, especially since he was going to have to break their date with the caterers tomorrow.

***

When Mia opened the door to greet him, Ron was amazed how she could still take his breath away with her smile. He loved the dimple that suddenly appeared and how her eyes crinkled with merriment. Not anxious to change that smile to a frown, he decided his news about driving to Ohio with his sister could wait until later.

Mia held up the Moscato she planned to take along. "I have a bottle of white, but would you like me to grab a red for you?"

"No, the white is good." Ron usually preferred a red wine but took an occasional step into the lighter grape. "Are you ready to go?" They were headed for one of Mia's favorite restaurants, The Moonlight Café, and having her favorite wine. Ron hoped all this would play in his favor. At least she would be in a good mood.

It wasn't until they had enjoyed the crab dip appetizer, another of Mia's favorites, and were digging into their entrees that Mia forced him into breaking the news.

"We're meeting with the caterer at eleven in the morning, so I doubt we'll need lunch after sampling all the goodies."

"About that..." Ron saw Mia stop midair with her forkful of chicken marsala. This wasn't going to be easy. "I'm afraid I'm not going to be able to make it tomorrow."

The marsala didn't make it to Mia's mouth. She put the fork back on her plate, wiped her mouth with her napkin and stared at him in disbelief. "Why not?"

"We have a lead on finding Robin's kidnappers... the men who murdered our parents." He watched his fiancée's face for understanding, but she seemed to be struggling.

"And you have to follow that lead at eleven o'clock on Saturday morning? You can't wait until maybe two?"

"I'm sorry, but it's actually going to take pretty much all day." Ron watched Mia put down her napkin and drop her hands into her lap. As much as he wanted to dig back into his lasagna, he didn't dare. "Look, Robin remembered the name of the grocery store where they used to go, and I tracked it down. We know the name of the town now, and she thinks once we locate the store, she might be able to find their house."

"That's... that's really good." Mia picked up her fork. "I'm glad." She pushed the food around her plate.

"It is, Mia. It really is." He could see her softening, but all the joy seemed to have drained out of her. "Maybe Julie could go with you tomorrow." That didn't have the desired effect. "Honestly, I don't need to be there. I trust your judgment, so whatever you decide. It's just food." He was doing all right until the last statement. Now he was looking into glassy eyes that threatened to overflow.

"But it's not *just food*. It's for our wedding."

"I'm sorry." Ron knew it sounded lame, but it was all he had.

Mia took a deep breath. "No, I'm the one who should apologize. Picking out food certainly isn't as important as finding murderers." She gave him a little smile that looked like it took some effort. "Besides, Julie's my maid of honor *and* she loves to eat. I'm sure she'll go."

"Thank you, sweetheart. I love you." He had never meant it more, and he felt blessed when she smiled back and said what he needed to hear.

"I know." She smiled. "And I love you."

Chapter Nineteen

"Are you all right?"

"Yes, Julie. I told you I'm fine." It was the third time her sister had asked, and Mia was getting tired of the question. "Why wouldn't I be all right? I'm planning my wedding, and I can't wait to be Mrs. Mia Reed Bishop." She knew it was true, she should be walking on air.

"True, but you'd rather be planning it with him, not me."

"Hey, you might be my second choice, but I love having you come with me, and I appreciate you... really. Now stop asking me if I'm okay and get ready to taste."

They arrived shortly before eleven, and Sarah was already there waiting for them by her car. "I'm so glad you included me, sweetie." She hugged each of her daughters and they all headed inside. "So, what's going on with Ron that he couldn't be here?"

"He had to go out of town. It was extremely important, or he would have been here for sure. I'll fill you in on the details later."

The three Reed women thoroughly enjoyed all the food and said what they liked best while leaving the final decisions to the bride-to-be.

"Oh my gosh, I can't decide between all these appetizers. I wish Ron was here to help." She regretted saying it as soon as the words were out of her mouth.

Julie bit her lower lip, and Sarah looked concerned.

"You never did tell me what was so important that it couldn't wait until Monday." Sarah put her fork down and waited.

"It's about Robin." Mia sighed. "No, I'm not being fair. It's not just Robin. The people those men killed were both their parents. And now, after all these years, he might finally catch them." She explained the latest developments, and she watched Sarah's expression wondering what was going on with her.

"That would certainly be a huge relief for Robin."

It took Mia a moment before she realized why her mother had that reaction. "Oh, that's right. I had forgotten. She's your client!"

"Shh, Let's change the subject, shall we? Or tell us more about this new lead."

Mia filled them in on where Ron and Robin were going and what—or who—they hoped to find when they got there.

With choices for the appetizers, like baby lobster rolls and a fruit and cheese spread, entrees like beef wellington, chicken topped with crabmeat, and a pasta dish, sides galore, and a spread of tasty dessert treats, Mia wondered if she had gone overboard, but Sarah chided her for worrying about the cost.

"Don't be silly, sweetie. With the wedding at church and since you decided to have the reception in the fellowship hall, we didn't have an expensive venue to worry about, and besides, I want to make this day perfect for you."

"Yeah, but what about Dad? What is he going to think when he sees the bill for all this?"

Sarah laughed. "Don't you worry about your dad. You're his little girl, and he's certainly not going to cheap out on you."

"Yes, but don't forget, you've got two other daughters' weddings to worry about one of these days." Mia looked at her sister. "Right, Jules?"

"Sure, one of these days... maybe."

"Speaking of which, how is Dr. Curtain?"

"He's fine. Actually, he's really fine." Julie winked, and pulled out her phone. "As a matter of fact, he's coming by tonight, sis. Do you have any plans?"

"Is that your way of asking me to make myself scarce?"

"No, not at all. I think we'll probably watch a movie in the den. You can join us if you want."

Mia doubted very much if that was what her sister really wanted. "No, thanks. I don't want to be a hindrance to this blossoming relationship. Oh, look who's blushing now!" Mia and Sarah laughed at Julie's denial.

"Holy macaroni, I take it back. You're not invited to join us… well, yeah, you are… but only if you promise to behave."

"Thanks Jules, but Ron said he'd call if they got back early enough, and no offense, but given a choice between spending time with you or him, I choose Ron."

After they finished up, finalized all the choices, and signed the contract, Sarah checked her phone and discovered she'd gotten a text from Cody. "Oh no."

"What is it?" Mia asked.

"It's your brother, Cody. You know that body they found out by the lake the other night?" When Mia and Julie both nodded, Sarah told them, "It was his friend, Matt… Matt Markle." Cody and Matt had been friends since grade school. Sarah shook her head in disbelief. "Cody said he never knew him to use drugs, but he died of an overdose of pain killers. Excuse me a minute. I'd better give him a call."

For the few moments Sarah was gone, Mia found herself wondering about that picture she'd drawn the night before Matt's body was found… wondering if she had missed something, if somehow, she could have stopped it from happening.

Sarah returned shaking her head in disbelief as she took her seat.

Julie reached over for her mother's hand. "Is Cody okay?"

"I guess, but he was pretty shaken. Cody and Matt were such good friends, and Matt had confided in him that the sarcoma in his leg had come back. The doctor told Matt they would have to amputate his leg."

"Oh, how awful." Mia was horrified and couldn't imagine how such devastating news would affect him, but she wished she could have somehow prevented the suicide.

Sarah took a deep breath. "Cody said Matt was seeing a psychiatrist, and maybe he could have gotten through that somehow, but then his girlfriend said she couldn't handle it."

"Oh my God," Julie said. "Do you mean she broke up with him and left him to handle all that on his own?"

Sarah nodded.

"Well, I hope she can live with herself now."

The joy of the day evaporated, and Mia was reminded of something her client, Adam, told her he'd learned from his first therapist. *Suicide is the thief of all hope.*

Chapter Twenty

The long drive to Ohio had given the twins plenty of time to talk. They reminisced about childhood memories—mostly the good ones—their present lives, and much of what had gone on in between. Robin had already told Ron all she was willing to share about the worst six years of her life and the main highlights of the twists and turns her life had taken since, but she didn't know much about his life during those fifteen years—all those years she thought he was dead. Even now she could hardly believe he was alive and sitting next to her as they covered the miles back to a past she'd never wanted to revisit.

"You never mentioned how you and Mia met."

Ron told her the story of Claire Alessi's murder and how Mia's drawings had helped solve the case. He shared how he and Mia wound up in a room with the murderer and his enormous relief that nothing happened to the woman with whom he was falling in love. "And as they say, the rest is history."

"But how in the world did you wind up in the Madison area?"

"What can I say? When the woman you love buys a house and moves to Sweet Glen, what choice did I have? It was either move here or spend half my life on the commute." With a sidelong glance he added, "Besides, I didn't believe for a minute that the therapist at Mia's Center and your waitress had both jumped to their death. It didn't add up."

They crossed the state line. Robin read the sign, "Welcome to Ohio," and her breath caught.

"Hey, it's okay, little sister. You're not alone."

Robin smiled and hoped her appreciation showed. "So can you tell me more about the way she draws stuff... the way she did my picture?"

"The way I understand it is, the first time Mia or anyone else realized she had this gift was when she was about fourteen. Mia told me she was pretty gullible. This guy she'd gotten to know online said he was going to take her and her art to meet some big shot agent. So, she went with him. It turned out it was all a lie. Instead of taking her to see this agent, he kidnapped—"

"What?" Robin had no idea and was shocked to think Mia had been through the same ordeal.

"Yeah, it must have been terrifying for a fourteen-year-old... Jeeze, Robin, I'm sorry."

"It's okay. Keep going. What happened?"

"It's important to understand it was nothing like what happened to you. I mean apparently the guy wasn't wrapped too tight, and he was trying to hurt Mia's mom by kidnapping her kid." Ron took his eyes off the road long enough to look at his sister. "This man took her to a cabin up in the mountains and locked her in a cage. Are you all right?"

"Yes, but oh God, in a cage?"

"Yeah, some kind of big dog crate. But I guess she was pretty lucky. He didn't do anything else to her. I mean she said she was definitely traumatized, but at least it only lasted a few days. Nothing like what you went through."

"But how did she get away?" Robin had often wondered if there wasn't something more she could have done to escape from her captors.

"That's the crazy part. She had done a drawing of a cabin, and this little kid, her name was Betsy, had a dream about that very same cabin and that Mia was in danger. So, when Betsy saw the picture of the cabin on Valerie Reed's wall—Val is Mia's grandmother—she kind of freaked and told them about her dream."

Robin listened, trying to follow but finding the story hard to believe.

"There was some other stuff—I don't remember all the details—but something about one of Sarah's clients being this crazy guy's ex, and she got involved, recognized the cabin, and was able to lead the police there. As a matter of fact, my partner, Jason, was one of the detectives. He said it was the craziest case he ever had."

The GPS broke in, taking them off the highway, and Ron said, "It shouldn't take long now. How are you doing? Still okay?"

"Yeah," she answered in barely more than a whisper.

Ten minutes later the voice of the GPS said, "You have arrived at your destination."

Robin stared at the sign. Nothing had changed. She looked to the right and saw the furniture store. "This is it."

"Okay, do you remember how you got back to the house from here?"

"I know we turned right off the parking lot."

Ron steered the car in the direction she said.

Robin was hypervigilant and after a few miles she saw a familiar landmark. "That's where they stopped to get beer. I don't think it's much farther."

They rode in silence for a couple more miles.

"There, at that gas station, turn right again." It all came back. It was like she'd been on this ride just yesterday, not nine years ago. She directed him through several more turns then finally whispered, "This is the street. It's right down there past the red barn."

They passed the barn and the wide empty expanse leading to an overgrown yard that looked like it hadn't had any attention in years. Sitting back from the road, there it was. Her old prison.

"Wait here." Ron hopped out pushed the button to lock the car doors.

Robin watched as he cautiously approached the run-down house. She saw him put his hand on his revolver as he banged on the door. Nothing happened. Charlie didn't come out. Ron banged on it again then walked around and peered in the windows.

When he returned to the car, he told her there was no sign of life, but he wanted to check with the neighbors and see if they knew anything.

"I doubt it. I was here all that time, and they never saw me. Never helped me." Robin could taste the bitterness as she spit out the words.

He checked with the neighbor up the road, and Robin recognized her as the same woman she'd seen so often hanging clothes on the line. This time she got out of the car in time to hear her say, "From what I can tell, nobody's been there for weeks."

"I guess that explains why it's so overgrown." Ron glanced back at the high grass.

"No, it was just as bad when they were there. Look at it. I called the city twice about that overgrown lawn, if you can even call it a lawn. It didn't make no difference."

"Ma'am, there were two men living there, right?"

"Yeah... and my name's Shirley. But actually, there was three of 'em. Two men and a girl."

"Do you remember me?" Robin asked thinking the woman was talking about her.

"No, should I?" The neighbor tilted her head and looked at her through squinted eyes.

"Robin, let me." Ron gave her a look that begged her not to interrupt his questioning. "Ma'am, I mean Shirley, can you tell me the last time you saw the girl?"

"I told you, a few weeks ago. I'm guessing it's been maybe three, maybe even a month. It's not my job to keep track of that trash. That's what they were, you know. Good riddance. I hope they never come back."

"But 'the girl' left a long time ago." Robin looked at her brother.

Shirley looked at Robin then Ron. "I don't know what this woman's talkin' about, but I'm telling you, all three of 'em was still living there until a little while back."

Robin turned and stumbled back to the car with Ron right on her heels. “Are you all right?”

“Ron, what is she talking about? Do you think they were holding another girl prisoner?”

“I don’t know, but I intend to find out. Let’s go have a talk with the local sheriff.”

The sheriff was able to give them three important facts. One, these two guys were known as bullies and thugs and their last name was Jenkins; two, Charlie Jenkins was in hospice care dying of lung cancer; three, Buddy Jenkins took off, just disappeared as soon as the old man’s cancer got really bad. Nobody had seen or heard from him since.

“What’s going on with the house where they lived?” Robin had an inexplicable urge to see it.

“Nothing that I know of. Technically I guess it’ll belong to Jenkins, the son, after the father passes, but it’s been sitting since the old man was taken out in an ambulance. As far as I’m concerned, the place looks like it ought to be bulldozed.”

On their way back to the car, Robin turned to her brother. “I need to see it. I need to see the inside of that house.” She could see by his frown that Ron had serious misgivings, but she didn’t care. “Ron, please...”

“Let me see what I can do. Wait in the car, okay?”

Robin nodded, got in, and locked the door.

The nearly twenty minutes it took for Ron to return felt like forever to her, but as he approached her, he gave a little smile and a nod.

Robin was simultaneously relieved and terrified.

When they got back to the house, Robin stepped through the threshold and stepped back in time. Making her way to the kitchen, she saw the same table and chairs where they’d eaten so many suppers, the same ratty and now filthy curtains she had looked through a million times while doing their dishes and searching for freedom. She looked at the gas stove she’d wiped clean each night now covered with so much grease and grime it turned her stomach. The counters even showed evidence rodents had taken up residence in the Jenkins' absence.

"My God, the smell is atrocious, Robin. Are you ready to get out of here?"

Robin's head jerked up, and she looked at her brother who she'd nearly forgotten was there. "Not yet." She let her gaze go toward the door that led from the kitchen to the basement. "I need to see the basement."

"Are you sure?"

Robin nodded. She'd never been more sure or more insecure in a decision.

"Be careful... Wait, I have a flashlight in the car. Let me go get it."

"Okay." It was obvious the utility bill hadn't been paid, and with no electricity the stairs were even darker than she remembered, but she put one foot in front of the other and was on the bottom step by the time Ron returned.

He hurried down the steps and flooded the room with light.

"Turn it off. Ron, turn it off."

He did as she asked.

Robin was mesmerized as she looked at the gray walls and floor lit only by the little bit of light coming through the tiny window near the ceiling. She couldn't move as she looked at the bed, still there as though nothing had been touched since the day she managed to escape. But upon closer examination, she realized someone else had been there.

"Turn it back on, Ron." With the bright light shining on the bed, she extended her hand toward an article of clothing.

"Stop!"

Robin was startled and jumped back.

"I told the sheriff we wouldn't touch anything. That could be evidence. And if there is another girl in trouble, that evidence might help us to find her."

"Ron, if they have another girl... if they've hurt someone else, it's my fault."

"No, no it's not. None of this is anybody's fault but the two murdering bastards that held you here."

Robin knew what he was saying, yet if she had gone to the police instead of just running away... if she had done something to stop them, then they couldn't have hurt anyone else. "Ronnie, I need to know. I need to know if Buddy has... I mean if there is a girl being held. You've seen this place now. And I know what it was like to be their prisoner. I know what Buddy Jenkins was like. How cruel, especially if his father wasn't around."

"Don't worry, sis, we're going to get him. But we don't even know for sure he had a girl or woman. We've just got the neighbor's word."

"But I need to know. We need to find out." Robin waited while her brother got the sheriff on the phone, jotted down a number, then called to arrange a visit with Charlie Jenkins.

"Are you sure you're up for this?" Ron's question caused her to pause, but she simply had to find out, and this was the quickest and best way to do that.

"I'm sure."

When they arrived at the hospice house, they were told Charlie was very near the end and heavily medicated for the pain.

"Are you a relative?" the woman who let them in had asked.

"No!" Robin's skin crawled at the very idea.

Ron showed the caretaker his ID and said they wouldn't be long. He just had one question to ask Jenkins.

"All right, but I'm not sure how coherent he'll be. Like I said, he's sedated to deal with the pain."

When they were alone in the room with the patient, Ron shook his head in disgust. "He doesn't deserve to have anyone ease his pain."

Robin stared at the frail man lying in the hospital bed, ugly memories rushing back. His breathing was labored and raspy.

"Hey, Jenkins. Charlie, can you hear me?"

Charlie opened his eyes a crack and gave an almost imperceptible nod. “Something for the pain?” It was barely more than a whisper.

“No, Charlie. Nothing for the pain. Where’s your son?” There was no response. “Charlie, where’s Buddy?” Charlie opened his eyes a bit wider in an attempt to look around for his son. “No, Charlie. Buddy isn’t here. Do you know where I can find him?”

“Little prick,” he muttered. “Took... off... took her... with–” Charlie coughed, gasped for air, and collapsed back into the pillows. “Gone,” was all he said before closing his eyes.

“Is he?” Robin thought he might have died.

“No. He’s still breathing.”

“Who’s there?” the old man asked, opening his eyes with great effort. “Who is that? Vanessa, is that you?”

“No, Charlie. It’s me, Robin. Remember me?” She wanted to hurt him somehow, like he’d hurt her. Like he had destroyed her family and stolen her childhood. But he was beyond that. Charlie didn’t respond. Didn’t seem to recognize her... or care.

“Who is Vanessa, Charlie?” Ron asked.

“She’s gone.” There was another pause. “Buddy. Took. Her.”

He seemed to be finished talking but Robin had to try one more time. “Charlie, who is Vanessa? Where did Buddy take her?”

“She was mine...” Charlie gasped again, then he was gone.

As the caretaker rushed in, Ron and Robin stepped back out of the way, and when they knew Charlie would never be able to answer another question, they quietly left the room.

Seconds later, as they were about to exit the building, they heard a voice calling them back. “I know he has a son, but I don’t know how to get in touch with him or any other relatives. Do you have his contact information?”

“No, but if you find out anything, would you let me know?” Ron handed over his card and ushered his sister out of the building.

Robin had spent six years of her life living in this man's house. She wondered if she should feel sorry for him. If she should mourn his death. But she only had one thought. *May he burn in hell.*

Chapter Twenty-one

"Now what?" Robin fastened her seatbelt and Ron could see she was ready to get away from that town and all the ugly memories it held.

"Now your detective brother gets to work finding this Buddy Jenkins and having him face the consequences for everything he's done. I'm just sorry the other one's dead."

"Why?"

"Because he never paid for killing Mom and Dad or for what he did to you."

"You're right." Robin stared out the window then muttered, "But maybe he's paying now."

Ron wasn't sure how to respond. He wasn't even sure he believed in a heaven and hell. Unlike his fiancée whose faith seemed unshakeable, all his beliefs seemed to be in flux lately. If there really was a God and each of us had to go before him, then maybe Charlie Jenkins had left this world and gone before God's judgment. But Ron still wished he could exact his own justice on this disgusting excuse for a human being.

"So how do we find him?" Robin's question interrupted his thought. "Where do you even begin?"

"We have a name, we have a picture—not just the sketch artist's rendition, but the sheriff had a mug shot from one of his arrests for petty crime—and we know he's driving a red pickup. I'd say we have a lot to go on."

"So now will you put out one of those APBs like they do on TV?"

Ron laughed at the way she asked, but she had it right. "Actually, it's already done. There's nowhere for him to hide."

Whether it was the early morning start they'd gotten or the fact she hadn't been sleeping well, Ron could see his sister was fighting to keep her eyes open. "You look exhausted, Robbie. Why don't you close your eyes? Maybe you can catch a couple Zs."

When he glanced over at her, he saw a curious little smile. "I haven't heard that nickname in more than fifteen years."

Ron wasn't even sure why it had come out of his mouth, but seeing his sister's reaction and glassy eyes, he had to swallow the lump in his own throat.

When he was able to speak, he said, "Funny how easy it is to be that person again. I mean the one who teased his sister." He turned and gave her a wink. "Now close your eyes. Try to get some rest and I'll wake you when we get to a rest stop."

Ron was amazed when he heard a soft snoring within moments. His mind wandered as he rode along for the next fifteen or twenty miles, and eventually his thoughts went to where he had originally planned to be this Saturday. He looked over to check Robin again, and she was breathing deeply enough that he was pretty sure he could make a call without waking her.

Mia answered on the second ring. "Hey, you. How did it go?"

"Pretty good I guess, but I'll fill you in when we get back."

"Why are you whispering?"

"Sorry, but we're on the road, and Robin's sleeping. Can you hear me all right?" Mia told him she could. "Okay, I just wanted to check in with you. How did the tasting go?"

"It was great. Mom and Julie came along, and we had a good time... but I missed you."

"I'm sorry. You know I would have been there if—"

"I know. Don't worry about it. It's fine, and I think you'll approve of all the choices I made for us. It's going to be delicious."

"I think you're delicious." Ron could almost hear her smiling. "What are you up to now?"

"I'm at the house. Oh, and you know that guy you found at the lake? Turns out it was one of Cody's best friends. After hearing about that we all decided to head home."

Ron told Mia how sorry he was and wished he had been there to be more supportive. "Is Cody all right? Is there anything I can do?"

"No, he's pretty shaken, but Mom and Dad are there for him. I'm just hanging out trying to recuperate from eating too much, and I'm getting ready to head downstairs and relax with my sketch pad."

"Okay, well I'll give you a call as soon as I drop Robin off. Maybe we can go get some dinner. All right, love you... bye."

Seeing that his sister was still sleeping peacefully, Ron decided to place one more call to his partner. "Hey, yeah Jason. Sorry to bother you on a Saturday but thought you might want to know the latest." He briefly filled Det. Evans in on what they'd learned in Easterberg and that they were looking for one suspect in the cold case of his parents' murders. "Yeah, the other one is dead. Lung cancer, and I wouldn't say this about anyone else, but he suffered, and I'm not sorry."

Ron ended the call and twenty minutes later he pulled into a roadside diner. As soon as he cut off the engine, Robin's head popped up, and she appeared startled and disoriented.

"Hey sleepyhead, are you okay there?"

Robin looked around uncertainly. "Where are we?"

"We're still a couple hours from home, but I thought you might be hungry... and I know I am."

Once inside, Robin excused herself to use the restroom, and when she returned, she shook her head in utter disgust.

"It's places like this that give diners a bad name. That bathroom is filthy."

Ron laughed but agreed this diner didn't compare to the Sweet Glen when it came to cleanliness. And after one quick look, Robin also sent her utensils back.

"Do you want to go somewhere else?" Ron could see his sister's displeasure.

"No, this is fine. I mean it's not actually fine, but it will do for a quick bite to eat. It's just that if it were mine, I would make sure the staff shaped up."

Ron understood his sister's aggravation, but at least the waitress was friendly and provided them with excellent service. "Hey, look," Ron pointed to the dome-covered pie sitting on the counter. And he enjoyed the smile that lit her face. It was as if the last fifteen years had been erased and he saw the very same smile he'd seen on his sister's face every time their mom made lemon meringue pie.

"Yes please," she said.

Ron chuckled. "Some things never change."

Chapter Twenty-two

Mia was halfway down the stairs when the doorbell rang. "Who in the world could that be?" she asked the feline in her arms. Simmie didn't answer but jumped to the floor when she got back to the top of the steps.

"Betsy!" Mia looked beyond the younger girl for her mother. "It's so good to see you, but how did you get here?"

"I drove."

"No, that can't be possible. How could you possibly be old enough to drive already?" Mia embraced her snickering young friend. "How's your mom?"

"Great, but so busy. Between her job at the hospital and all the work she does with AA, she doesn't have much spare time, but that's good for her. And Dad's still busy with his practice, so you know..."

Betsy Walter's mother, Susan, was a recovering alcoholic herself who thought she'd lost her nursing career forever because of the bad choices she'd made years ago when she was drinking. But with a lot of hard work and staying clean and sober for ten years, she had won back the respect of everyone who knew her, even Mia's Grandma Val who had more reason to dislike her than most were aware.

"I need to give your dad a call. Now that I've moved back, I'm hoping he can be my dentist again. Do you know if he's taking new patients?"

"I don't know, but he'll make room for you. I'll see to that."

"Thank you, Bets, and by the way, you look amazing. I love your hair." Betsy's strawberry blonde hair had always been curly, but she had used a flatiron to get the neat pageboy style she was sporting today.

"It's my new 'adult' look. I just had my eighteenth birthday, you know."

"Oh, that can't be true. I go away to school, and you do all this growing up. Wow, you are all grown up, aren't you?"

"Indeed," Betsy said grinning. "So, Mom said you wanted to talk to me."

"I did, and I'm glad you came over, but you didn't have to."

"Oh, so you want me to leave?" Betsy turned like she was heading for the door.

"No, brat. Get back here. Gosh, I've missed you." Mia pulled her over to the sofa and they plopped down on either end, each with one leg tucked under them facing one another like a pair of bookends. "Not to be sappy, but you know how special you are to me, right?"

Betsy nodded. "Of course. Everybody knows that... I *am* special." Mia saw the mischievous grin she loved.

"Well, first of all, I wanted to let you know I'm getting married." After Betsy jumped to her end of the couch and nearly strangled her with a huge hug, Mia added, "and I wondered if you would be in my wedding?"

Betsy agreed and bounced up and down like the little girl Mia remembered.

After lots of wedding talk, Betsy asked if she could see some of Mia's recent artwork. "It's been so long since I've seen anything of yours." They were in Mia's studio when Julie came down followed by the groom.

"Look who pulled in right behind me," Julie said, then laying eyes on Betsy, she squealed, "Oh my gosh, I don't believe it. It's been ages! How are you?" When they finished their hugs and giggles, Betsy broke away and gave Ron a look up and down, then turned to Mia and raised her eyebrows. "And who is this?"

Mia put her arm through Ron's. "This is my fiancé, Detective Ron Bishop."

"Damn! Good job, Mia!"

"Betsy!" Mia felt the heat creeping up her neck and into her face, while Ron chuckled.

"Sorry, Mia, but you've got to admit, he's hot. Well, I guess I should go."

"You don't have to leave on my account." Ron winked at Mia.

"Yeah, I really should. Mom still isn't crazy about me driving at night. Even after a year she still thinks of me as a new driver, you know."

"You're driving? Holy macaroni! Now I feel old." Julie groaned.

"Thanks for letting me see your new stuff, Mia," Betsy said looking around again. She stopped when something caught her eye. "Hmm, you didn't show me that one. Who is that dude?"

"Oh, that's Dr. Block. He's the psychiatrist at the center."

"I don't like it. Sorry... bad vibes." Betsy shuddered. "Okay, gotta go, but thank you, Mia. I'm so excited. Let me know when you need me to go find my dress. This is so cool!"

Mia stared at the portrait of Dr. Block long after saying goodbye to Betsy and watching her and Julie head upstairs.

"What's wrong?" Ron asked.

"Oh, it's nothing really, but Betsy tends to have a sixth sense about things... never mind. How about that dinner you promised me?"

"You've got it. Shall we ask Julie to join us?"

"No, tonight I want you all to myself." She put her arms around his neck and pulled him down until his lips met hers. After a long, slow kiss, she said, "We'd better get going. I'm starving."

"I'm hungry too, but not for food," Ron said going back for seconds of what he really desired. When he finally released her, Ron asked, "Do you mind if we sit and relax for a few minutes before we head out?"

"Sure, come, sit." Mia finally noticed the deep lines in his forehead and his slightly bloodshot eyes. "You must be exhausted."

"A little tired, maybe. It's been a long day."

Without another word, Mia grabbed her phone and scrolled to a familiar, often used number in her favorites. "Yes, I'd like one order of General Tso's chicken, one order of steamed shrimp and broccoli, and two egg rolls." She gave her name and ended the call. "Now you sit tight and I'll go grab our dinner. It will be ready in fifteen minutes."

"You are an angel. But I'll come with you."

"Yes, I am, and no you won't. Oh crap, I don't know if Julie's eaten yet. I'd better check with her and see if she wants Chinese too." Mia hurried up the steps with Ron right on her heels.

"She must be up in her room." Mia shot her sister a text and got an immediate response, then called in the addition to her order and grabbed her keys and jacket.

"Before you go, I'm curious. Is the girl I met tonight the one you told me about? The one who had the dream that helped save you?"

"One and the same. We seem to have a special connection." Mia remembered how close they'd become when Betsy was only five or six years old. She had stayed with Mia's grandparents while her mother was incarcerated for driving under the influence and causing an accident that could have killed both her and her child. Mia had always felt a need to protect the little girl, and Betsy had adored her from the day they met. "She's like a little sister." And it was Betsy and her dream that helped rescue Mia when she had been a captive in a cage.

Chapter Twenty-three

Ron gave in to Mia's insistence that he stay there and wait while she picked up their Chinese food, and after a few minutes, he went back down to Mia's studio. There was one picture in particular he felt drawn to look at yet again.

The portrait she'd done of the psychiatrist was an excellent likeness—the very image of the peculiar man—but Ron's fascination derived from Betsy Walter's reaction to it. He had seen the way she shuddered. *"Bad vibes,"* she had said. And Ron had to admit the man gave him "bad vibes" as well.

Returning to the living room, Ron checked the time. It would be at least another fifteen to twenty minutes before Mia could get back with the food, so he collapsed on the sofa, put his head back and closed his eyes to rest until then.

"Wake up, sleepy-head." Mia's voice startled Ron awake, and it took him a moment to remember where he was. "Wow, you were sound asleep. I'm sorry I woke you." Mia was pulling out little white cartons of rice and containers of food that made Ron's mouth water.

"No, I wasn't sleeping. I was resting my eyes." Mia's laughter said she saw right through his lie. "All right, so I might have dozed off a little. It's been quite a day." Ron joined her at the table. "Made for some weird dreams. They were all mixed up with that horrible house in Ohio where they held Robin and a red pickup, and then that Dr. Block."

"What's that about old blockhead?" Julie had come rushing down the steps as soon as she got her sister's text saying the food had arrived.

Ron and Mia laughed at her name for the good doctor. "I was telling Mia about my crazy dreams when I dozed off. Your Dr.

Block was sitting in his big ol' black leather chair, rocking back and forth with a grim smile."

"Grim smile? Those two words hardly go together." Mia brought plates and utensils to the table. "That is a weird dream."

"Yeah, well when you woke me, I remember hearing this mirthless laughter. It was eerie."

"I don't know if I've ever seen the man smile, much less heard him laugh. At least not at the office. He really is an odd duck."

"Quack, quack," Julie piped in.

Though she laughed, Mia corrected her sister. "But he's not a quack. He's a very good psychiatrist from what I understand. He's well published and highly respected in his field. And speaking of ducks, could you pass me the duck-sauce, please?"

"Yeah, but from what Mom says, he can be a bit of a douche." Julie handed her sister the packet and grabbed two hot mustards for her own eggroll.

Ron grinned. "I can't imagine your mom saying that."

"Okay, so I'm paraphrasing."

Ron was becoming more curious about the man he had interviewed. "What do you think of him, Mia?"

She shrugged. "We honestly haven't had that many interactions. But I'll tell you this. If he thinks my client attacked him, he's the one who's crazy."

Though Ron appreciated how Mia defended her client, he wasn't convinced of the man's innocence. "Your guy isn't the only one we're looking at, but there were only four male clients seen that day... well, it would be five if you count the guy who was there with his wife for marriage counseling, except he's got a solid alibi since they drove home together." Ron took a big bite of his egg roll. "Thanks for doing this, sweetheart. I'm sorry I didn't take you out like I promised."

"Don't be silly. We eat out all the time, and I love Chinese."

"And I got a free meal out of it!" Julie grinned. "No, how much do I owe you?"

"Nothing. My treat tonight," Mia said.

"Let me get this." Ron felt guilty enough for not going with his fiancée to the caterers on top of not taking her out to dinner. He didn't want to add not paying to his tab.

"Absolutely not. You need to save your money for our honeymoon."

"We honestly need to sit down and go over our finances so you stop worrying about money, Mia." Ron wondered what she would think when she finally saw his net worth and realized money would be no problem… even for the new house he hoped to buy for them.

"Okay, you two. This brings me to a rather important question." Julie put her fork down, put her elbows on the table, and rested her chin on her folded hands. "Where are you planning to live after you're married? Here?"

Ron looked from Julie to Mia and back again as they both stared at him expectantly. He and Mia had discussed wanting to have their own home, but neither of them had broached the subject with Julie. It was obvious that his fiancée was hoping he would handle the delicate situation. "Well, not really. I mean we were actually thinking about house hunting."

"I'm sorry, Jules. I hate to leave you in the lurch, but—"

"Yeah, right," Julie interrupted with a look of indignation. "It seems to me when we decided to buy this place you were worried about me getting married and kicking you out… now look."

Ron watched the sisters, wondering where this was going. Mia appeared to be near tears, but he detected more mischief than annoyance in Julie's eyes. He was right on the mark.

"Good grief, Mia, did you really think I didn't know you'd want your own place?" Then she chuckled, and Ron saw relief sweep across Mia's face. "Besides, speaking of finances, I have news of my own." Julie's smile broadened. "Earlier today, I signed a contract for my book!" she said triumphantly.

Julie's news had both women on their feet and hugging as Ron had seen them do so often. He simply leaned back in his chair and enjoyed the scene.

"Oh my gosh, my sister is soon to be a published author. I mean, I know you're already published, but your novel... wow! When did you find out?"

"Yesterday. I was waiting for the right moment to share it. This seemed to be it."

"Did you tell Mom?"

"Nope, you're the first to know. I was thinking I'd make a big, dramatic announcement at dinner tomorrow. What do you think?"

"I think that's a great idea."

"How about if I bring the champagne?" Ron suggested.

"That would be great," Mia said. "With all the family there, you'd better bring two bottles, if that's okay."

"Oh yeah, and I invited someone to join us."

"What? Who?"

Julie smiled shyly. "That would be our veterinarian, Dr. Drake."

Mia's jaw dropped then she slowly started to grin. "Hmm, Drake... tall, dark, and handsome's first name is very sexy.

"Ahem." Ron decided it was time to remind his girl he was sitting right there.

Both women thought he was hilarious, but when they stopped laughing and finished putting their leftovers away, Julie went upstairs to "make a call" and Ron took his girl into his arms for a kiss that proved she indeed had not forgotten him.

Chapter Twenty-four

Sunday dinner at the Reeds' turned out to be a full house and a fun-filled day.

"You must be exhausted, Mom." Mia was helping to load one of the dishwashers with Julie, while their mother and father worked together to load the other one.

"Not really. Your dad always helps, and with you guys pitching in to clean up, it gets done lickety-split. Just put that platter by the sink, Destiny," Sarah said to her youngest while Julie began filling the sink to handwash a few bigger items.

Craig pushed Julie aside, and took over washing while she dried and put things away. When he finished the last pan, he said, "My work here is done!" and headed back to join the rest of the gang.

Mia followed right behind him and found Ron in a serious discussion with her brothers about the Steelers and their chances of making it to the Superbowl. Bobby's girlfriend, Megan, who had joined in the discussion, had an opposing view. She was apparently an Eagles fan, and Mia could foresee many contentious moments ahead... but hopefully all in good fun. At least she was still sitting with Bobby's arm draped around her shoulders.

Dr. Drake Curtain was sitting quietly, watching with obvious amusement, and Mia saw his smile broaden when Julie came back into the room and joined him. It seemed strange to Mia that Julie had introduced him to the family so early in their relationship, if there was even to be a relationship. But she had to admit, they made a cute couple.

Mia looked around at how many people were there for a simple Sunday dinner and it made her think of the upcoming holiday. "Have you figured out how big of a turkey we need for Thanksgiving, Mom?"

Sarah rolled her eyes. "Let's just say it's going to have to be a big boy."

"Is it going to be all the usual people? Plus a few?" Mia was thinking of Ron and Megan when she said it but noticed Julie take Drake's hand.

"Yes, I figure around twelve to fifteen people at least. I told your grandma I'd like her to extend an invitation to Aunt Bonnie. I know the holidays are going to be difficult for her having just lost Joe."

"You don't think she'll be going to visit one of her kids for Thanksgiving?"

"Possibly, but I wanted to put it out there just in case. After all, she's family. Besides, at the Reed house, there's always room for one more."

Mia knew it was true, and she looked forward to this holiday almost as much as Christmas. Then she noticed an odd exchange between Bobby and Megan. Her brother slid forward in his seat, glanced back at Megan then said, "Mom, about Thanksgiving. Megan's Mom and Dad were kind of hoping we'd spend the holiday with them."

"Oh," Sarah said. Then after a brief pause, "Sure. Do they live in the Philadelphia area?"

"No, they're actually over in Delaware... Rehoboth Beach."

"Nice," Julie said.

Sarah had taken a seat next to Craig and snuggled in close. He put his arm around her. "We'll miss you, Bobby... both of you. Won't we, guys?"

Mia watched the scene, realizing Bobby was Sarah's baby boy, named for his father whom she had loved and lost to brain cancer when Bobby was too young to remember. Mia knew her mom was a therapist and could handle it, but her baby birds were starting to leave the nest, and Mia thought it must be hard.

"But you'll be here for Christmas, right?" Mia asked hopefully.

"Wouldn't miss it for the world."

Sarah's face brightened.

Mia decided this would be the perfect moment to mention something that had been on her mind since the night before. "Getting back to Thanksgiving, you said there's always room for one more. How about three more?" She looked at Ron and saw that he recognized where she was going with this. "I'd like to ask Robin and Kevin to join us if that's okay."

"Okay? Of course!" Sarah's big smile was evidence of her sincerity. "They're family, and we'd love to have them. I was sorry they couldn't make it today." Robin had called the night before explaining that her little one had an ear infection and apologizing for having to cancel.

"Oh good, because I already invited them."

Amidst the laughter, Mia noticed her sister raise her eyebrows in a silent question. "We have so much to be thankful for this year, don't we, Julie?" Seeing that Julie apparently got her drift she whispered to Ron, "I think it's almost time for the champagne."

"What? Oh, yeah. I'll go get it." He quietly slipped out of the room and went to his car to grab the bubbly.

Julie cleared her throat and sat up straight in her seat. "Mia is right. We've had a crazy few months with lots of changes, mostly good, some scary. So today I want to share some good news." After a long pause for dramatic effect, she raised her voice and exclaimed, "I sold my book!"

Everyone began yelling their congratulations at once, and as the cheering, hugs and applause settled down, Craig shouted, "I wish we had some champagne on hand to toast your good news."

"I'm way ahead of you." Ron held up two bottles, and Sarah jumped up to get the champagne flutes.

Watching the festivities that followed, Mia couldn't help reflect on all that had happened since she moved back to the area. Her sister could occasionally get on her last nerve, but she couldn't love her more if they'd been born of the same parents. They had been sisters since they were five years old, and Mia couldn't remember not having Julie as part of her life. Yet she'd nearly lost her to a maniacal serial killer. Mia shivered when she thought how close he had come to pushing her over the edge of that cliff.

Ron's arm encircled her and pulled her close. "Are you okay?" he asked softly.

"Yes, just glad she's alive. Glad we got there in time."

"Yeah, I still shudder when I think what could have happened to you both. You saved her life, but you could have lost your own. I could have lost you."

"But you didn't."

"What are you two whispering about?" Sarah asked, handing them each a glass.

"Just counting our blessings."

When Craig had filled all the glasses—even Destiny got a little splash of the bubbly—he held his glass high. "To my daughter the author, congratulations, and may you remember us all when you become a rich and famous bestseller, as I know you will."

There were many shouts of "Here, here!" and Drake added, "I had no idea I was in the presence of such greatness."

Mia noticed the way he looked at Julie when he said it. *Wow, he's got it bad.*

Chapter Twenty-five

"Hi, Adam. How are you doing?" Mia had been worried about Adam Grant ever since his last appointment. He hadn't called and she hadn't heard any more about him being a suspect in Dr. Block's assault, but his usual smile was missing.

"Okay," was his only answer.

"Yeah? No episodes since the last time we talked?"

"Well, no. I woke up in the middle of the night a couple times, but I couldn't remember what I'd been dreaming about. Sleeping isn't as much of a problem as being awake."

Mia watched him wringing his hands. "Tell me about it."

Adam didn't answer right away, and when he did, it was hesitantly. "I've been struggling, you know?" Mia waited for more. "You know... I stopped in at the Wildhorse, and I, um, I ordered a shot."

The Wildhorse Tavern was a dive and Adam's old hangout. He'd told Mia a few of the stories of things he'd done there when he drank himself into oblivion. Mia wanted to scream *Nooo!* but instead she simply said, "Okay, and?"

"I... I sat there staring at that whiskey for a while. I even picked it up and smelled it. I was so close." He shook his head then started rubbing his forehead.

When he finally looked up, Mia recognized his desperation. She knew he was losing his grip. "But you didn't drink it, did you?" she said confidently. He shook his head again. "You're a lot stronger than you realize, Adam. To get that close and walk away... that took a lot of strength."

"You're giving me too much credit. You don't know what happened next."

"Okay, tell me."

"So, I was sitting there... staring at the stuff... and I felt a hand on my shoulder. When I looked up it was my sponsor."

"Really? What was he doing at the Wildhorse?" It didn't seem likely that an AA sponsor would be hanging out in a joint like that unless he had fallen off the wagon himself.

"He was driving by and thought he recognized my bike parked in the front of the lot. We've been talking, and he knows I'm struggling, so he came in to see if I was there. Mia, it was like my higher power stepped in to stop me. I seriously think I would have had that drink if he hadn't shown up when he did."

"But. You. Didn't." *There are angels among us.* "Let's talk about why you're struggling."

Adam flopped against the back of the chair and looked up at the ceiling. "I'm not sure how to explain it," he said meeting her eyes again. "It's just that ever since that cop questioned me and told me what this was all about, I've had this feeling—this really bad feeling—that I'm going to get blamed for attacking Dr. Block. And I mean I don't like him much, I'll admit that, but it's not like I hate him or something. Why would I want to hang around and hit him on the head?"

"I understand—"

"Do you? Seriously? Then maybe you can explain it to me. Tell me why they think I did it. You know, I almost canceled my appointment for today. I just didn't even want to come to this place."

"I'm glad you came. And you need to know, you weren't the only one the police questioned. They talked to all the male clients who were here that day." Mia leaned forward in her seat. "They really didn't single you out." But she wasn't sure that was true.

Adam was young and, according to the detectives, the most likely suspect. Now, looking at what their suspicion was doing to her client, Mia was livid.

She was almost glad she wouldn't be seeing Ron for a couple of days. Almost.

When she got home, Mia did the only thing she could think of to try to prove Adam Grant was innocent. *I have to find the real culprit.*

She picked up her watercolor pencils and sat with her hand poised in front of the easel, waiting for inspiration... but nothing. When she thought to draw a person, she simply didn't know where to begin. Exasperated, Mia put the pencils down and raised her eyes heavenward. "I could use a little help here."

"Who are you talking to?" Julie had quietly come down the steps and looked around. She spied Simeon curled up in his favorite spot. "Oh, Simmie, is she talking to you? Sorry to interrupt. I just wanted to tell you we can eat in about twenty minutes, okay?"

"Sure. Nothing's happening down here."

"Oh, I know that feeling. Nothing like staring at a blank page and not knowing where to start. With writing I've learned to use any gibberish that comes to mind in order to get into the flow. I don't know if that works with what you do."

"Not so much." Mia stared at the blank canvas. "Maybe I should try fingerpainting."

Julie laughed. "Sounds kind of fun. Anyhoo, I'll call you when it's ready."

Mia seriously considered the fingerpaint idea before picking up a pencil and doodling. Still nothing. By the time Julie called her for dinner, she was totally frustrated and discouraged.

With little to say, Mia allowed Julie to carry the conversation, which was easy since Julie had plenty to talk about, but by the time they were clearing the table her sister had apparently noticed how unusually quiet Mia was.

"What's up, sis? Are you that spent or is something wrong?"

"Just tired... mostly."

"Okay, and what else?"

"I'm worried about one of my clients. He was questioned about the assault on Dr. Block—I guess he's a suspect—and he's been going downhill since." Mia closed the dishwasher and leaned back against the kitchen counter. "I know he didn't have anything to do with it, but I wish he didn't think the police were looking at him for this. It's making him a wreck."

"Well, did you ever think maybe he's worried because he did it?"

"No! He didn't!" Mia hadn't meant to raise her voice, but her sister's comment added to her irritation. "I'm sorry. I just know better."

"Hey, don't worry about it. By now I should know not to doubt my psychic sister." Julie gave her a quick hug.

"But I'm not psychic. I wish I was." Mia finished wiping the counters and threw the dishcloth over the side of the sink. "I keep hoping to draw something that will help clear him, but I can't seem to do it."

"It doesn't work like that, does it?"

"What do you mean?" Mia followed her sister who walked out of the kitchen and headed for the stairs.

"I mean, you don't get inspiration on demand, right? It happens when it happens." She stopped at the bottom of the stairs. "Do you want to talk?"

"No, not really," Mia said sullenly.

"Okay, then I'm going up to my room to read until *my new beau* calls." With a wink she turned and trotted up the steps.

Mia's own beau hadn't yet called or even promised to call tonight, so she flopped onto the sofa and flipped on the TV. Scanning the guide and finding nothing of any real interest, she turned it off again and retreated to her studio once more.

"I need some help, Lord." She picked up her sketch pad and let her intuition—or whatever it was—take over. When she'd completed her sketch, Mia said, "Great... you again." She crumpled up the paper and tossed it in the trash. She certainly didn't need another picture of the quirky Dr. Block.

Chapter Twenty-six

The memory of Charlie Jenkins's gaunt face haunted Ron. It was true that the man he saw was frail, dying... then dead, and maybe that was a kind of justice, but it wasn't the justice he had been seeking, and he felt cheated.

Buddy Jenkins, you're not going to get off that easy.

Determined to finally find the man who had murdered his parents, kidnapped his sister, and destroyed the life he once knew, Ron followed every lead, working day and night. He owed it to his parents. He owed it to his sister. He owed it to his own peace of mind to catch this poor excuse of a human being and put him in a cage. Or worse.

So far, though, every lead had been a dead-end. Ron grabbed the vibrating phone from his desktop and saw it was Mia calling. Though it wasn't a good time, he decided he'd better answer since he hadn't spoken with her since Sunday.

"What's up, sweetheart?" Ron continued scanning some of the messages that had come pouring in since they'd put their wanted man's picture on the news.

"That's a fine way to greet the woman you love."

"Sorry, we're kind of busy, but how are you doing?"

"Not great. I'm really worried about one of my clients."

Ron didn't have time for chit-chat, but said, "I'm sorry to hear that. I'm sure with you as his therapist he'll be all right."

"Maybe... maybe not. Thanks to being considered a suspect in the attack on Dr. Block, he's in a really bad place. I'm afraid of what he might do." There was a long pause in which Ron didn't know what to say, so he said nothing. "Ron, are you still there?"

"Yeah, sorry, I'm not sure how I can help you though."

"Well, what would help is if you'd find out who really did it so he could be cleared."

"Seriously?" Ron dropped the pen he'd been holding onto his desk, leaned back in his chair, and shook his head. "Well, we'll get right on that, okay?" He heard the sarcasm in his own voice and knew he'd better walk it back. "Listen, Mia, right now I've got another case that's a little more important than some guy hitting a shrink on the head. We're trying to track down a murderer who might be holding a girl captive and doing God knows what to her."

There was silence on the other end of the line.

"Mia, sweetheart, I'm sorry—"

"Hey Bishop, we might have a real lead." Det. Jason Evans was getting up from his chair and grabbing his jacket.

"Mia, I've gotta go. I'll call you later." Not even waiting for a response, Ron disconnected then grabbed his own jacket and followed his partner out the door. "Where are we headed?"

"That motel out by the Wildhorse Tavern. That clerk we talked to before, he says the guy is registered there again."

***

Ron checked the parking lot for a red pickup, and seeing none he jumped out of the vehicle and hurried into the motel with Jason right behind him.

"Sorry, he left, but his girl is still here."

They got the room number and key but knocked on the door when they located it. Ron didn't know what he'd expected, but it wasn't what he found. A woman, probably mid-thirties, with an abundance of makeup, cherry red lipstick, and badly bleached hair opened the door.

"What?" was all she said.

"Is Buddy here?"

"No, who's askin'?"

Ron and Jason flashed their IDs, and Ron managed to get his foot and his shoulder in the door before she could slam it in his face. "Sorry ma'am, but we'd like to ask you a few questions. Do you know when he'll be back?"

"No. Why? What do you want with him?"

"What's your relationship to Buddy Jenkins?" Ron asked as they pushed their way inside. The shabby room reeked of stale cigarette smoke and beer.

"I don't know that that's any of your business." The woman turned to walk away from him, and Ron grabbed her by the shoulder.

"Hey," she shouted. "You better get your hands off me."

Det. Evans, who hadn't said a word until now, put his hand on Ron's shoulder. "Take it easy, Bishop." Then he turned to the woman. "Ma'am, you can answer our questions here, or we can all take a ride back to the station." Seeing her subdued reaction, Evans decided to keep going. "First of all, what's your name, ma'am?"

"Vanessa."

"All right, Vanessa. Thank you. Can you tell me your relationship to Jenkins?"

"He's my old man."

Ron decided to get back in on the conversation. "How long have you and Jenkins been together?"

"I guess about a year." Vanessa took out a cigarette, but when Evans shook his head, she put it back in the pack. "Why are you looking for him, anyway?"

"We'll get to that. So, did you know his father, Charlie Jenkins?"

"Buddy's father? Know him?" She laughed, ending in a cough. "Yeah, I guess you could say that."

"What do you mean?" Jason asked.

"He's the one what picked me up. I was with him for a while, but man, he was getting disgusting. All that coughing and he could hardly get around after a while. He was old and sick, and Buddy was young and virile, if you get my drift."

Ron was filled with revulsion. "He's dead, you know." He watched to see what kind of reaction he'd get and wasn't surprised at the lack of concern she showed.

"Yeah, we figured he wasn't going to last too much longer." Vanessa's head popped up, "Oh, is that why you want Buddy? You want to let him know his old man died." After another cynical laugh, she added, "Like he'll give a damn."

Jason sat down on the foot of the bed. "Well, I think we'll hang around and let him know just the same. Ron, can you move our car from where we're blocking the entrance?"

Ron dashed out and drove around to the back of the building. When he rounded the corner on his return, he saw him. There was no mistaking the resemblance to the sketch artist's picture. Buddy got out of his truck carrying a couple six-packs, one in his hand and one under his arm, and entered the motel. Ron watched from a safe distance, noticed the clerk didn't tip him off, then followed him inside, still keeping his distance. He didn't know how the man would react when he saw Evans, but Ron was going to be ready.

Buddy moved the one six-pack from under his arm and now had one in each hand so he kicked the door with his foot. "Hey, Nessa, it's me. Open up."

The door opened, and Jenkins must have spotted Evans. He dropped both six-packs, turned to make a run for it, and came face to face with the barrel of Ron's revolver.

Chapter Twenty-seven

Robin kissed her sleeping child on the forehead, tiptoed out the door, and rejoined her husband in the living room.

"I think you got a text, sweet cheeks."

Robin grabbed her phone off the end table and checked the message.

"What's wrong?" Kevin asked.

Robin slowly moved her gaze from her phone to meet her husband's questioning stare.

"They got him." It came out almost as a sigh. Relief washed over her like a tsunami, bringing with it a flood of tears.

Kevin rushed to her side and took her in his arms. "It's over, babe. It's okay now. It's over."

She heard his words and wanted to tell him she was all right—better than all right—but all she could do was sob. He held her until the deluge subsided. It was some time before the calm that comes after the storm settled on her. She sat there with her husband, barely able to move but content to simply be.

Kevin finally lifted her chin, and looked into her eyes. "Are you all right now?" The love and concern she saw there overwhelmed her, and she was struck with the realization of how much she truly did love this man.

"I really am." Robin put her hand on his cheek, enjoying the soft stubble. "And I really, really love you." She curled into his arms, feeling safer than she ever had in all of her adult life. A cricket sound stirred her from her peaceful pose as another text came in.

Are you okay?

"Oh, my goodness. I never responded to Ron's text." She quickly replied.

Better than OK, thank you. What about the girl?

Not a victim. His girlfriend.

Thank God! R U OK?

She got a thumbs up emoji in reply and turned to her husband, "Do you think I should call him?"

Kevin's advice was to wait until morning which sounded good to her.

"Good idea. I was totally wound up, but now I'm exhausted. I feel like a limp wash cloth."

"Would you like me to carry you into the bedroom?" Kevin asked with a come-hither look.

They both got to their feet, but Robin declined his offer. "No sense having you throw your back out."

A little while later, as they were lying in bed, Robin had an unusual urge, but after a little more cuddle time, Kevin had promptly fallen asleep. Restless and unable to ignore the urge, she slid out of bed and slipped out of her pajamas, then crawled back between the covers. She was tempted to wake her husband, but she had never in their married life been the one to initiate sex and was suddenly too shy to even consider it.

Yet, the longer she lay there, the more her desire grew. She decided she had two choices. She could put her PJs back on, or she could wake her husband. Then she thought of a compromise. Kevin was lying on his side with his back to her, so she moved closer and curled into him, spooning her naked body against his.

Nothing happened, no response as he continued to breathe evenly, so she snuggled closer, moving gently until he responded. Kevin, though groggy and seeming confused at first, finally understood, rolled over, and though surprised, gladly answered her need, and the two were united as never before, but as they were meant to be.

***

At 10:00 A.M. the next morning Robin walked into the police station. Ron hurried to meet her and after a quick hug, walked her back to the holding cell where they found Buddy Jenkins sitting, head in hands. He looked up at the sound of them approaching.

He jumped to his feet, glaring at the man who had arrested him. "You'd better let me out of here. You don't have any proof on these trumped-up charges." Noticing Robin walking slightly behind her brother, he asked, "Who's this?"

Robin moved closer, rubbing the goosebumps on her arms. "Remember me?" she asked somewhat timidly.

"No, should I?"

Unable to believe her ears, she moved closer, timidity subsiding. "Take a good look." Her cheeks on fire with fifteen years of fury, she stared him down.

Buddy took a step back, hesitated, and turned to face Ron. "Who is this? What's going on here?"

"You said we had no proof. You were wrong. Our proof is standing right in front of you."

Robin knew she barely resembled the waif she'd been when this creature had stolen her life, but how could he possibly not recognize her? Even with the change in her hair and the changes nine years of aging and healthy living had brought, he had to know her.

Then she saw it... the dawning of recognition on his vile face.

He gasped, his eyes grew wide, and his jaw dropped. "Those eyes... It's you!"

"Yeah Buddy, it's me." She felt her lips curl into a sneer.

"But how..." He looked from her to her brother and back.

"Yes, you see it, don't you? This detective is my brother, the man you told me was dead. And as you can also see, as you *always knew*, he is quite alive, and now you're going to finally pay for killing our parents." Robin spat the words as her rage burned within.

Silence.

Robin saw that he recognized defeat. "I want a lawyer."

Ron's arm went around his sister's shoulders. "Good idea. You're going to need one," he said turning and guiding her away from her nightmare.

Robin turned back once, saw him locked up—imprisoned—like she'd been when she was at his mercy. It was good to see him in a cage where he belonged, and she even got some satisfaction when she thought of how attractive he might be to some of his fellow prisoners.

Your turn, Buddy!

Chapter Twenty-eight

Thanksgiving Day had turned into a huge gathering with all of Sarah and Craig Reed's family, Grandma Val and Grandpa Andy, the Longs with their little boy, Aunt Bonnie who had decided not to travel to her daughter's house until Christmas, and Aunt Bonnie's neighbor and friend, Edna Schmidt. The only ones missing were Bobby and Megan.

There were people everywhere in the house, and thanks to the unusually warm weather for late November, they even spilled out onto the patio.

The highlight of the day was when everyone gathered together, finding seats on every available piece of furniture as well as the floor, to give thanks for the blessings of the year, and there had been many.

Valerie and Andy Reed gave thanks for Andy's complete recovery from his stroke. Sarah and Craig gave thanks for all their family being healthy and happy, and especially for Ron and Mia saving Julie's life. Julie said how grateful she was to be alive and to have Drake by her side, while he said he was grateful for finding her and being part of this family's Thanksgiving Day celebration. Destiny thanked the Lord for having two wonderful parents (and was later asked if she was kissing up because Christmas was coming), and Cody echoed his little sister and added thanks for meeting someone special (for which he'd be questioned endlessly later in the day).

Edna Schmidt gave thanks for being invited to be with such a wonderful family and having such a special friend in Bonnie, and Aunt Bonnie said how grateful she was for all the love and support she'd had since losing her husband Joe.

Robin and Kevin gave thanks for their little boy who was now sleeping in the guest room and for finding Robin's brother—or being found—and Ron gave thanks for finding his sister, finding the men who had done so much to hurt them and especially for the woman he was going to marry.

Mia Reed was overwhelmed by all she heard, and by the time it was her turn, she wasn't sure she'd be able to swallow the lump in her throat in time to speak, but taking a deep breath, she found the words.

"I am grateful for being raised in a family so filled with faith and love and trust, and especially this year for my roommate and sister, Julie, being in my life and, of course, for my fiancé, Detective Ronald Bishop."

When all the thanks had been given, there were lots of hugs and a few tears before Sarah gave Julie the secret signal, and she called out, "Holy macaroni, let's eat!"

Amidst much laughter everyone followed their noses to the wonderful aroma of the turkey and all the fixin's and piled their plates high. And they ate, and ate, and ate, until they were as stuffed as the turkey had been coming out of the oven.

That's when Sarah said, "Is anyone ready for dessert?"

There were groans and protests, as there were every year, until she said, "All right, you have one hour to let it all settle. By the time we've cleared this and the dishes are done, I expect you'll be ready for the pies." And there were plenty of pies... pumpkin, sweet potato, apple, and pecan. Edna had even brought cookies. There was no chance of anyone leaving this house hungry.

Sarah allowed Aunt Bonnie, Edna, and Grandma Val to help carry dishes from the dining room to the kitchen but then shooed them away, insisting they go and relax while the younger folks took care of cleanup.

"I'm not that old," Grandma Val said giving her daughter-in-law a wink and a kiss on the cheek, "but this is one time I don't mind playing the old lady card."

Aunt Bonnie laughed and hooked arms with her dear friend. "Yes, Val. There are certain advantages to seniority. Let's go sit and chat."

There were still a lot of people in the kitchen, even for a kitchen as large as this, stumbling over each other, until Julie took command. "All right, nothing warms my heart more than seeing a man help in the kitchen, but you guys are just getting in the way now, especially you two," she said to Ron and Drake. "You don't know where anything goes. Why don't you guys get outta here? You too, Dad. We've got this."

"Are you sure?" When Craig was certain he was dismissed, he made a quick exit.

"Uh, sorry, there's too much estrogen in here. You can't leave me alone with all these females." Cody hastily followed his father from the room.

"Now we can get something done." Julie wiped her hands clean and laughed, but she was right. Sarah, Mia, Julie, Robin, and Destiny made fairly quick work of even this gigantic cleanup and enjoyed their time together doing it.

The conversation turned nostalgic as so often happens when families gather for the holidays and Sarah asked, "Do you remember when we all used to gather around your grandparents' table for Thanksgiving? I'll never forget the first year I joined you all there—all but you, Destiny... you didn't join us for the holidays until a few years later."

Mia did remember. She remembered many big gatherings for Thanksgiving dinner at Grandma Val's. One in particular popped into her mind. "Do you remember the year Betsy was living with Grandma and Grandpa?" Sarah's head snapped around, and Mia thought she had the strangest look on her face. "What, Mom?"

"Oh, nothing." Sarah went back to washing the pan in the sink. "I just hadn't thought about that in a long time. Whatever made you bring that up?"

"I don't know. Maybe because I just talked to Betsy about dress shopping for the wedding. She's been on my mind a lot lately."

"I was surprised you asked her to be a bridesmaid."

"Why? You know she's special to me. She's like a little sister."

Sarah didn't answer but handed Robin a pan to dry. "Did you tell your grandparents she was going to be in your wedding?"

"No. We haven't really talked about the wedding party. Why?"

"No reason, but I know your grandma is interested in all the details."

Mia had no doubt that was true. She and her grandma had shared a special bond that grew out of the time they'd spent together after Jenny Reed, Mia's biological mother, had been killed in an accident on the way home from one of their Bridge nights, and until her father had remarried and Sarah became a part of their lives.

It was when they'd all gathered around the table for dessert that Mia brought up their wedding plans.

"What time are we meeting Saturday?" Julie put the time in her phone. "Is it just going to be the five of us?"

Mia nodded.

"Five?" Grandma Val asked. "I thought it was just going to be Julie, Destiny, and your old roommate, Morgan." She looked curious. "Who is the fifth? Your Mom?" She turned to Sarah who shook her head.

"No, I asked Betsy to be in the wedding, too." Mia saw her grandparents exchange a look and wondered if they disapproved. "She was thrilled, and you know how close we've always been. I told Mom, she's almost like another little sister."

As soon as Grandpa Andy finished his pie, he suggested they head home. He said he was a little tired. Mia had never known her grandparents to leave the Thanksgiving festivities so early, but then even though he appeared to have fully recovered from his stroke, she realized he might still have some residual effects like tiring easily, and it had been a long day.

As her grandma was saying goodbye to Aunt Bonnie, Mia heard her apologize, "I hope you understand." Her dear friend said she understood perfectly and glanced at Mia, then she walked out with her.

"Did that seem strange to you?" Mia asked Julie.

"What? Oh, yeah, I guess. A little. Did you want more pie?"

"Good grief! You've got to be kidding. I need to walk off what I've had." Mia looked across the room at Ron who was chatting with Kevin and Drake. "Want to go for a walk?" she mouthed the words, not wanting to shout over other conversations and mimed the walking with her fingers.

He gave a quick nod, excused himself, and escorted her out the front door. Andy Reed was already sitting in the car while Val and Bonnie stood in the driveway having what looked like a serious conversation. They stopped talking and smiled when they saw the young couple coming their way.

"Is Grandpa okay?" Mia asked.

"Yes, yes, he's just a little tired. We're not getting any younger, you know."

Mia did know that, but still, it all seemed a little odd.

Chapter Twenty-nine

"There's not going to be a trial, sis." Ron hadn't been looking forward to telling Robin the latest news primarily because he hadn't been sure how she would take it.

"What? But why not?"

"They offered him a plea bargain, and he took it. He's pleading guilty to everything in exchange for life in prison without parole. He was afraid with your testimony he'd get the needle, and he was too scared to face that possibility." Ron waited for a reaction as his sister sat motionless beside her husband.

It was Kevin who spoke first. "Sweet cheeks, at least you won't have to testify."

"Yeah, I know."

Ron watched her and could almost see the wheels turning as she processed this new information.

Finally, she looked up, first at her husband then Ron. "I have mixed feelings, you know? I mean, part of me thinks that's not fair. He should die. Mom and Dad didn't have a choice," she said looking at Ron. "And part of me wanted to face him in court." She took a deep breath. "But then that would have been horrible... having to relive it all... and God only knows what kind of questions they would have asked. So now I don't have to put myself through that, right?"

"Right." Ron was relieved his sister wouldn't have to go through that humiliation.

"And we'll avoid all that publicity and everybody in this small town knowing everything."

"That's right, Robin. And you never have to lay eyes on him again unless you want to."

"Why on earth would I want to?"

"You probably won't. But they told me if you wanted to sit down across from him and say whatever you wanted to say, you have that right." Ron waited for a response but knew if she decided to face Jenkins, he would be right there beside her. He had a few words he wouldn't mind saying himself. But he was afraid if he spent too much time in the same room with that man, he might not control the fury that threatened to erupt. If Ron did what he wanted, he'd lose his badge and possibly wind up in prison... though he couldn't imagine anyone would blame him.

"You know what?" Robin said putting her hand on her husband's knee. "I think I'll be satisfied enough to know he will finally have some idea of what he put me through. Although I'm sure the prisoners are treated better than I was and have better accommodations, maybe he'll have night visitors for many, many years... for the rest of his worthless life."

The reminder of what his sister had endured nearly crushed him, but then when he looked at her face, free of worry lines and smiling lovingly at her husband, he vowed not to dwell on the past... neither hers nor his own.

Ron walked with a lighter step returning to his vehicle. As he pulled out, he placed a call to Mia who finally answered on the fourth ring. "I was about to hang up. Are you busy?" He heard women's laughter in the background.

"Yes and no. We just left the dress shop and we're getting ready to have lunch. Would you like to join us?"

"Me and five women? No, I don't think so. Those don't sound like good odds to me." He heard his fiancée relay what he'd said to the rest of the group and more laughter followed. "Was the shopping trip a success?"

"Definitely. They're all going to look absolutely gorgeous in their red dresses. They're all the same color but different styles, and they're beautiful."

"But not as beautiful as the bride, I'm sure."

He heard the amusement in her voice when she answered, "Well, I certainly hope not."

"Okay, I won't keep you, but I wanted to let you know, I told Robin about the plea bargain, and she's okay."

Ron headed home, looking forward to seeing Mia later. It would have to be a late dinner since she was having a leisurely late lunch with the girls, but that gave him time to hit the driving range. Craig, his future father-in-law had invited him to play golf sometime soon, so Ron thought he'd better hit a bucket of balls. Maybe even take a lesson. He hadn't played much golf and didn't want to make a fool of himself when the time came.

Ron didn't even own any clubs, but his partner had been kind enough to lend him a few out of his bag. Ron's first couple swings were sad to say the least. He even whiffed a couple. But once he got in the groove and relaxed, it got better. Not good, but better.

When he hit the last ball in the bucket, he'd had enough and headed back to the clubhouse to get a beer before going home. He saw a familiar face sitting alone at one of the tables in the 19th Hole, hesitated, but then decided it might be worthwhile to stop and say hello.

"Dr. Block, how are you?"

"Oh, Detective, hello," he said as though surprised. Ron was certain the man would have spotted him coming across the parking lot from his seat by the window. "I don't remember seeing you here before. So you're a golfer?"

"I'm not sure I'd say that, but I enjoy playing a round now and then, and since my future father-in-law is a golfer, I thought it might be a good idea to work at my game. How about you?"

"Me? It's the best relaxation in the world to take your mind off your troubles. Your fiancée's grandfather and I play every Thursday... at least we used to before his stroke." The doctor looked out the window and adjusted his glasses then turned and smiled. "He swears he'll be back on the links by spring. He's no quitter."

"He seems like a good man. I suppose you'll be looking forward to that." Ron noticed a faraway look in the doctor's eyes and wasn't sure what he should say. He didn't know Andy Reed very well, but he certainly seemed like one of the good guys. "Well, good talking with you." Ron turned to leave.

"Detective, have you made any progress on my case?"

"I'm sorry, no, not yet. But we're not giving up."

"Oh well, maybe this is one of those cases that will never get solved. Not your fault, I'm sure. I know I wasn't much help. *C'est la vie.*"

"Well, don't give up hope. We haven't. Now, if you'll excuse me," Ron checked the time, "I have a hot date, and I'd hate to keep her waiting."

The doctor was very kind to let them off the hook for not solving the case and finding out who attacked him. Most victims were not so kind. They were hurt and angry and quite often took their anger out on the police who were trying to help them. The strange Dr. Block was uncharacteristically understanding.

***

Two hours later, after a shower, shave, and change of clothes, Ron was at his girl's front door, and when she opened it, seeing her in an emerald green dress that fell softly off her shoulders, he forgot everything else.

"You look amazing!" And he meant it. He could hardly believe she was his. Or at least she was going to be.

"Why thank you, Detective Bishop. You don't look so bad yourself. Come on in."

Ron followed her and was surprised to see Drake Curtain sitting on the sofa with Julie.

He greeted them then asked Mia if she was ready to go. "Our reservation is in half an hour."

"It only takes ten minutes to get there. Why don't you sit down? Would you like a glass of wine?"

Ron noticed the others were all enjoying some but turned down the offer. "Maybe when we get to the restaurant."

"Can you call and change the reservation from two to four? I asked Julie and Drake to join us if that's all right."

“I hope you don’t mind,” Julie said.

“Of course not. It shouldn’t be a problem.” Ron did enjoy Julie with her inimitable personality and Drake seemed like a decent enough guy—could even become a friend down the road—but he had been looking forward to having Mia all to himself tonight.

“We’re all set,” he said after placing the call.

Each of the men helped their ladies into their coats, and as the girls headed out to the car, Drake nudged Ron. “Sorry about this, man. They’ve been hanging out all afternoon and sprung this on us both. Hope you don’t mind.”

“Hey, it’s all good.”

Chapter Thirty

Mia thought they had been having a perfectly good time until Ron ruined it by bringing up a sore subject.

"Guess who I ran into today."

Mia had no idea. She shrugged.

"Dr. Block from the center. He is an odd one, isn't he?"

"Who's that?" Drake had never heard of the man so Julie filled him in.

"He seemed quite nonchalant about the case." Ron put down his napkin and shook his head. "Unusual. Most victims harass us until we solve their case, but when I said we were no closer to closing it, this guy actually said, *'C'est la vie.'* Can you believe that? It's like he doesn't even care if we catch the guy who hit him."

"Does that mean you can drop the case now?" Mia thought that would at least keep Ron from harassing her client anymore.

"What? No, absolutely not. Someone assaulted a man. Besides that, he stole drugs and a prescription pad. How are we supposed to ignore that?"

Mia couldn't believe Ron would bring this up at dinner and spoil a perfectly good evening. "Well, he didn't do it, you know."

"What? Who didn't? What are you talking about?"

Mia noticed Ron wasn't the only one staring at her. Julie and Drake looked puzzled too. "You know I can't say his name in front of them." She pointed her wine glass toward the couple across from them who suddenly took great interest in talking to each other about something else.

"Oh, I see." Ron smiled and nodded his head in what Mia saw as a most condescending manner. "Why don't we change the subject then, sweetie?"

"You don't have to talk to me like I'm a child."

"That's not what I'm doing, Mia. But this doesn't seem to be a good topic for dinner conversation. Maybe we can discuss it another time when we're alone, and perhaps when you haven't had so many glasses of wine."

Mia couldn't believe her ears. Was he actually insinuating she was drunk? She knew she'd had a little more wine than typical, but she certainly wasn't drunk. "I resent your insinuation." Mia pushed her chair back to leave for the bathroom in a huff, but the room tilted ever so slightly and she grabbed the edge of the table until it straightened itself again.

"Are you all right?" Ron jumped to his feet and took her elbow to steady her which infuriated her even more.

"Of course! I'm fine." She pulled away from him and made her way carefully to the restroom. *I didn't think I had that much to drink.* She was still steadying herself when Julie popped in.

"Are you sure you're okay, sis?"

"Yes. No. I don't know. I didn't think I drank that much, but I guess I shouldn't have had that last glass of wine."

"You are a bit of a lightweight."

"I... I want to go home." Mia suddenly felt sick. "Oh no." Rushing into the stall, Mia lost the beautiful dinner she had just enjoyed, and when she came back out Julie was still there, waiting.

"Are you gonna be okay?"

Mia shrugged. "I'm not sure."

Julie assured her she would live and said, "I'll go tell the guys you aren't feeling well so they can pay the check, and we'll get out of here."

"Don't... don't tell them, you know."

"Mum's the word."

Mia wasn't sure she believed her sister. She imagined they would all have a good laugh at her expense, but she took the next few minutes to freshen up and meekly returned to the table.

"Ready to go?" Ron sounded very matter-of-fact, but she saw a twinkle in his eye that totally irked her. He was amused, and Mia saw nothing at all funny about feeling as miserable as she did.

She grabbed her water glass from the table and took a quick sip to get rid of the foul taste in her mouth then brushed past him toward the exit.

By the time they pulled up in front of the cottage on Glen View Court, Mia was queasy again, and the last thing she wanted was to have anyone with her. Ron came around and helped her out of the car, and they followed Julie and Drake to the front door.

The two of them went straight inside, but when Ron and Mia got to the entrance, Mia said, "It's been a long day, Ron. If you don't mind, I think I'd like to call it a night."

"Oh... Okay, sure. Whatever." Ron turned to walk away.

"Ron, I... I'm sorry. It's just—"

"Hey, no worries." He was already heading for the car. "Whatever," she heard him mumble. She watched him pull out of the driveway without looking back.

Miserable, she walked in the house alone, and Julie said, "Where's Ron?"

"I told him I was ready to call it a night."

"Oh." Mia saw Julie look at her new boyfriend with raised eyebrows before she added, "Drake and I will go down to the den then."

"No. You don't have to do that. I'm going up to bed."

"At nine o'clock?"

"Yes, at nine o'clock." She hadn't meant to use that tone of voice and was surprised it came out that way. She continued up the steps but heard the couple downstairs giggle and could have sworn she heard the words "pass out" as she reached the top.

I am not going to pass out. And she didn't, that is, until she had managed to slip into her pajamas and crawl into bed.

***

Sunday morning Mia woke to a rainy day, a dry mouth, and a terrible headache. When she stumbled downstairs to the kitchen, Julie was already sitting at the table with her big mug of coffee.

"Good morning, sunshine!"

"Ha ha. Not funny." Mia stuck her tongue out at her sister which evoked laughter from both of them. "Oh, don't make me laugh... it hurts."

"I didn't do it. You did. Here, sit down and let me get you some breakfast." Julie headed for the stove.

"No. No breakfast. Not yet. But a cup of tea would be nice."

"You got it." Julie set about brewing the tea and asked, "So, are you and Ron okay?"

"What? Of course. Why would you ask that?" Mia thought back on the night before and wondered if they were indeed okay. She felt somewhat ashamed for how she had treated him.

"Sorry. No reason... except, you know, he usually comes in for a while. But I'm sure it's fine. We all knew you'd had enough."

"Yes, and I guess you all had a good laugh at my expense," Mia snapped.

"Hey, chill. We've all been there. But you've got to admit, it doesn't usually happen to you." Then she laughed. "I don't remember seeing you get drunk since we went to that party when we were both too young to even be drinking."

Mia couldn't help but laugh again, in spite of the repercussions in her aching head. "Yeah, we were both kind of messed up that night. I thought Mom and Dad would kill us!"

"Yeah, instead they said how disappointed they were in us. God, that was worse!"

"For sure. Man, you'd think I would have learned my lesson. I didn't ever want to feel that bad again."

"Don't be so hard on yourself. Once every five years isn't too bad. Besides, last night you weren't totally wasted like that vodka night." Julie set the cup of tea in front of her sister. "And yesterday was a big day. A day of celebration. You just aren't used to celebrating all afternoon and into the evening."

"But you were celebrating right along with me, right? How come you're so chipper this morning?"

"Practice." Julie opened the refrigerator. "Are you sure you don't want some eggs?"

"Yuck, no eggs."

"All right, how about French toast?"

"Okay, I guess I'd better eat something. French toast sounds pretty good."

"Are you going to church this morning?"

Mia groaned and checked the time. "Of course... but do you think we could tell the organist to keep it down?"

Julie laughed. "Carol? Not hardly. You'd better take something for that headache." Julie turned and looked at Mia. "Is Ron going to church with you today?"

Mia hadn't thought about it. He had been coming to church with her every week, but last night neither of them had said, "See you tomorrow," and she suddenly wasn't sure. "Hmm, I guess so, but maybe I'd better check."

She thought for a minute before sending him a hasty text.

Do you want to pick me up for church?

He didn't answer as quickly as usual, but the answer finally came in the form of a question.

Do you want me to?

Yes.

"Everything okay?" Julie asked.

"I hope so." For the first time since she and Ron had started dating, she wasn't so sure of herself. *Did I totally mess things up?*

An hour and a half later, stomach full and settled, Mia hurried to answer the door when Ron arrived. The drive to church was quieter than usual, and when they finally slid into their usual pew, Mia felt awkward and a little bit scared.

Unable to stand it any longer, right before the opening hymn, Mia leaned in close and asked Ron, "Are you angry with me? Did I mess this up?"

He turned to her and whispered back, "I thought you were upset with me. And you could never mess *this thing* up."

His words were followed by the blasting of the organ, and she saw Julie, who was sitting further down the pew, peek over at her and roll her eyes. Mia discreetly rubbed her head. It was going to be a long service.

Chapter Thirty-one

Ron knew things had been too quiet lately, and had a bad feeling when he got the call about another overdose… another young person. Arriving at the morgue, he got all the information he needed to confirm it was probably an accidental overdose, but he had to follow up with her parents. This was the worst part of his job, and each time he sat with a victim's family—whether murder, suicide, or accident—he questioned his choice of professions. This wasn't going to be easy.

He sat across from Mr. and Mrs. Burke and waited.

"But I don't understand," Mrs. Burke finally managed. "She wasn't on any medication like that."

"Do you know if she had any recent injuries, or even older ones, that might have been giving her pain?"

"What kind of injury? How would she get injured?" Mrs. Burke blew her nose. "What do you mean?"

"Has she possibly been in a car accident or maybe had a sports injury?"

"She doesn't play any sports, and no, she would have told us if she'd been in an automobile accident," the girl's father said.

"And she was here for dinner last weekend. Her and her boyfriend."

"What's her boyfriend's name?"

"David," the mother said.

"David Sipe," her father added.

"And do you have an address or phone number where I could reach him?"

The victim's parents hadn't been much help, but at least he had a name. Ron figured he would find something in the apartment with an address or phone number. He definitely wanted to talk to David Sipe.

It didn't take long to locate the boyfriend, but he wasn't any help at all. He was dead. Another OD... same stuff. Oxycodone. Ron had gone to the address he found–it was a Motel Six with weekly rates–where he had expected to ask Sipe some questions about the girl. Instead he found David on the floor outside his door.

At first, he thought the young man was sleeping, or rather, passed out. One does not usually sleep on the floor outside of their place. But when Ron shook him by the shoulder and tried to rouse him, the boy fell the rest of the way over. An immediate 9-1-1 call got the EMTs there within minutes, but it was too late, and they said he had probably been dead for hours.

Knocking on a few other doors to ask if the neighbors had seen anything brought no results. It wasn't until Ron went down to the front desk that he got any answers at all. The clerk said the cleaning staff had finished up by two o'clock which explained why no one had discovered the body. The other rooms in that hall were vacant except for an elderly woman he described as being "bats" and who Ron figured was probably schizophrenic from the way she was portrayed.

The bottle of pills was in Sipe's pocket, and the prescription was written by the same doctor as the first victim... Dr. Douglas Block.

It took a while to get answers to the questions burning in Ron's mind.

"Hi, Ann," he said into the phone. "Is Dr. Block available to take my call?" The receptionist explained that he was with a client and had one more after that. Then he would be through for the day. "Great. Would you ask him to give me a call back as soon as he can?"

It was more than an hour later when Block finally returned the call, and after much hemming and hawing, he admitted Sipe was one of his clients, and yes, he had seen him the day of the attack.

"What about Carol Burke?"

"Who?"

"Carol Burke. Is she also one of your clients?" The good doctor said he'd never heard of her, took a few moments to check his newer cases, and repeated that she was not one of his patients... and yet she also had a prescription from him.

"Are you absolutely sure? It seems she had oxycodone which had been prescribed by you."

"And she said she sees me?"

"No, doctor. She didn't say anything. She's dead."

There was a long pause before the doctor asked, "How..."

"Apparently she took too much oxy."

"And my patient? David Sipe?"

"Also dead."

The doctor seemed genuinely sorry to hear that. "He must have been the one... the one who took the drugs and the scrip pad."

Yet it simply didn't add up. Ron took out the evidence bag and looked at the pill bottle again. He checked the date on the girl's pill bottle. According to that, it had been filled two days prior to Block being assaulted and the prescription pad stolen... and David Sipe's name did not appear in the appointment book at RMH.

It was time to find out more about this Sipe fellow.

Three overdoses this close together—all with the same drug—and in this small town where drug use wasn't known to be a major problem... or at least it hadn't been until now. *What are we missing?*

All his years on the job had taught Ron one thing. You've got to connect the dots, so starting at square one, he went back to the body they'd found by the lake. Matt Markle. He had thought that death to be suspicious partly because of where they'd found him, though that didn't rule out suicide or accidental death, but also partly because of Mia's drawing before it happened.

A visit to question the coroner had determined Markle died after the mysterious drawing was done by his fiancée. But how? Why?

Chapter Thirty-two

"I met someone."

Adam's shy smile warmed Mia's heart. "That's wonderful, Adam. When was this, and where did you meet?"

"Well, you know how I've been feeling really funky lately... and I hadn't been looking forward to spending Thanksgiving with all the relatives."

"Why is that?" Mia couldn't imagine spending Thanksgiving without her family.

"I guess it might sound silly to you, but you know, it's Mom and Dad, and my sister and her husband and kids, and my brothers and their wives and their kids." Adam shook his head. "And they're all settled down in their successful marriages and have these great careers... and then there's me. Single. Lousy job. Alone. And pretty much a failure in life."

"Adam, stop." Mia wanted to remind him that at least he had a job and he'd turned his life around.

"No, let me finish. I was feeling lousy, like I said, so the night before, Wednesday, I went out, and I was driving around—not knowing where to go or what to do—and I came to my old hangout." He had been looking at the floor but peeked up at his therapist and added, "Yeah, I should've learned my lesson by now."

Mia held her breath, half afraid of what he was going to say next. As an alcoholic, meeting a girl in a bar would not bode well for their future together.

"But hey, don't look so worried."

Mia hadn't realized her concern was showing and tried to erase the frown lines that she realized must be there.

Adam went on. "I guess I actually did because, even though I slowed down and started looking for a parking place, at the last minute I thought of a better place to go. There was a meeting nearby at the church a few blocks away."

Relieved, Mia let her breath out slowly. "Is that where you met her?"

"Yeah." The small shy smile from earlier had now blossomed into a full-toothed grin. "Actually, I didn't just meet her. I mean we've seen each other at meetings before and we've chatted over coffee and snacks after the meetings, but we'd never really talked. You know what I mean?"

Mia nodded and smiled, delighting in the change in her client's affect as he talked about this girl. "Okay, so you talked more and got to know her a little better?"

"Yeah, and we went to the diner with a bunch of other people after, and when they had all headed home, we were still there, still talking, you know?"

Knowing that the road to recovery can be rocky and difficult, especially in the early weeks, months, and years, Mia had to ask. "Has this girl been in recovery long?"

Adam flashed the big grin again. "She's got three years clean and sober, and she has a name. It's Melody. Isn't that perfect?"

Oh boy, is he smitten! Mia smiled and nodded. "That's a beautiful name."

"Yeah, and she's cute and funny... and calm. Yeah, calm. And she makes me feel calm." Adam leaned back in his chair and heaved a big sigh. "So, I asked her if she would come to Thanksgiving dinner with me at my house."

"And did she accept?"

"Funny thing, I didn't think she was going to at first, and she said she should go to her folks', but once we figured out that her mom did dinner at one o'clock and my mom doesn't have ours until four, she agreed. So, short story long, I had a date for Thanksgiving."

"And how did that go? Your mom didn't mind having to set an extra plate?"

"Nah, there's so many of us that we sit everywhere, and a couple years ago we finally got her to switch to those heavy-duty paper plates. Makes cleanup a lot easier… and you don't have to worry about any of the rug rats breaking dishes. Actually, I think Mom and Dad were happy to see me with somebody, and Melody was a hit. Everybody likes her."

"So, have you seen her since Thursday?"

And there was that big grin again. "Yeah, we went to the Friday night meeting, and went to the diner again and talked for hours. Then we spent Saturday together. Rode our bikes on the trail and stuff."

"Sounds like you like her a lot."

"Yeah, I know it seems like we're moving kind of fast, but we talked about that too, and we're not going to do anything stupid, but we just really seemed to click."

"And do you know much else about her? Like where she works? What are her hobbies?"

"She studied meteorology and she's been on the local news for almost a year now. I never watched that channel so I didn't realize that." Adam laughed a little. "I could've been watching her all this time. And now I can see her when I tune in."

Mia had a sudden realization. "Oh, I think I've seen her on the morning weather report."

Adam nodded. "Yeah? What do you think?"

"I think she is pretty. I like her. She seems very personable."

"And she's hot!" Adam laughed.

"Will you be seeing her again soon?"

Adam's smile faded. "I thought so, but now I'm not so sure. I texted her this morning because I was going to ask her if she planned to go to the Tuesday night meeting at the Fellowship House tonight, but she hasn't answered."

"Well, she's at work, right?"

"Yeah, but she was off the air by seven o'clock, and she should have had time to text by now."

Mia lifted his spirits when she reminded him that people get busy, but she also spent some time establishing that he would be okay even if this blossoming romance didn't blossom. Even though Adam hadn't had a drink in eighteen months, after all he'd been through lately, she didn't know if he was strong enough in his recovery to withstand another huge disappointment.

It wasn't until after Adam's session ended and she was writing her notes that she remembered something. Only giving it half her attention this morning, Mia had watched the local news and weather before coming to work. Now she remembered, the weather had been given by the usual weekend girl. For some reason the regular weekday morning meteorologist wasn't on.

Where were you this morning, Melody Sipe?

Chapter Thirty-three

David Sipe's parents were like so many Ron had met under similar circumstances. They had been worried sick about their son because of his drug use, but they could not believe he was gone. They were adamant that he would not have overdosed on purpose. Even his sister, who looked awfully familiar, declared her brother was in no way suicidal.

"He was here for a little while on Thanksgiving, and he had a new girlfriend. He seemed to like her a lot, and he was looking healthier." The sister he learned was named Melody dabbed at her eyes.

David's father coughed, blew his nose, and cleared his throat. "This is my fault."

"No," his wife said. "You can't blame yourself."

Ron's curiosity was piqued. "What makes you say that, Mr. Sipe?"

"He got it from me. They both did," he said nodding toward his daughter.

"Stop it, Dad!" Melody looked hurt and angry. "You haven't had a drink since we were in grade school. If anything, you showed us how to overcome addiction."

Ron looked from Melody to her father who was having a hard time keeping it together. "Mr. Sipe, you were aware then, that your son was using drugs?"

"Yes, he's been getting high since he was in high school, you know, smoking weed, and then he started playing around with pills, and he got hooked."

"And forgive me for asking," Ron said turning to Melody, "but do you also use?"

"No!" Melody and both parents all answered at once.

"I started drinking in college, and it got out of hand, so I'm a recovering alcoholic, but I haven't had a drink in three years. I still go to meetings and stay involved with my community. Please... I'm afraid if my alcoholism and past problems come out, it could cost me my career."

"Don't worry, Miss, there's no reason for that to happen. But you were aware of your brother's addiction?"

"Of course. I tried to get him to go to NA meetings, and he actually did a few times, but he didn't think he was like the others there because he didn't use that much."

"Did your brother ever happen to mention where he got his oxycodone?" Ron was still trying to connect the dots, but no one in the family seemed to have any idea.

"We assumed he got them on the street, but he wouldn't talk about it," David's mother choked out.

"And you said he was here Thursday and seemed okay?" When they all nodded again, Ron asked, "And did he say anything before he left about where he was going next or who he might be seeing?"

Melody looked at her parents and back at Ron. "Not to me. But I left before he did. I was going to a friend's house for a second family celebration."

"He and the girl just thanked us and said they had to get going. I asked them to stay for more pie," Mrs. Sipe said, "but they said they were meeting some friends to watch the game."

"And what was the girl's name?"

"Oh gosh, I don't remember, do you Melody?"

"It was Carol," she said. "But I don't remember her last name."

Ron flipped the pages in his notepad. "Could it have been Burke?"

"Yes, yes, that was it. Carol Burke. Oh, poor girl. I wonder if she knows."

Ron shook his head. "I'm afraid she's gone, too." He thought of the devastation he'd seen on the Burkes' faces that he now saw mirrored here. "We found her body a few hours before we found David."

"Oh no." This news brought fresh tears from Mrs. Sipe, and her husband asked, "Did she... do you know if she got the drugs from our boy?"

"No sir, she did not. She had her own prescription." Ron saw relief sweep across his face. Then he saw a question forming.

"Prescription? You said 'her own prescription.' Does that mean David had a prescription too? He didn't get drugs on the street?"

"No, sir. He did indeed have a prescription from his doctor."

"What doctor is that? I didn't know he was seeing a doctor."

"Dr. Douglas Block was the prescribing doctor." Seeing the questioning look on the three faces in front of him, Ron decided to tell them more. But first he had a question for them. "Did you know he was seeing a psychiatrist?"

"He never said a word." Melody looked at her phone which had binged several times since Ron arrived. She grabbed a tissue and excused herself.

"Can't that wait?" her father said indignantly.

"It's Adam. He's been trying to reach me all day," she said sniffing. "I'll only be a minute."

"I'm sorry, Detective. You were about to say something?" Mr. Sipe put his arm around his wife who looked like she was barely holding it together.

"Well, this may not be related at all, but I thought you should know. The doctor I mentioned denies writing either prescription, your son's or the girl's."

"I don't understand." Mrs. Sipe was suddenly more alert.

"The doctor was assaulted not too long ago, and whoever knocked him on the head also took some things from the office... including prescription pads."

"You aren't accusing my brother—" Melody had just walked back into the living room.

"No, ma'am. Not at all," Ron said. "But I thought you might want to know that whoever is responsible for the attack on the doctor might be writing out prescriptions."

"But you don't think our son did that?"

"In all honesty, I have to rule out the possibility, but we didn't find any evidence of that where he was staying." Ron actually still considered Adam Grant as his major suspect. Then a thought crossed his mind. "Miss Sipe, you said someone was trying to reach you on the phone?"

"Yes, it was a friend."

"And what was his name?"

"Why?"

"Just dotting all the Is and crossing all the Ts."

"I don't know what that has to do with anything, but his name is Adam. Adam Grant."

Bam!

Chapter Thirty-four

When Mia arrived home from the center Wednesday, she collapsed onto the couch where Simeon immediately joined her.

"You okay?" Julie asked from the kitchen.

"Just tired," Mia said stroking her Persian's silver-gray fur.

"Long day shrinking heads, huh?"

Mia heard her sister chuckling from the next room and would have thrown something at her but couldn't quite muster enough energy. "I guess," she said. "I feel like my own brain has shrunk."

Julie walked in and sat on the other end of the couch with a dish towel over her shoulder. "But it's Humpday! And if a good meal would help, you're in luck. I've got my famous pork chops supreme in the oven, and they'll be ready in half an hour."

"Bless you. That sounds good." Mia loved their arrangement of Julie doing the cooking on Mondays, Wednesdays, and even on Thursdays, the night she had her critique group, Julie would make something in the crockpot and leave it for her sister before she headed to the library. Tuesdays Mia worked until nine and ordered supper delivered or ran out for a quick dinner at the diner. And of course, Friday was date night.

"My last client of the day has bulimia, which is one of the most difficult disorders to resolve. She wouldn't touch your pork chops, or anything else. I feel so bad for her, but I'm going to refer her to someone who specializes in eating disorders. We've got someone new coming on staff. I'll have to check with her, but I don't remember hearing that she specializes in that area."

"Yeah, Mom told me you're actually hiring two new people. The practice must be doing well."

Mia stretched and yawned, then she and her sister both laughed when Simmie decided he'd better also stretch. "Yeah, and now that Grandpa is cutting back and only working two days a week and no evenings, we really need them."

"Have you met either of the new people?" Julie got up and headed back to the kitchen and Mia followed, taking a seat at the island.

"Yes, and they both made a good first impression." Mia accepted the snack of cheese and crackers her sister set before her. "Thanks, I'm famished. So, the woman is actually a psychiatrist, which means we'll have two psychiatrists on staff, but she's willing to do a lot more therapy than just med checks like the Block does."

Julie laughed at the nickname which she said suited the odd doctor quite well. "What's her name?"

"Dr. Lois Finney. She had been practicing in the Philadelphia area, but her husband had a great career opportunity in little old Madison, so they decided it was worth the move."

"What does he do?" Julie asked tearing up the lettuces for their salad.

"He's an attorney, but he has accepted a judgeship here."

"Wow, impressive. What about the other new person? I thought Mom said you all hired a man. What did you think of him?"

"He'll be a perfect fit for our agency. His only problem might be with his patients and transference. I mean that's always a thing, but with a looker like him, I imagine all his female clients will think they're in love with him." Mia rolled her eyes. "But I suppose he's learned how to deal with that. Anyhow, he starts Monday. He's coming in tomorrow to get his office ready and start familiarizing himself with a few of the clients he'll have right away. He'll be getting a lot of the new ones too... and maybe my eating disorder girl, I hope."

Julie's latest splurge had been a lift-top coffee table so when everything was ready the girls fixed their plates and carried them into the living room to watch the news while they ate.

When the weather came on, Mia was reminded of what Adam told her the day before, and she wondered if he had heard from his new weathergirl friend. Then the news anchor came back on the air and announced, "The identities of the two latest drug overdose fatalities have now been released. They are David Alan Sipe and Carol Marie Burke. No further details have been released at this time. And we would like to send our condolences to the families of those lost."

"Well, that's odd," Julie said turning to look at her sister. "They don't usually do that, do they?"

"No, no, I wonder if..."

"If what?"

"Well, he said the man's last name was Sipe, and do you remember the girl that does the weather in the morning?"

"Yeah, sort of. Why?"

"Her name is Melody Sipe. Do you think they might be related? Her brother, maybe?"

"Oh, yeah... that makes sense. Wow!"

Yeah, that makes sense, but I hope it's not true.

"It's like an epidemic all of a sudden around here. I don't get it."

Knowing Melody and Adam were both recovering alcoholics, Mia prayed they were in no way involved and that if the victim was Melody's brother, that it wouldn't threaten her sobriety... or Adam's.

Adam wasn't scheduled for another session until the following Tuesday, but she wondered how he was doing. Did Melody ever get back to him? It was obvious now why she hadn't returned his text Tuesday. She'd probably just learned of her brother's death. But how was she doing now? And more importantly, to Mia, how was Adam?

When she and Julie finished their dinner, Mia cleaned up the kitchen and loaded the dishwasher while Julie flipped on a movie on Netflix.

"Do you want to watch something?" Julie asked.

"No." Mia dried her hands and headed downstairs. "You go ahead," she called back to her sister. "I want to do a quick sketch. Maybe I'll join you after a bit."

The itch had come on suddenly after she'd made the possible connection between one of the overdose victims and her client's new friend. Now she needed to find out why.

Her pencil flew, and when she was done, she sat back and looked at it with disgust. "You again. What the heck?" She looked heavenward. "I need your help clearing Adam. Why do you keep giving me this Blockhead?"

The next morning, Thursday, Mia hoped she was wrong but searched and found the obituary. She read the parents' names and one sister, Melody Sipe. *Nuts!* There was to be visitation and a funeral Friday morning.

When Mia got to the center, she checked her schedule for the next day then picked up her phone and called the number of her first client Friday morning who was scheduled for eleven o'clock. Fortunately, she had an opening later in the day, and also fortunately the woman on the other end of the line had a flexible lifestyle and an easy-to-get-along-with attitude. That left Mia free to discreetly attend the visitation, or at least observe from a distance, and see if Adam was there with Melody.

***

By ten o'clock Friday morning, Mia was at the funeral home listed in David Sipe's obituary. The parking lot was already packed with cars and there were people in somber clothing standing in groups of three or four as they moved toward the entrance. She waited a few minutes before venturing into the small crowd of mourners as unobtrusively as possible.

Once inside Mia inhaled the familiar scent of lilies, carnations, and chrysanthemums, and saw countless arrangements sitting on every available surface, but what struck her most were the clusters of young men and women caught in tearful embraces. She searched the crowd and finally saw Adam standing near the casket next to the lovely weathergirl. He had his hand around her waist, and she appeared to be leaning on him for support. Next to Melody, Mia saw a middle-aged couple—obviously the parents—accepting condolences with a mix of smiles and tears, barely holding their grief at bay. The characteristic solemnity one expects in a funeral home's atmosphere, is magnified when the life of a young person has been cut short, and David Sipe's age along with the circumstances of his death could be seen in the desolation of so many faces.

Having seen what she'd needed to see, Mia turned to leave, but someone else caught her eye. Standing in the corner was a man she knew quite well. Detective Ronald Bishop. He seemed to have seen her at the same moment and followed her outside.

"Hey, hi," he said when he caught up with her. "Did you know David Sipe or a member of his family?"

Mia thought about how to answer and wanted to choose her words carefully. "Well, yes, indirectly."

Ron wrinkled his brow. "What does that mean?"

"I can't really say." Mia took several steps in the direction of where she was parked. "I really have to get back to the center. Talk to you later, okay?"

"Whoa... hold up there. Don't I even get a kiss?"

Mia took the few steps back to answer his request, and with the touch of his lips, she wanted more. "I love you," she said hurrying away in spite of her desire. It was the best way to avoid any further questions, and she really did need to get back.

When she heard him say, "I love you, too," she turned back and flashed him a warm smile, waved and wondered why he was there. *I hope you don't suspect what I think you do.*

Chapter Thirty-five

Mia always enjoyed Saturday lunches at Ron's apartment and spending the lazy afternoon watching a movie, talking, or on nice days, going for a walk. Today wasn't providing that kind of weather though. Gray skies and twenty-five MPH wind gusts did not beckon, so Ron turned on the TV and checked the time while Mia settled in on the couch.

"Hey, do you want me to do some popcorn before we get into a movie?" she asked.

"Um, nah, maybe later. I'm still full from breakfast."

"Seriously? You? Too full for popcorn?" Mia laughed. "That's a first."

Ron had settled in next to her while checking Netflix and taking forever to decide on a movie, when Mia got a text.

She groaned and pulled out her phone to check it. "Oh crap! We've got to go."

"What's wrong?"

"It's Julie. She said something's wrong with the dishwasher, and it's leaking. She's afraid the water might go through to the downstairs and ruin stuff in my studio." Mia already had her jacket on and Ron was right on her heels.

"Do you want me to drive?"

"No, hop in." She appreciated that he had automatically come with her because she had a feeling she and Julie were in over their heads and would need his help. She pulled out in a hurry and lead-footed it until the cop in the passenger seat warned her to slow down.

"You don't want to get pulled over for speeding and take even longer to get there. Take it easy. It's going to be all right."

"Easy for you to say." But she let up on the gas, grateful they were so close.

Minutes later she was pulling into the driveway. The garage door was up, so Mia hopped out of the car and dashed to the door with Ron following behind.

When she opened the door, she stopped short.

"SURPRISE!" came the shouts from a crowd of people standing before her. Confused, she stared blankly until gradually, amidst the laughter and cheers, it began to sink in. She saw streamers, heart-shaped balloons, and a huge white banner with gold letters that read "Future Mrs. Bishop," and she was suddenly surrounded by friends and family taking turns embracing her. Mia never imagined this many people would even fit in her little house.

"So, the dishwasher is okay? There's no water?" Howls of laughter gave Mia her answer. She turned to Ron who stood cross-armed leaning against the wall. "You brat! You knew!" She gave him a friendly punch on the arm.

"Hey, blame your maid of honor. She's the brat who arranged the whole thing."

But Mia didn't punch Julie. She hugged her and whispered, "I really do love my sister."

Julie led her to one of the dining chairs that had been adorned with white tulle, situated next to a table covered in a champagne sequin tablecloth and piled high with gifts. Then everything started to register as she looked at individual faces and realized how many people had come to share in her bridal shower. She spotted both her parents and grandparents, then her little sister, Destiny, Ron's sister, Robin, Gabby and Ann from the center, and... "Morgan! Oh my gosh you drove all the way out here!"

"Of course. I wouldn't miss it."

Then Mia saw two more faces... two lovely ladies sitting quietly watching all the excitement and smiling. "Aunt Bonnie! Miss Edna! Oh my gosh." So totally overwhelmed by all the love, she had to bat back the tears that threatened.

Julie led her to the seat of honor, and still flabbergasted, Mia began to take in all the rest. The decorations, the food, the stack of beautifully decorated gifts. "How in the world did you do all this? I just left here a few hours ago."

"Don't I know it! I didn't think you'd ever leave," Julie said. "I texted Mom the minute you were out the door, and she and Dad and Destiny lugged all the food over. Oh, and I called Morgan at the hotel and she picked up Betsy and came right over to help decorate."

"Betsy! Oh my gosh, I didn't even see you sitting down there in the corner!" Mia was suddenly at a complete loss for words and was relieved when Julie invited everyone to fix themselves a plate and get ready for the games.

Ron looked at Craig and Andy.

"Games? I've got a better idea," Craig said. "I happen to know there's a TV in the den downstairs, and we could watch some golf."

Mia was reading a question on her fiancé's face, so she gave him a nod of permission, and he joined his future father-in-law and grandfather-in-law in filling their plates and escaping to the basement. But Ron did set his plate down to give Mia a kiss before fleeing to the temporary mancave.

"Aw..." came a chorus of voices in the estrogen-filled room.

"Okay, yep, I'm outta here. Have fun, sweetheart."

The food was delicious, the games were fun, and the gifts were delightful. From the beautiful set of four champagne flutes, to the engraved silver-plated photo frame that would soon hold their wedding picture, to Julie's snarky gift of a cookbook, which brought another round of hilarity.

The most laughter though, probably came when Mia opened the gift tagged from Aunt Bonnie and Edna. It was a skimpy, red and black, Victoria's Secret number, and Mia's face turned almost as red as the teddy.

"You should have seen the looks we got in there making the purchase," Edna said to more hilarity.

"Sounds like you ladies are having way too much fun." Hearing Ron, who had come up to grab a few more sodas for the menfolk, Mia quickly put the lid back on the box which amused her guests even more. "I don't even want to know," Ron said before making a hasty exit.

"I bet he would!" Julie winked at her sister.

When the final gift had been opened—a gorgeous white, diaphanous peignoir from her parents—and Mia was making her rounds thanking people and catching up with them, she caught something strange going on in the kitchen area. Sarah and Val were standing side by side facing Betsy, and all three, especially Betsy, looked stunned. *What in the world?*

Moments later, Betsy got her coat, gave Mia a hug, and said she had to be going.

"Wait. What's going on? Is everything all right?" Mia asked.

"Yes, I just told Mom I'd be home in time to help her out with something." Betsy turned toward the door, but turned back. "I'll call you, okay? Maybe we can get together... and talk." Before Mia could even respond, Betsy was gone.

It was many hours later after the last of the guests had gone, that Mia got the call. "Betsy, what's wrong?"

"Has everyone gone? Are you there by yourself?" Betsy asked.

"Pretty much. Ron's still here, but he'll be leaving soon, why?" Mia saw Ron give her a look figuring he was being invited to leave.

"I need to talk to you if I can, and... I need a place to stay tonight."

"A place to stay? Why? What happened?"

"I can explain when I get there, but if you don't want—"

"Of course, you can stay here. But you sound really upset. Are you coming over by yourself? Are you okay to drive?" She ended the call after Betsy assured her she would be fine, she'd be careful, and she was on her way... but Mia was concerned.

"What's going on?" Julie asked from the couch where she was sitting with Drake who had arrived moments earlier.

"I don't know. Betsy is upset about something, and she asked if she could stay here tonight. She seemed disturbed earlier, but she sounds worse now."

"I better get going then, but I rode here in your car," Ron said. "Do you have time to run me home or should I get an Uber?" Seeing Mia's hesitation, Ron reached for his phone.

"I have a better idea," Drake said. "Would you like to go for a ride, Julie? We can drop Ron off at his place on the way."

"Sure thing." Julie got her jacket and gave Mia a hug. "I hope everything is all right. I'll be home later, but call if you need me."

Mia had no idea what to expect when Betsy arrived—no idea her own world was about to be rocked—but she knew it was bad as soon as she saw the other girl's red swollen eyes. She took Betsy in her arms and held her as she shed a few more tears, then led her to the couch.

"Where's Julie?" Betsy asked.

"Out with her new boyfriend. We're the only ones here. Now what's going on? Did something happen to upset you at the shower this afternoon?"

Betsy nodded weakly.

"I'm so sorry. What was it?"

"I saw your mom and Grandma Val talking quietly in the kitchen. I didn't think, I mean... I didn't mean to eavesdrop... but I heard my name. And then your mother said, 'I can't believe how much she looks like Andy.' And Grandma Val said, 'I know, but she's never suspected a thing, and Susan would never tell her'."

"What... what were they talking about?"

"That's what I wanted to know. So, I went home and confronted my mom. Mia, it was awful. At first she acted like she didn't know what I was talking about, and we argued, and I finally screamed at her to tell me the truth." Betsy took a big breath. "That's when she started to cry. And I felt horrible. I love my mom. I didn't want to make her cry, but... anyhow she finally told me the whole story."

"What whole story? Tell me!" Mia had started putting the pieces of the puzzle together, but they just didn't fit. She didn't want them to fit.

"The whole story of how I was born, and who I am. And how my whole life has been a lie." Betsy paused, then finally took a deep breath and said, "Grandpa Andy is my biological father."

Mia stared at her friend with disbelief. "What?" Her mind reeled in the endless silence until she finally found words. "No! That's not possible. I mean, how? Why?" Mia was stunned. None of it made sense. How could her grandpa possibly be Betsy's father?

"Can I get some water?"

"Yes, of course." Going to the kitchen gave Mia a minute to gather herself, but it wasn't enough.

"Well, the best I can understand," Betsy said after taking a sip, "is back before I was born, my mom and your grandfather had a little fling—"

"Grandpa cheated on Grandma?" Mia couldn't grasp it. She heard the words, but they didn't make sense.

"Yes, and I guess your grandma forgave him because by the time Mom found out she was pregnant, your grandparents had reconciled." Betsy took a deep breath. "As it turns out Mom and Dad had been trying to have a child and couldn't, so Mom decided to keep the baby—me—and make Dad think I was his."

"So, Grandma knows all this?" Mia's mind was whirling.

"Yep. Apparently, everybody does. Well, your grandparents *and* your parents *and* my father. That is, the man I always thought was my father. God only knows who else."

"I can't believe it." Mia could think of nothing else to say. Her grandfather was a rock. Her rock. He was the head of their family. Her very faith had grown out of the steadfast Christian faith of her grandparents and her parents. How could this possibly be true? Was it all a lie?

Betsy's phone had been pinging repeatedly. She finally took it out and turned it off.

"Your mom?" Mia asked.

"My dad. He's worried about me. He tried to stop me from leaving, but I couldn't stay in that house with her for one more minute."

"I understand, but do you mind if I just let your dad know you're okay?" When Betsy gave the go ahead, Mia sent Dr. Walters a quick text.

"Would you like a cup of tea? Or hot chocolate?" Mia decided they both needed something to warm them.

"Tea would be great. You always have the best teas."

Mia suddenly laughed, and Betsy's head snapped around to see what was funny.

"I just realized something kind of amusing. I mean, I know it's not funny, but..."

"What? I could use a laugh right about now," Betsy said.

"Well, it seems I should be calling you Aunt Betsy!"

Chapter Thirty-six

The next morning when Mia awoke, she went straight to the guest room to check on Betsy and found her already up, dressed, and sitting cross-legged in the middle of the bed scrolling through her phone.

"You okay? Did you sleep?" she asked.

"Yes, I think all that bawling I did last night must have worn me out because I fell right to sleep. Only problem was, I kept having stupid dreams that woke me up. I finally surrendered about an hour ago."

"What kind of dreams?" Mia sat on the side of the bed, much like she had when Betsy was a frightened six-year-old staying with Grandpa Andy and Grandma Val. It occurred to Mia that the little girl had actually been staying with her father back then.

"Nothing that made any sense," Betsy said. "It wasn't about Mom and Dad or Grandpa Andy." Betsy rolled her eyes when she said his name. "How am I going to face him now? Damn, I don't even know what to call him."

"I don't know, Bets. I don't know." Mia wasn't even sure how *she* was going to face him. Everyone was bound to find out the truth now. "I guess it's going to be awkward for a while."

"That's an understatement. And I was thinking how I hardly ever see most of your family anymore. But with the wedding coming up..." Betsy looked thoughtful then asked Mia, "Do you still think I should be a bridesmaid?"

"Yes! Of course I do. Unless—"

"Unless what?"

"Unless it would be too hard for you."

"No, I'm in. After all," Betsy flashed a sly little smile, "I want to be there for my niece."

"Oh lordy, this is crazy. I don't know whether to laugh or cry about the whole relationship thing." But Mia realized it was Betsy she should be thinking about, not herself. "What can I do? I mean, how can I help, Bets?"

"You've already done it. I needed time. Time away from Mom. And you gave me that. And you gave me your shoulder to cry on."

"Anytime."

"Yes, I know. You've always been there for me for as long as I can remember, but I'm not a child anymore, and I think I'm ready to deal with this head on." Betsy sounded so brave, but Mia detected the slight quiver in her chin.

"What are you going to do now?"

"I'm going to go home and talk to Mom and Dad. I need to apologize for the way I lashed out at her."

"Seriously... no one can blame you after what you'd just discovered and the way you found out." Mia didn't deem Betsy the one who ought to be apologizing. "Your mother should certainly understand."

"Yeah, probably. I wish I did. But all the same..."

Mia realized little Betsy had truly grown up, and she was handling this whole thing much better than Mia presumed she would. "Okay, kiddo. But first, I'm going to get dressed and make us some breakfast."

When they got to the kitchen, they found Julie dressed and ready for church. She looked from Mia to Betsy and back again. "Everything okay?"

"Getting there," Betsy said.

"How about some pancakes?" Julie was already mixing the batter and soon had the cakes stacked high.

"There are only three of us. Looks like you're cooking for an army, Jules."

"Might as well. You know when he gets here, Ron will eat some if we've got them."

"Oh, I should text him. I don't think I'm going to church this morning. I'm sure he won't mind."

Julie was refilling her coffee mug and stopped mid-pour. Mia thought she looked as though she was dying to find out what was going on. "Oh," was all she said.

Half an hour later, after a big hug and promise to talk again soon, Betsy hopped in her car and headed home. As Mia watched her drive away, and she was about to close the door, she saw Ron's vehicle turn into the cul-de-sac.

"What's going on?" he asked as he got out of his car. "Aren't you feeling well?"

Mia gave her fiancé a warm greeting, holding onto him a little longer than usual, long enough that when she stepped back, she could see the concern in his eyes. "I'm feeling fine... better now that you're here."

Once inside, Ron proved Julie's earlier prediction, filling a plate with a short stack of pancakes. While he was eating and Julie had a second coffee, Mia filled them both in on all she'd learned from Betsy.

"Grandpa Andy? No, I don't believe it. He would never."

"I can't believe he would either, but obviously we don't know him as well as we thought."

"So, you're saying this eighteen-year-old girl is actually your aunt, and your grandfather once cheated on your grandmother?" Ron seemed dumbfounded.

"Yes, and I'm not ready to see him in church this morning looking all righteous. They've been lying to us all these years." The more she talked about it, the angrier Mia became.

"I hear you," Julie said, "but it's still Grandpa. And if Grandma knows and she's okay with it, maybe we should—"

"Maybe we should what? Act like it doesn't matter?" Mia, who had been sitting across from her sister, pushed away from the table and got to her feet. "That might be easy for you. He's not *your* grandfather!" Mia saw the look of shock on Julie's face but she couldn't stop the glut of emotion. "And you didn't all of a sudden find out that Betsy is literally your aunt. I did." Mia's chest moved in and out with each breath coming faster and her heart pounding. She could barely breathe.

She didn't see him move, but somehow Ron was holding her, and had his arms around her. He murmured in her ear, "Calm down, sweetie. Don't cry. It's going to be all right."

"No! It's not all right!" She pulled away from him. "And I'm not crying. I'm mad!" She felt like she had to get away from Ron, away from Julie, and headed for the stairs to her studio. But as she passed Julie, she saw the pain in her sister's eyes and realized how much her words must have hurt. Andy Reed had after all become Julie's grandfather too. "I'm sorry," she choked out as she swept by.

When Mia reached her studio, she stood in the center of all of her work and felt lost. Her gaze fell on the portrait of Dr. Block, and something snapped. In three steps, she reached the sliding door to the backyard and threw it open, storming out into the brisk morning air. She moved forward, and when she reached the middle of the yard, she felt someone watching her and turned in time to see Ron viewing her from an upstairs window. *Why didn't I grab my jacket?* The early December air might have felt crisp and refreshing had she been dressed for it, but she suddenly shivered.

Seconds later the patio door slid open. Ron approached with her jacket in his arms. When he reached her, he placed it around her shoulders without a word and turned back toward the house.

"Wait! Ron... I'm sorry."

He said it was okay, but Mia knew she had been unkind to him as well as her sister. They weren't even the ones she was really angry with. It was her grandparents, her parents... and even God.

Ron put his arm around Mia and guided her back inside and up to the kitchen. She expected to see her sister, to whom she believed she owed an apology, but the kitchen was empty.

Mia turned to Ron. "Do you know where Julie is?"

"When you headed downstairs, she grabbed her jacket and said she was going to church." Ron checked the time. "We can still make it if you've changed your mind."

"No, not today. I just can't." Mia saw the look of confusion on Ron's face and wanted to explain, but how could she when she didn't understand it herself? All she knew was that all of a sudden everything was off. All the things that seemed so simple and made perfect sense were suddenly complicated.

"I've always thought God answered my prayers, yet now He doesn't seem to be listening."

"What are you talking about? Your grandfather? What prayers aren't being answered?"

"Well, it's not just this. I know you may not believe it, but for one thing, I am absolutely certain Adam Grant had nothing to do with the assault on Dr. Block." She heard Ron sigh. and knew he didn't put any stock in her belief in Adam... and now even she began to wonder. But she still believed in him. "So I've been praying about it, and I thought I could draw or paint something that would help us find the real culprit."

"Us?"

"Yes, Ron. Us. But even when I thought I had the itch that might give us some answers, all I drew was the victim. I have two pictures of Dr. Block... and I don't even especially like him."

"Is that why I saw you at David Sipe's visitation? Were you aware he was a friend?"

"Yes and no."

"What does that mean?"

"I knew he was a friend of *Melody* Sipe, not David." The look on Ron's face said it all. She hadn't helped Adam's case. But still, she knew he was innocent.

Chapter Thirty-seven

When Mia revealed the connection between Adam Grant and Melody Sipe, it didn't surprise Ron. He had watched Adam support Melody during her brother's funeral, and when it was over, Ron knew Adam went to the Sipe residence and remained there for at least thirty minutes, long enough to establish he was more than a casual friend.

Because he loved Mia, Ron had hoped his hunch was wrong, but from what she was saying, she had nothing to back up her belief in Adam.

Then again, Ron had no proof of his guilt. Sure, Adam had been there the day Block was attacked and fit the very general description the doctor had given them. He was actually the only young male client who had been seen at the Reed Mental Health Center that day. The other men could not be described as young.

When Ron had discovered David Sipe was a patient of Dr. Block and had filled a prescription from him, the detective wondered if the dead man could also be a suspect, but after double checking, he established Sipe hadn't been seen that day. And there was no sign of a prescription pad at either his or his girlfriend's residence.

He was mulling all this over while driving Mia to her parents' home for Sunday dinner and had plenty of time for thought as Mia wasn't her usual talkative self. Any other day she would have been chatting about the wedding.

"Did you have fun at your bridal shower?" he asked.

"Yes, but Betsy didn't," Mia responded sullenly.

No more needed to be said. They drove in silence. Ron wondered if the usual fun-filled Reed Sunday dinner would be the same.

"Are you ready?" he asked Mia, helping her out of the car.

She smiled—a smile he would have totally believed if he hadn't known her better—and assured him she was ready. As soon as they were inside, Ron saw her make a beeline for Julie. Though he couldn't hear what they were saying, it was obvious by their embrace that Mia was mending fences.

"Hey Ron, how's it going?" Cody said. "Has my sister driven you crazy yet?"

"Not yet," Ron said patting his future brother-in-law on the back.

"I heard you were there yesterday. I bet that was crazy."

You have no idea. "Let's just say from downstairs we heard a lot of laughing." That part was true. Too bad the day had ended with tears.

Chapter Thirty-eight

Mia sighed with relief after apologizing to Julie, but sitting down at the table with her parents promised to be challenging. Certain family members probably still didn't know anything about Betsy's true parentage. Dinner would not be the time or place to bring it up. However, Mia had made up her mind there was a conversation to be had... and it wasn't going to be pleasant.

She was on her way to the table when Cody asked, "Hey, where were you this morning? I didn't see you in church."

"I, um—"

"My fault," Ron interjected. "I was running late. Sorry."

"Oh, I thought Julie said—"

Cody was interrupted once again when Sarah said, "Cody, come help me carry the food in, please."

"Oh okay, sure." Cody looked back over his shoulder, and Mia saw that her brother was suspicious. Unfortunately, he was no dummy.

"Thank you," she whispered to Ron. "Cody seems to be a bit of a detective like somebody else I know."

With all the family gathered around the table, Craig asked who would like to say grace.

"I will," Sarah said quickly. "Dear Lord, we thank you for your many blessings and especially for your forgiveness. You taught us to pray, 'Forgive us our trespasses as we forgive those who trespass against us.' We pray for the strength to forgive others as you forgive us. Bless us, Lord, and bless this food we are about to receive. Amen."

Mia felt the heat growing in her neck and ears. Her mother was obviously talking to her and telling her to forgive her grandfather, and all the rest of them, she supposed. But that only amplified Mia's anger. *How dare she!*

As they shared their Sunday dinner, everyone seemed quieter than usual, and conversation was rather stilted.

"All right," Destiny said putting her fork down on her plate with a clank. "What's going on?"

"What do you mean, Squirrel?" Craig asked.

"Something's not right and you know it. You're all acting weird, and I don't like it." Sarah and Craig looked at each other, then both shifted their gaze to their plates. Destiny looked around the table. "Is anybody going to tell me what's wrong?" When no one answered, she pushed her chair back and stormed out of the room. Seconds later Mia heard her bedroom door slam.

"She's right," Cody said. "And I'm getting the distinct impression that everybody here is in on it except Destiny and me." Still, no one said anything. "Okay, I get that Destiny is still a kid, and maybe you're trying to protect her or something, but I'm not, so... what gives?"

After a long pause, during which Cody continued to look from one to another of his family members, it was Craig who finally spoke. "Cody, your sister," he nodded his head in Mia's direction, "well, she found out something—a family secret I guess you could call it—about someone and it upset her. Your mother and I had kept the person's secret, so I think she's angry with us, too. Right, Mia?"

Now Mia's whole face felt like it was on fire. "What do you think!" It wasn't a question.

Silence.

But the silence didn't last long. "Well, somebody better tell me the rest of it. Who's been keeping a secret? Julie?" he asked looking at her. She shook her head, and her eyes filled with tears.

"All right, that's enough," Craig said slamming his fork down on his plate. "I'm not going to let this tear our family apart. It's about your grandfather, Cody."

Cody's eyes widened in disbelief.

"Yes, my father made a mistake, a big mistake, a long time ago. I learned about it much later, and it was difficult," he said looking at Mia and Julie. "But in time I came to accept it and forgive him. More importantly, the most important person—the one he hurt most—your grandma forgave him."

"The one he hurt most?" Mia said. "Seriously? What about Betsy?"

"Betsy?" Cody's head snapped around to look at Mia. "What does Betsy have to do with it?"

"Betsy was the result of Grandpa's 'mistake'," Mia said throwing up air quotes. "Grandpa is actually Betsy's father!"

Mia regretted the bitterness with which she'd blurted out the truth and the shock on Cody's face. But then she noticed his jaw drop as he gazed toward the doorway through which Destiny had exited moments earlier.

Mia swung around in time to see her little sister turn and rush out of the house through the patio doors.

She jumped up from her seat. "I'll go after her."

"No! I'll handle this. You've done enough." Sarah hurried out after Destiny.

"It's all right, Mia. Let your mom talk to her."

"I'm... I'm sorry. I didn't mean to..."

"Wow," Cody finally said. "Grandpa. Who would've thought...?"

"Listen, kids. Your grandfather is a good man. He was the best father I could have ever hoped for, and he's been a damn good grandfather to you kids. All of you. But he's human. And a long, long time ago, yes, he was unfaithful to my mom, to your grandma. And they went through some difficult times, but eventually your grandma told me how he had begged for forgiveness, not only from her, but from God. She said he got down on his knees in church and..."

Mia saw her father gulp and swipe at the tears. She couldn't stand to see the pain in his eyes. Jumping from her seat at the table, she rushed to where he was sitting and threw her arms around his neck. "I'm sorry, Daddy. I'm so sorry."

"It's okay, baby girl."

Mia couldn't remember the last time he had called her that. She thought it might have been after she'd been rescued from her kidnapper.

"I'm sure this has been a terrible shock. Maybe we shouldn't have kept it from you, but to tell you the truth, I never thought this was my secret to share. And after all these years, I never imagined Betsy would find out."

"How did she?" Cody asked still looking stunned.

"Apparently your grandma mentioned to your mom yesterday that Betsy bears a striking resemblance to your grandpa when he was a young man. She didn't realize Betsy had come in behind her. Now your grandma feels dreadful, and as you might imagine, your grandfather is devasted too."

Mia hadn't even thought about how this would affect Grandpa. She'd been so focused on Betsy—the truly innocent victim in this situation—that it hadn't occurred to her that the girl's biological father would also be distraught knowing of her pain.

"I don't know what to do." Mia moved back to her spot at the table. "Should I leave?"

"What? No, please don't Mia," Craig said.

"But I've made such a mess." She sat down next to Ron who hadn't said a word through the whole fiasco, and he put his hand on her knee. "Do you think she's all right?"

"Destiny?" Craig asked. "I'm sure she will be. Your mom will know what to say... but it might take some time. She idolizes her grandpa."

The crushing guilt Mia felt at hurting her little sister was the ultimate low. She felt helpless to do anything about it. "You know I would never do anything to hurt Squirrel. I don't know what to do."

Ron put his arm around her and she rested her head on his shoulder. Then he gave her the answer. “Do what you do best, sweetheart. Just pray.”

Chapter Thirty-nine

Ron dragged himself out of bed Monday morning. He had stayed with Mia late into the night, and wouldn't have left when he did had she not pushed him out the door. Even later, when he should have been exhausted and sleeping soundly, Ron lay awake worrying about her.

He had never seen his fiancée so utterly devastated, nor had he ever felt so powerless to help. His efforts to convince Mia she wasn't responsible for hurting her little sister or anyone else did not appease her.

He had tried to make her see how much her support for Betsy must have meant to the young girl. Yet, in spite of anything he said, Mia's anguish didn't appear to diminish. There was something more bothering her. Ron was sure of it, yet he couldn't quite put his finger on it, and Mia wasn't talking.

Although he drank two big mugs of coffee before leaving his apartment, Ron stopped in at the Hav-a-Cuppa Cafe downstairs and grabbed another joe to go—no cream or sugar—just good strong coffee. He would need all the caffeine he could get to make it through the day.

First stop, meet up with Evans at the station and compare notes. *What are we missing?* Still convinced Adam Grant was probably their guy in the Block case, he searched for the missing link, the piece that would tie it all up so he could put a ribbon on it and give more attention to the other cases begging for his attention.

It hadn't escaped his mind that Mia wouldn't be happy about it, but once the young man's guilt had been proven, she would have to accept it. She had admitted last night that she actually asked the powers that be—whoever gave her the gifts in her art—to give her a clue, to help her to draw the guilty party, but each time she prayed for it, all she got was a picture of the victim, Dr. Block.

Once he got to the station and he and Jason poured over all they knew, Ron decided on his next steps. Since Adam, a tech wizard, often worked from home, that's where Ron decided to start.

"Why don't you take care of this one?" he said pointing to another case file. "I'm going to swing by Grant's and ask a few more questions."

When he got to the man's house, Ron rang the doorbell and knocked on the door a couple times. He had all but given up and was turning to leave when the door opened. Adam was in sweats and bare feet. *Must be nice.* Ron thought he'd rather enjoy wearing sweat pants to work, but he was pretty sure that wouldn't wash with the captain.

The earbuds explained why Grant probably hadn't heard him knocking, and he started to apologize until he recognized Ron. "Oh, it's you. What do you want now?"

"Just a couple of questions. May I come in?" Adam opened the door wider and stepped back out of the way. "Thanks."

Ron expected the young man to offer him a seat, but Adam stood facing him with no such offer.

Since the front door opened right into the living room of the small house, Ron took the few steps over to the nearest chair and asked, "May I sit?"

"Sure, I guess." Adam remained standing.

Ron noticed a picture of a little girl—looked to be four or five years old. "Cute kid. Yours?"

"Yes, my daughter."

"So, you're married?"

"Divorced." Adam took a seat on the edge of the sofa. "But I'm sure you're not here to ask me about my marital status or family. How can I help you, Detective?"

"I saw you at David Sipe's funeral. You were a friend of his?"

"No, I never met him." Responding to the detective's raised eyebrows he added, "I know his sister." Ron pulled out his notepad and jotted something down, and Adam responded by sitting down and slumping back against the sofa cushions. "Why? Is there a law against being friends with the deceased?"

"No, of course not. Have you known her long?"

"Not really. We met the day before Thanksgiving."

"Is that right?"

"Well, no, not exactly. I was acquainted with Melody, but we became friends after a meeting that night."

"A meeting? What kind of meeting?" Ron noticed a moment's hesitation before his suspect answered the question. It made him wonder if the answer was going to be a truthful one.

"You know, I don't think it's any of your business... and it's supposed to be anonymous, but I guess if I don't tell you, you're going to suspect me of something. AA. I'm a recovering alcoholic. I go to meetings, all right?"

"Yeah, that's not a problem." Ron wrote AA in his notepad. "So, Melody is an alcoholic too, huh?"

"What do you think? But like I said, it's called Alcoholics *Anonymous.*" Adam leaned forward. "If you blab this it could hurt her. She's a meteorologist. She's does the local weather."

"I know who Melody Sipe is."

"Yeah, of course you do."

Ron noticed the bitterness in Adam's voice.

"Can you just leave her out of this?"

"Out of what? Is there something you want to tell me?"

"No," Adam said indignantly. "Would you quit playing games and get to it, man? Are you here to accuse me of something else?"

"No, sir. I'm simply trying to put the pieces of the puzzle together. I got a young guy dead from an overdose of a prescription drug, and when Dr. Block was attacked, blank prescription pads were taken. You were known to have been at the Reed Mental Health Center the day of the assault, and now I discover you are friends with the dead man's sister. Does that sound about right?"

"I told you, I never met Melody's brother. Do I need a lawyer?"

"I don't know. Do you think you do?"

"I think you need to get out of my house." Adam jumped to his feet and was at the front door in two long strides. "If you're not arresting me, please leave." He pulled the door open and stood back.

Ron could see by the man's flushed face and gritted teeth that he was extremely agitated. "I'll be in touch," he said before the door shut in his face.

Back in the car he couldn't help wonder if Adam was displaying the agitation of a guilty man who realizes he's going to be caught or of an innocent man wrongly accused. He was leaning toward the former, but he knew Mia would believe the latter.

For her sake he wished the evidence didn't point to Adam's guilt, but it did. Yet it was still all circumstantial. He grabbed his phone and placed a quick call.

"Yeah. I'm going to need a search warrant."

Chapter Forty

Mia hurried to the waiting room to get her next client. She was anxious to see how Adam Grant was doing. He had been on her mind ever since she saw him standing with Melody Sipe four days earlier at her brother's funeral.

"Adam, come on back." She saw his agitation immediately.

Once in her office, Adam flopped onto the chair, squeezed his lips together, and shook his head. "That detective... he's trying to pin that attack on Dr. Block on me."

Mia knew who Adam meant. "Did he question you again?" She had expected Ron would after seeing the suspect at the Sipe funeral, but that certainly didn't prove anything.

"Yes! But that's not all. He was asking all these questions about Melody's brother and if I knew him and stuff. And I answered everything. Then I finally asked him to leave, but that wasn't the end of it."

"What do you mean?"

"He showed up again a couple hours later with a search warrant and some helpers, and they tore my place apart." Adam was hitting his fist into his other palm. "You should've seen the mess they left me."

"But did they find anything?"

"What? No... of course not! Do you think I did it now, too?"

"No! No, Adam, I definitely do not." *I should never have asked that.* "But that's good, isn't it?"

"You would think so, but I heard that Bishop guy say something to his partner about how maybe I got rid of it."

"Do you know what they were looking for, Adam?" She was pretty sure she knew.

"They wouldn't answer me when I asked, but when he questioned me earlier, he said something about missing prescription pads. I'm sure that's what they were looking for since Melody's brother overdosed. But I. Didn't. Do. It."

"I believe you, Adam, honestly I do. And they didn't arrest you... and I know they can't prove you did something you didn't do."

"Yeah, but this detective, I think he's trying to build a case out of circumstantial evidence. What if he talks to Melody and she believes him? What if she thinks I'm somehow responsible for her brother dying? And what about my little girl?"

Mia was appalled by what her fiancé had put Adam through and what he still might do to make it worse. At the end of Adam's session, she had to ask one thing.

"Are you okay? Are you secure in your sobriety right now?"

"I am not going to drink today, Mia," he assured her. "I'm going to my home meeting in a couple hours. That's what I need right now. That and for the cops to find the real guilty person."

Mia limped through the rest of her day, giving her full focus to each of her remaining three clients, then headed home. All the anger and frustration she'd been pushing down for the past three hours came bubbling to the surface, and by the time she entered her house she was fuming.

Julie was finishing up an early dinner before heading out to meet with her critique group, so Mia said a quick hello with the briefest small talk, then excused herself. Mia didn't anticipate it getting any better when she glared at her portrait of Dr. Block in the studio. *Why can't he just remember and identify the man who really did this to him?*

With no answer to her rhetorical question, all Mia wanted to do right now, and the only thing that might stop the pressure from building, was to speak with Detective Ronald Bishop.

Chapter Forty-one

After taking a timeout to journal her resentment then eating a quick dinner, Mia retired to her studio. She lined up her drawings of Dr. Block—she had four of them now—and studied the man's facial expression in each one, noticing the slight changes in his eyes and around his mouth. The first one she had drawn was virtually expressionless, looking much like a man posing for the camera. In the second, he no longer wore the "say cheese" smile, and the third picture seemed to show a mix of fear and anger. In the final one there was definitely a sneer... a smirk.

The sound of a male voice made her jump even though she'd been expecting its owner.

"You know you shouldn't leave your house wide open when you're down here alone," Ron said. "Anybody could wander in off the street."

"So I see." Mia strolled over and gave him a casual peck, then turned back to her drawings. "Look at these," she said turning back to the four shades of Dr. Block. "What do you think?"

"I think my fiancée is a very talented artist."

"No, I mean do you notice anything strange?"

"Other than you becoming obsessed with the good doctor? Why do you keep drawing him, anyway?"

"I'm not obsessed, and it's not my idea." Mia noticed how his brow wrinkled then gradually smoothed as he caught on to her meaning. Understanding, he scrutinized the row of images more carefully, looking from one to the next to the next... going down the line and back.

"Well, he looks a lot like a balding Christopher Walken—which I never noticed before—but other than that it just looks like you're doing the many moods of Dr. Block. Is that right?"

"Yes... I mean, that's not what I intended, but yeah, he has different expressions in each one."

"Yes, and that one on the end is downright creepy. Why do you think that is?"

Mia scratched her head and moved in closer. "I don't know. Maybe because he is creepy... but what is it trying to tell me?"

"Maybe he's angry that we still haven't locked up the guy who he now thinks assaulted him."

Mia's head snapped around, and she glared at her fiancé. "If you're talking about Adam, he didn't do it."

"I didn't name names," Ron said throwing up his hands in self-defense, but after a short pause, he added, "but you know all evidence is pointing that way, and now that Block may be remembering—"

"I don't care! I *know* he's innocent."

"All right, all right. Calm down—"

"Don't tell me to calm down... I think maybe you should leave."

Ron's jaw dropped. "What?"

Mia saw the look of disbelief on his face and knew she was being unreasonable, but she couldn't seem to help herself.

"Let's be rational," he added with an effort to smile. "I don't know why you're so angry."

"I'm not angry," Mia lied, turning her back to him. "I'm tired, and I have a headache. It's been a long day, and I just want to have a cup of tea and go lie down."

She trudged up the stairs, uncomfortable with how closely Ron followed, and went straight to the front door. Mia sensed Ron wanted to say something more as he hesitated before leaving. His eyes seemed to be searching her face for some explanation, but then he simply kissed her on the forehead and left without another word.

"What was that all about?"

Mia was startled by her sister's voice.

"Does he have to go back to work or something?"

"Huh? Oh, no, we just decided to make it an early night. I think I'll get a cup of tea and head upstairs and lie down." *Well, that makes two people you've lied to tonight.*

Once on the way to her room, tea in hand, Mia saw the skeptical look on her sister's face.

"Hope your headache goes away," Julie said. "I'll be here if you want to talk."

"Okay, thanks."

Mia pulled her phone from her back pocket and sat on the side of her bed sipping tea and wondering what to do next. She wasn't a bit tired and unexpectedly wished she was in Ron's arms. She also wished she hadn't sent him away. *What is wrong with me?* She stared at the phone in her hands, then finally texted.

Sorry about tonight.

She sat staring, waiting for those little dots that signaled he was typing a response. Nothing.

Five long minutes passed before he finally replied with the "okay" emoji. Nothing more. No heart emoji. No "talk to you tomorrow" or "I love you." Mia's heart sank, and she laid the phone on her nightstand.

What have I done? But seconds later her concern reverted to anger once again. She seized her phone and punched in the words "But Adam is innocent," then turned it off and crawled under her comforter.

***

The house was quiet when Mia awoke confused and shaken. Still fully dressed, she slid out from under the covers and into her slippers. Discovering the house was dark, and Julie's door closed, Mia realized she had no idea what time it was. She got her phone and was surprised to see it was only eleven-thirty. At that hour Julie was probably still awake reading or working since she tended to be a night owl. Mia considered knocking on her door and taking her up on the offer to talk.

On second thought, though, she decided she wasn't ready to speak to Julie or anyone else. She crept down the stairs using only the flashlight on her phone, then flipped on the basement light and hurried to her studio. The four faces of Dr. Block greeted her—mocked her—from where they sat lined up like an enemy force. *But why do I see you as the enemy? I need answers!*

Chapter Forty-two

After driving around mindlessly, Ron found himself pulling into his sister's diner. He didn't recognize either of the two waitresses who looked his way when he entered, but he did notice one of them checking the clock on the wall. As she approached, he was pretty sure she was going to let him know they were closing in twenty minutes, so he decided to beat her to the punch.

"Hi, I know you're getting ready to close, but I wondered if Rachel might still be here." The single customer sitting at the counter—obviously the driver of the truck pulled alongside the diner—picked up his check and headed for the register.

"No, but Kevin's in the back. Do you want me to get him?" Before Ron could answer, Kevin emerged from the kitchen, greeted him with a hearty handshake and asked what he could do for him.

"I was actually looking for my sister."

"Is anything wrong?"

"No, not at all. Just thought I'd stop in and chat." Ron made a show of checking the time. "Wow, I didn't realize it was this late, though," he lied.

"She's at home. Why don't you stop by? I know she'd love to see you."

"But it's late. I shouldn't bother her."

"Are you kidding? She'll be glad to see you, and by now Ronnie's probably asleep, so you might actually be able to talk. Go ahead over, and tell Rache I should be home in about an hour."

Back in his vehicle, Ron tried phoning Mia, but since the call went straight to voicemail, he shot his sister a quick text, and getting her immediate response, went directly there.

A quarter of an hour later, sitting across from Robin with his head in his hands, he mumbled, "I don't know what to do about it." He had explained Mia's conviction that their suspect was completely innocent. "I know she's upset, but I'm just doing my job, you know?" It was good having someone to talk to... someone who cared.

Robin leaned forward in her chair. "Listen, Ron. You can't beat yourself up. She's the one being unreasonable."

"She seems so damned certain he didn't do it." Ron shook his head. "I don't get it. All the evidence points to this guy, but Mia simply isn't buying it."

"So? I mean, that's not your problem."

"Yeah, well it sure felt like my problem tonight when she kicked me out."

"You're the detective; not her. Maybe Mia needs to butt out and let you do your job."

Ron leaned back into the couch and blew out a breath of frustration. "Hold on, though. It's not like she has nothing to base it on. She knows the guy. She knows him really well... and she's pretty intuitive."

"Are you saying you think she might be right?"

"To tell you the truth, I don't know what I'm saying." Ron pulled out his phone. Still no more word from Mia. "It's getting late. I'd better get going," he said getting to his feet.

Robin jumped up. "Are you sure? Kevin should be here any minute."

"I'm sure. I'll catch up with you guys this weekend, okay?"

"Absolutely. Little Ronnie keeps asking for Unca Wonnie."

"He's a pretty cool little guy. All right, it's a date. If it's okay, I'll bring my fiancée along." *If she's still my fiancée by then.*

"Of course." After a quick embrace, Ron left feeling no less bewildered by the evening's events, but determined to somehow get some answers.

Examining his phone and seeing no return call from Mia, he tried to reach her again. Straight to voicemail. "Hey sweetheart, guess maybe you turned your phone off. I, uh, I hope your headache is better. Talk to you tomorrow... love you." *If you even had a headache.*

Chapter Forty-three

Mia woke early in spite of a restless night haunted by the four faces of Block mixed with eerie appearances of Christopher Walken battling James Bond and doping horses. Shaking off the last of the blurring images, she sat on the side of her bed and stared out at a gray sky. The first big flakes of early December snow floated to rest on green grass that would soon disappear beneath a blanket of white.

Her first client was scheduled for nine o'clock, so even allowing for the possibility of slow traveling if the white stuff was sticking to the roads by then, she had plenty of time for a leisurely breakfast.

"You're up early," Mia said finding her sister already in the kitchen.

"Yeah, it was so quiet around here I fell asleep reading last night. Slept like a rock. How 'bout you?"

"Same... well, not really. I was kind of restless." Mia took the quick and easy road, grabbing a Keurig cup of Earl Gray instead of her usual loose tea. "Have you checked the forecast for today? Am I going to need my boots?"

"Let's see." Julie opened her weather app. "Yep, it says six to eight inches. I don't plan on going anywhere except to shovel off the sidewalk and your side of the driveway later."

Mia laughed. "Maybe the neighbor will plow it out for you." Taking her tea to the living room, she flipped on the TV in time to see Melody Sipe pointing to the map showing the same accumulation while school and community closings and delays scrolled across the bottom of the screen.

Seeing Melody made her mind fly to Adam and she wondered how he was faring, which in turn made her think of Ron and the way she'd left things last night.

“Penny for your thoughts.”

“What?” Mia had been so absorbed she hadn’t been aware Julie had joined her. “Oh, I was just thinking.”

“Yeah, I could see that. Is everything okay?”

Mia deliberated before answering. “I’m not sure. I guess so. It’s just that Ron and I disagree about a case he’s working on—Dr. Block’s case—and I don’t know how to convince him he’s wrong.”

“And what if you’re the one who’s wrong?” Julie asked with raised eyebrows.

“I’m going to make breakfast... and I’m not wrong.”

***

With almost two inches of snow on the ground there was a quiet stillness in the parking area by the time Mia got to the center. Each shrub was adorned with white splendor, and she stood savoring the beauty of it until the cold urged her inside. With one more quick look back from the entrance, she captured the image in her mind to put on canvas sometime later.

“Oh, you’re here,” Ann said. “I was just going to call and tell you to take your time. Your first client called a few minutes ago and canceled.”

“I kind of thought she might. That’s all right. I can catch up on some paperwork,” Mia said.

“I’ll let you know if I hear from your next one. I wouldn’t be surprised if we have lots of spare time today.”

The receptionist was right in her prediction. Mia’s second client, a rugged mechanic afraid of his wife but with no fear of the elements, showed up right at ten o’clock for his appointment, but her eleven o’clock canceled. She looked out at the snow piling up then wandered out to the empty waiting room and found Ann on the phone.

“Sure, I can understand that. I’ll have Sarah call you to reschedule, and you stay safe.” After jotting down the message, the receptionist filled Mia in on the other cancellations. “Do you have anyone else this afternoon?”

"Just one." Mia had reviewed her book and all had canceled except her two o'clock.

"Hold on a sec," Ann said putting up one finger. After a quick conversation on the phone, she blew out her breath. "That was Sarah. She, Dr. Reed and Dr. Block had a pow-wow and decided we're going to close. Do you need help calling anyone to cancel?"

"No, I can take care of it." Her two o'clock client sounded both disappointed and relieved about having to reschedule, so Mia squeezed her into the next day's busy schedule. *Lunch breaks are overrated anyway.*

Mia, reached for her phone, then laid it back on her desktop. *What would I say?* She had finally turned it back on in the morning and listened to Ron's voicemail, and he said he'd talk to her today, yet he still hadn't called.

Then Sarah popped in. "Hey, did you hear? We're closing."

"Yes, Ann told me. Thanks, Mom."

"Okay, I'm out of here. Be careful driving home," she said.

Standing in the middle of her office, immobilized by indecision, Mia decided it wouldn't hurt to have a sounding board, and she couldn't think of a better one than her mom. Sarah had a unique ability to combine her therapist and mother's hats, thus being a good listener... she listened with love and answered with wisdom.

Mia hurried down the hall to Sarah's office, but she was too late. When Sarah said she was out of here, she'd meant it. On the way back to her own office, Mia noticed Dr. Block's door was ajar. Deciding to be more sociable than she felt, she poked her head in to say goodbye and tell him to be careful driving home. She stopped short at what she saw.

There, reclining in his big black leather chair, sat the good doctor, mouth wide open, arms hanging at his sides. It didn't look right. Mia hesitated. Was he sleeping... or something much worse?

If he was asleep, she didn't want to embarrass him—or herself—by waking him. But what if he was ill? What if he'd had a heart attack or stroke? She couldn't just walk away. *What if he's...*

"Excuse me," she said softly. He didn't move. Mia raised her voice and tried again. "Excuse me, Dr. Block?" Still nothing. Moving closer, she nearly shouted, "Dr. Block, are you okay?"

Panic crept up her spine as she put two fingers on his carotid, and relief swept over her with the feel of his pulse.

The doctor's head jerked up. "What are you doing, girl?" he asked groggily.

"Oh, I'm so sorry." Mia had jumped at his sudden movement and the sound of his voice, and she could feel the color rushing to her face. "I... I... you must have dozed off. I tried to wake you, but I guess you were pretty sound... I mean when you didn't wake up, I was afraid you might be ill or—"

"I'm not ill! I was relaxing! Get out!" He sounded angry yet still quite bleary.

Mia scurried out of the doctor's office, glancing back once. Block looked like he was already out of it again, so she quickly jerked the door closed behind her, and fell back against it. Her face burned, perspiration seemed to erupt from every pore, and her heart pounded in her chest. She had the sudden desire to run outside and fall face first into the snow. Instead, she dashed to her office, hastily pulled on her boots, and with her coat thrown over her arm breezed past Ann and out the front door.

Rushing into the sudden blast of cold air, it didn't take Mia long to cool down, and she was both relieved and gratified to discover someone, probably Sarah, had cleared the snow off her car so she could hop right in.

She started the engine, and listened to it racing almost as fast as her mind. Allowing time for the vehicle to warm up, she reflected on her discovery of Dr. Block *sleeping*.

He was totally out. And the way he reacted was... crazy. What a jerk! It's no wonder somebody hit him over the head... But it wasn't Adam. I just know it.

Chapter Forty-four

Mia took her time driving home, grateful there was little traffic and that the five or six inches of snow had been plowed from all the roads she had to travel. She wondered if Julie had managed to clear her side of the driveway, and when she turned onto her street, she was relieved to see the entire thing had been plowed, and from the thin layer of white covering it now, it hadn't been long ago.

Mia took off her boots, and once inside, found her sister curled up on the couch with a book and a hot drink.

"The driveway looks great." Mia hung her coat on the hook by the door. "Don't tell me you shoveled all that out by yourself."

"Hardly. I was shoveling the walk, and the guy two doors up, his name's Paul by the way, was finishing up his driveway so he bopped on over here with his snow blower and got ours without even asking. He just grinned and waved. Nice guy." Julie took a sip of her hot chocolate. "All I had to do was dig out the mailbox and sidewalk."

"I thought you'd wait until it stopped." Mia fell onto the other end of the couch, and Simmie immediately curled up on her lap.

"Yeah, I thought about it but figured it would be easier doing it twice than waiting until it was really deep and heavy. You're home early. Did everybody cancel on you?"

"Pretty much, then Grandpa made the call to close for the day. Evidently, Dr. Block must have been glad to shut it down early."

"What do you mean?"

Mia told her sister how she'd found the doctor so sound asleep she had trouble waking him. Julie laughed and suggested it might be time for the old guy to retire.

"But you know, he's not actually that old," Mia said. "I think Mom said he was only in his mid-fifties. I don't know... maybe he's coming down with something. I do know this; he wouldn't be missed—at least not by me. And now that we have Dr. Finney on staff, I think we could manage without The Block." Absently stroking the silver-gray fur of her Persian had a calming effect, and Mia smiled as he purred his appreciation.

"Listen to that," Julie said looking around the room. "And I don't even know where Willie is." Right on cue her cat strutted into the room, hopped onto her lap and back down seconds later. "See that. Mr. Independent. But wait 'til I put a laptop on my knees, and he's right there. Can I get you some tea?" Julie asked getting to her feet. "Or hot chocolate?"

"Thanks, sis. That sounds good... hot chocolate and maybe some marshmallows?"

"You got it. Oh, and I've got some beef stew started in the slow-cooker. Drake's coming over. Do you think Ron would like to join us?"

"Yum, that's perfect for a day like this. I'll give him a call and see." Mia was thankful for an excuse to call Ron that didn't involve talking about Adam or their disagreement.

He answered on the first ring, "Yeah?"

Not much of a greeting. "Hi, I'm sorry to bother you—"

"No, no, it's okay. Sorry, we're on our way to talk with a witness. What's up?"

"I won't keep you. Julie's making beef stew, and we thought you might want to join us for dinner."

"Sounds great. Look, we just pulled up here. Can I call you back later?"

"Okay, sure." The call ended. There was no "love you" or even a goodbye. Mia was left staring at her phone no more certain of where they stood than she had been.

"Is he coming?" Julie asked, handing her a big mug of hot chocolate loaded with miniature marshmallows.

"Mmm, thanks. Yes, I think so. He had to go." Mia saw the quizzical look on her sister's face. "He's still on duty and they were getting ready to interview somebody," she explained. It was perfectly logical, yet the niggling doubt troubled her still. She had kicked him out less than twenty-four hours earlier. *Are we going to be all right?*

***

By six o'clock when Ron arrived, Drake was already there, and the delicious aroma of Julie's beef stew permeated the house, calling them to the table with little pause for conversation. Paired with a wedge salad topped with bacon and blue cheese and crusty French baguettes, it was the perfect meal for a cold snowy evening.

"Your girl really knows how to cook," Ron said looking at Drake.

The veterinarian smiled at Julie whose cheeks had a sudden rosy glow. "She sure does."

Mia didn't miss the intimate look they exchanged and thought the relationship must really be progressing. Maybe she wouldn't have to feel bad about marrying Ron and leaving Julie with the house... that is if she and Ron actually made it to the altar.

He had given her a kiss when he arrived—one of those quick ones—and each time their eyes met, he smiled, but Mia didn't see the usual "I love you so much" kind of look that she had come to expect. *Is it my imagination?*

"Who's ready for dessert?" Julie got to her feet to clear the table, and the others each grabbed their own place settings and followed her.

"Are you kidding? I'm stuffed." Ron put his dishes down and patted his stomach.

"Don't worry," Mia said. "I made the dessert so you won't be missing that much."

"Don't say that, sis. She made a Mississippi Mud pie this afternoon... homemade crust and all. And it looks delicious."

Mia appreciated her sister's support, but now that it seemed her novice baking skills might be judged against her sister's masterpieces, she wasn't feeling too confident.

"In that case, I think I can make room for a small slice." Ron's reassuring smile almost made up for all the unease she'd been feeling. She cut four slices and was relieved when everyone said how much they liked it, but Ron didn't finish his piece.

After two bites he excused himself and moved to the kitchen to take a phone call. "I'd better get this. It might be important." And evidently it was. He returned a few moments later. "I'm so sorry, but I've got to go."

"Really?" Mia had been looking forward to them finally having a conversation... finally knowing everything was all right between them.

"Yeah, it's Robin. Kevin is having chest pain and he doesn't think it's serious, but she wants to take him to get checked, and Ronnie's sick so she doesn't want to take the little guy out in this weather. I told her I'd be right over." One arm already in his coat, he said, "Sorry to eat and run. Everything was delicious."

"Do you want me to come with you?"

"No, you stay here and enjoy your pie." He put his hands on her shoulders, kissed her on the forehead, and was out the door with a hasty, "I'll call you."

Mia stood staring at the closed door for several seconds, then, remembering Julie and Drake were watching and waiting, put a smile on her face and returned to the table.

"Are you okay?" The concern in Julie's eyes told Mia she wasn't fooling anybody.

"Of course. I mean, I'm disappointed he had to leave already, but I think he liked the pie."

It was nearly two hours later when Ron finally called. Though invited to watch a movie with Julie and Drake, Mia had long since retreated to her studio. She wasn't in the mood for a rom-com, but neither was she in the mood to create, so she had spent most of the evening grooming Simeon and staring out at the snow.

"Hey there," Ron said. "It sounds like Robin won't be getting home for a while." He explained that after checking Kevin out, the doctor determined he didn't have a heart attack, but they were admitting him for observation and to run more tests. "I hated having to take off like that, and I hope you're not angry, but Robin didn't know who else to call."

"Don't be silly. I'm not angry. Just disappointed... and I hope Kevin's going to be okay."

"Yeah, me too. I thought I might come back over to see you, but now I have to hang out here until Robin gets back, and that might take a while. So, I guess I'll see you Friday night?"

"Okay. But Ron..." Mia hesitated unsure what to say.

"Yeah?"

"Nothing... just, I love you." Mia waited, holding her breath. Why didn't he say something?

"Glad to hear it." He laughed a little. "I was beginning to worry. I love you too, sweetheart. Maybe Friday we can... uh oh. I hear Ronnie... gotta go. Love you."

The call ended before she could respond. *Love you.*

Chapter Forty-five

Mia backed out of the garage and on to the cul-de-sac, then paused to look at the snow glistening in the morning sunlight. *What a difference a day makes!* With sun all day long and temperatures expected to climb into the mid-forties, the already plowed roads would have plenty of time to melt and dry before dark, and Mia's spirits lifted higher with each mile of beautifully snow-covered trees along the way.

Mia got to RMH forty-five minutes before her first client was due and was going through her usual morning readiness routine when there was a knock on her door. Before she could respond, the door opened, and she looked up at an unexpected visitor.

"Do you have a minute?" Dr. Reed asked.

"Sure, Grandpa. What's up?" Other than professionally, Mia hadn't spoken with her grandfather since learning Betsy was his daughter, and she hoped he only wanted to discuss the practice or a patient now.

"Mind if I sit down?"

"No, I mean I don't mind. Sit please." *Just don't go there.*

"So, Betsy came to see me Tuesday."

Oh crap, he's going there. Mia squirmed in her seat. "How is she?"

"Okay, I guess... all things considered. But it's you I want to talk about, not Betsy."

"But Betsy's the one who found out her whole life has been a lie. And besides, I, I really don't think this is the time or place, Grandpa. I have a client in half an hour."

"I'm sorry. You're right of course... but Mia, please, can we talk later?" Mia heard the pleading in his voice and was torn. "Please?"

"All right, but not now." Mia didn't have a six o'clock client so she agreed to stop in his office at five before grabbing dinner.

Andy Reed looked back over his shoulder as he was leaving. "I'll order dinner for us, okay?"

Mia noticed his slight limp, the only lingering evidence of the stroke he'd suffered earlier in the year… yet he suddenly appeared more fragile. She nodded agreement, though conflicted about spending that much time with him, then took a sip of her now cold tea and noticed her hand shaking. *Breathe.* She took three deep, relaxing breaths, picked up her first client's folder, and put her thoughts about her grandfather aside.

It was time to focus on Jasmine, the little girl she was about to see—a child who had suffered physical and emotional abuse at the hands of two angry parents—and the seven-year-old needed and deserved her total attention. Now in foster care, the little one rarely spoke, but after the first three sessions, she had finally been willing to draw, and in that first drawing, Mia saw the beginning of a breakthrough… the beginning of trust.

Today, as she brought Jasmine back to her office, Mia noticed the child's hair had been thoroughly brushed—no sign of the stringy, tangled mane she'd had at her first session—and she looked adorable in the rainbow-colored hair ribbons that matched her unicorn sweater. At least she'd been lucky enough to be placed with foster parents who seemed to care. The only detail in her appearance that hinted she wasn't like every other seven-year-old was the missing grin Mia's other young clients always greeted her with.

Showing no reluctance, Jasmine drew a picture of a figure with straight blonde hair—like hers—alone in front of what looked like a bench. When asked about her drawing, she explained it was her sitting on her bed.

"Are your parents there?" Jasmine shook her head. "Where are they?"

"Gone," Jasmine answered, staring straight ahead.

"And where are the Bensons?" Mia asked referring to her new foster parents. The only response was a shrug, and though disheartened, Mia decided to push a little further. "Jasmine, is there anyone else in the house?" Another shrug, but then the tiniest bit of a grin emerged and the child began to add to her picture... a body, a head, four legs, two eyes, two ears, and a smile.

"And who is this?" Jasmine didn't answer immediately. She studied her drawing, then hastily added a tail, and at last there was a smile... a real smile.

"Daisy."

It was obvious to Mia, this was a connection the child needed, and at the end of the session, she spoke quietly to Mrs. Benson. "Jasmine seems very fond of Daisy. I assume that's your dog and not her parents'."

"Oh, no. Neither. That's Daisy," she said smiling and pointing to the stuffed animal Jasmine now clutched tightly to her chest. "It's the only thing she brought with her from home, and she won't go anywhere without it."

It was going to be a long, slow process with Jasmine, but Mia was determined to help the little girl navigate her new world. Perhaps one day, she would be okay.

Mia had rescheduled one of her "snow-day" cancellations during what should have been her lunch break, so she worked straight through the day with only an apple and some peanut butter crackers between appointments. She was so busy and so focused on each of her clients, she hadn't thought about her meeting with her grandfather until her four o'clock person left the office.

A loud growling reminded Mia she hadn't eaten and that she had a "date" for dinner. Dr. Reed's office door was open and the scent of Italian food beckoned. As the founder and owner of the practice, Andy Reed had the largest and best office in the building, and Mia had always enjoyed being in the welcoming space he had created. Tonight, she wasn't so sure.

She did, however, appreciate her grandfather ordering from her favorite restaurant and was ready to dive in, but the food was still in the containers, and Dr. Reed jumped to his feet.

"I guess we'd better take this over to the lunchroom, but first... Mia, I just want to tell you how sorry I am... for everything."

"You don't need to apologize to me, Grandpa. You didn't do anything to me."

"That may be true, but I've seen the way you look at me since you found out. I know you're disappointed in me... and hurt."

Mia couldn't deny it. Everything he said was true. Finding no words, she stood silently looking down at the floor. She felt her grandfather's approach, and he put his arms around her, just as he had a million times before. "I'm so sorry I let you down. That I'm not the man you thought I was."

In the comfort of his arms, Mia wanted to let it go. She wanted to turn the clock back to the moment before Betsy had said the words that crumbled the pedestal she'd had him on.

"Mia, sweetie, I can't excuse my behavior all those years ago... and I can't ask you to excuse it. I can only tell you I'm not the same man. I've tried to make amends. And most importantly I begged for forgiveness."

Mia felt awkward. She felt like she should say something, but what?

After a moment, Dr. Reed continued. "I asked for forgiveness from your grandma and, more importantly, from God. And I can never express how grateful I am that I was forgiven, and I didn't lose all that really mattered to me." He stepped back. Holding her at arm's length, he looked her in the eyes and added, "But I wasn't truly free until now. Until Betsy knew the truth. What I have kept a secret at her mother's request for all these years has been a lie that kept me tied in knots I had no power to undo.

"I think Betsy is going to be okay. She's working through all this... with her mom... with her dad, and he *is* her dad in every way but blood..." Andy lifted his granddaughter's chin with his finger, and she looked at him through a blur of tears. "I hope and pray we're going to be okay, Mia. I don't think I could bear to lose the love of my favorite grandchild."

That did it. The damn broke. The tears fell, and Mia gratefully accepted the tissues her grandpa hurriedly got for her. Then, when the storm inside had finally subsided, she found the words.

"I love you, Grandpa."

***

It was hours later—after enjoying a delicious dinner with her grandpa and seeing two more clients—that Mia finally leaned back in her chair and had time for reflection. By now the last of the clients had left the center, and she knew the only other people still in the building would be Sarah and Ann. That's why, after donning her coat and heading down the hall, she was surprised to see Dr. Block's door ajar. He always closed and locked it before leaving for the night.

Remembering the last time she'd encountered The Block, she wanted to ignore the open door and leave, yet what if his mind was elsewhere and he forgot? Or what if he really was ill?

She considered getting Sarah or Ann to go with her to check it out, but decided that was ridiculous and quietly approached his office. Putting her hand on the doorknob, Mia was tempted to simply close it and dash out to her car, but something pressed her to peek inside.

There he was... exactly as before. Mia backed out of the doorway and hurriedly went to another open door down the hall.

"Mom, I think you ought to see this."

"What?"

"It's Dr. Block."

Chapter Forty-six

Ron knew Thursday was Mia's longest day at the center, but she usually called either on her lunch or dinner break just to say hello. Noting the late hour—nine-thirty—he wondered if she'd been too busy or if there was another reason he hadn't heard from her. *Is she still angry? She doesn't even care how Kevin is doing?* He tried to understand her loyalty to her client, but Adam Grant was the only obvious suspect, and Ron knew they would probably arrest him for the assault within the next few days.

He and Jason had been building the case against Adam, and though it wasn't open and shut, the circumstantial evidence pointed at him. Now, if the victim's memory became crystal clear and he could definitively identify Adam as the person who attacked him, Ron could finally close this case, and Mia would have to accept the truth.

He planned to interview Block the following morning to see where they stood. If the doctor identified Adam conclusively, Ron planned to take the man in and charge him, a necessary duty he didn't look forward to knowing how his fiancée felt about it.

He grabbed his phone then laid it back down. Two seconds later he picked it up again and tapped the top name in his favorites. Mia answered halfway through the first ring.

"Hi Ron, can I call you back when I get home?"

"Sure."

"Okay, love you!"

Ron laid his phone on the end table wondering what was going on with her. Though he had managed a few hours' sleep on his sister's sofa the night before, he was exhausted. He moved from the couch to his more comfortable easy chair, put his feet on the ottoman and rested his head on the soft cushion. He didn't think he'd fallen asleep, but the sound of his phone startled him to sudden alertness.

"Hello? Mia?" he said groggily.

"Hi, did I wake you up?" Ron didn't have a chance to answer before his fiancée went on. "Listen, I'm sorry I couldn't talk before. I was with my mom."

"Don't worry about it. I guess you must have had a busy day. I thought you might call today to see how Kevin was doing though."

"Oh yes, I'm sorry. It's been such a crazy day. How is he?"

Ron told her Robin hadn't gotten home until three in the morning after Kevin was settled in a room, and that they were going to run more tests. "Unless they find something serious, he'll probably be released tomorrow morning."

"Oh... good."

"So what's going on? Are you all right? You sound kind of odd."

"What? No, I'm fine... like I said, it's been a crazy day. I don't know, but I think there's something wrong with Dr. Block."

"What do you mean?"

"I'm not sure... it's just, I don't know... He's kind of out of it. Maybe that knock on the head did more damage than he thought."

Ron's curiosity was piqued, but fatigue was winning out, and he realized Mia must have heard him trying to stifle a yawn.

"I'd better let you get some rest," she said.

"Okay, but this thing with Block, you can fill me in tomorrow, okay?"

Mia assured him she would and said goodnight, leaving him to wonder exactly what she meant, yet too tired to think much about it before falling asleep right where he sat.

It was some time later that he woke with a start and a sense of uncertainty. He got his leftover pizza out of the fridge, ate it cold, and took his muddled brain into bed and into his dreams of the psychiatrist hiding in strange places.

At the end of a restless night, Ron rubbed his eyes, pulled his hands through his hair, and shook his head. *Okay, no more pizza in the middle of the night.*

Relieved that he didn't run into Mia in the waiting room, at ten o'clock sharp, Ron was directed back to Dr. Block's office. Remembering his conversation with his fiancée the night before, he was curious about the man's current state of mind.

"Good morning, Doctor. How are you feeling today?"

"I'm fine, Det. Bishop. Why wouldn't I be?" Douglas Block pointed to the chair on the other side of his desk, and took a seat in his own oversized leather monster. "I thought we'd covered everything, Detective, and I'm a busy man." He drummed his fingers on the desktop. "Could we get right to it? Why are you here?"

Ron was taken aback by the man's brusque manner. "I understand, and I'll be quick. We're hoping to close this case as soon as possible and give you some peace of mind, so can you tell me if you remember anything more—any more details—about the day you were attacked? Or about the person who assaulted you?"

"I've told you everything I know." The doctor was obviously agitated and took a handkerchief out of his pocket to mop his brow.

Ron thought he looked rather haggard.

"It was a young man, like I told you. He was big. Tall. Dark hair."

Ron flipped back through the pages of his notebook to the description Block had given him in his previous interview. "So, he was a big man? Exactly what do you mean? Was he stocky, overweight, muscular?"

Block hesitated, scratched his head, then answered slowly. "I guess muscular, like he probably works out."

Ron scribbled in his notepad, looked up and asked, "Anything else... scars, facial hair, glasses?"

"No, no, nothing like that."

"You're sure?"

"Yes!" he said adamantly. "Now, if you don't mind," getting to his feet he added, "I have patients to see."

Ron knew when he was being dismissed and left the man's office. However, he also knew there was one little detail he'd missed in his earlier examination of the evidence and the victim's description of his assailant. And that detail raised the first doubt about Adam being the perp. He pictured the young man, and there was one constant in his appearance each and every time Ron had interviewed him. Adam Grant was never without his wire-rimmed glasses.

Chapter Forty-seven

Though Mia usually finished with her final client at four o'clock on Fridays, today her last client canceled—for the third time—so she had an extra hour to play with. Glad she had learned her lesson with this woman and scheduled her at the end of the day, and noting it was time to remind her of their cancellation policy, Mia's first thought was to head home early. However something was still bothering her, so hoping to catch her mom between clients, she called Ann to see if Sarah was with anyone.

"You're in luck," the receptionist told Mia. "Her next client isn't until three-thirty."

Since it wasn't quite three yet, Mia slipped down to her mother's office and knocked on the open door. "Got a minute?"

Sarah looked up from her laptop, and with a big smile gave Mia her full attention. "What's up, sweetie?"

Mia parked herself on the edge of the nearest chair. "I wanted to ask your thoughts about Dr. Block. I mean, you saw him last night, and that's the second time I've found him like that. That's not normal, right?"

"No, not usually. I've never known Douglas to fall asleep in his office before, but like I told you last night, he's dealing with a lot right now." Sarah leaned back in her chair. "I'm not sure if you're aware that his wife is quite ill and has been for some time."

"No, I had no idea." That certainly might explain him being tired, but Mia thought this went beyond tired. "What's wrong with her?"

"Bone cancer... it's bad."

"Oh no. I've never met Mrs. Block, but I'll keep her in my prayers." She imagined a woman married to their quirky doctor must have the patience of a saint.

"That's a good idea. Karen is such a sweet and gentle soul. I'm not sure how much longer she has, and I understand she's in a lot of pain now... which reminds me, I really should stop in for a visit. And maybe we ought to cut Douglas a break, all things considered."

"Yes, of course. It must be horrible for him. Couldn't he take time off?"

"As a matter of fact, he's been turning a lot of his cases over to Dr. Finney so he can do just that. I think he's only planning to come in two days next week and that's it. He expects they will soon need hospice care for Karen."

On the ride home, Mia chided herself for all the mean thoughts she'd been having about the doctor, and promised herself to be more kind in her thoughts about him. *Lord, please help him through this difficult time.*

Once home, Mia put everything out of her mind but dinner preparations, and was leafing through one of her sister's cookbooks when Julie came bounding down the steps.

"Hey, you're early. I didn't hear you come in." Julie perched on the barstool at the kitchen peninsula. "I'm glad you didn't start dinner yet. Drake and I decided to try that new Mexican restaurant in town tonight. You and Ron want to join us?"

Mia stopped looking at recipes to consider the idea but decided having some time alone might be better. "I'll call Ron and see what he wants to do, but I think we'll probably stay in."

Not surprisingly, when she reached him, Ron agreed. "And since it's just going to be the two of us, let me pick up dinner from your favorite place. Do you want the chicken piccata?"

She didn't have the heart to tell him she'd had Italian with her grandfather the night before. Besides last night's entrée had been lasagna, so she decided she could go for the piccata. "And could you get some tiramisu?"

Ron promised to be there by six-thirty, so Mia put the cookbook back on the shelf. "Okay, my beau is bringing dinner, and that means I don't have to cook." Mia checked the time. "I can relax downstairs before I get my shower. When are you leaving?"

"Drake's picking me up at six."

"So, you two are getting pretty serious, huh?"

Julie's smile said it all, but she confirmed it. "Yeah, I think I found a good one this time. We're trying to take it slow, but I think we both know where this is going."

"I'm so glad." Mia gave her sister a hug before scooping up Simeon and heading for her studio. Once there, instead of picking up pencils, charcoal, or paint brushes, she grabbed a different kind of brush and began Simmie's motor as she pulled it through his long, thick fur.

The repetitive brushing motion, along with her Persian's purring, relaxed Mia and allowed her mind to wander. She thought about Dr. Block's wife slowly dying—which certainly could explain his strange behavior—and that reminded her of the assault and Ron considering Adam as a suspect. That train of thought ultimately led her to think about how much she disagreed with Ron. *Why doesn't he listen? Or could I be wrong? No!*

Mia was absolutely convinced of Adam's innocence, and though she had no idea how to prove he wasn't guilty, she was determined to sway Ron somehow. Armed with all the mental arguments she could conjure up, she was ready for battle and her strategy was to wait and visit the subject during dessert.

***

"This is delicious," Mia said after the first bite of her tiramisu. "Thank you."

Ron merely nodded as he also had a mouthful of the luscious dessert.

"So listen, I don't want to make you angry—and I promise not to get angry myself—but do you mind if we talk a little bit about your case against my client?" And, though she knew it might be difficult, Mia was determined to keep her promise.

Ron nodded and wiped his mouth with his napkin. "But before you start, let me ask you something. Your client, Adam, wears glasses, right?"

"Yes, but what does that have to do with anything?"

"Maybe nothing, but a funny thing occurred to me when I interviewed the doctor again this morning. In his description of the attacker, he has never mentioned him wearing glasses." Ron leaned back in his chair. "I mean, I even opened the door for him to mention it by asking if the guy had any scars, facial hair or wore glasses, and he said no. So now I'm thinking maybe it's possible that it wasn't Adam."

"I knew it!" Mia exclaimed. "Oh, thank goodness! Did you tell him yet?"

"Whoa, hold on. We're not there yet... but I do think we need to dig deeper and explore other possibilities. I have no idea where we go from here. I guess we need to push the doctor, and maybe other people working at the center, a little harder to see what we might have missed."

Mia was delighted with this new development, but then she remembered something. "That sounds like a good idea, but you may want to take it easy on Dr. Block right now."

"Why? What do you mean?"

"Mom told me today that Karen Block, the doctor's wife, is near death."

Chapter Forty-eight

Ron had a relatively relaxing weekend spending most of it with his future bride, and putting the Block case on a shelf in the back of his mind while he focused on Mia and their wedding plans. The excitement around the Reed Sunday dinner table was palpable as Sarah, Julie, and Mia discussed plans for the ceremony, the rehearsal dinner, and the reception. Even Destiny seemed to be caught up in it. Ron couldn't help thinking how different the atmosphere was compared to one week earlier.

"I think it's time we gentlemen retire to another room." Craig Reed looked to his wife. With no objection from Sarah, he got to his feet and said, "How about it, Ron?"

Not wanting his fiancée to think he was deserting her, Ron looked at Mia. "Do you mind?"

"Go on," she said. "You guys are no help anyway."

Ron was relieved to see the familiar dimple and the twinkle in her eyes when she said it. He didn't need to be asked—or given permission—twice before hastening to leave the table and join his future father-in-law.

"How's Cody doing?" Ron asked Craig as they settled into the much cozier den. The warm colors and dark furniture made this the manliest room in the Reed's beautifully decorated home. Mia had told him how close Cody and Matthew Markle were, and how devasted he'd been by the loss of his best friend.

"He's doing all right, I guess, but he's so quiet since, you know... I mean we're all used to his crazy, fun shenanigans. He seems to have lost that part of himself for the moment. It's like he grew up overnight... but not in a good way."

"I hear you. Death always hits hard—even when it's natural causes—but when it's suicide?" Ron shook his head.

"I guess you see a lot of death—murders and such. That must take a toll... or does it get easier?"

"Easier? No, I don't think so. Less of a shock maybe." Nothing would ever be as shocking and world-shattering as the night he'd found his own parents dead in their home. "The part that never gets any easier is telling the victim's family. Mrs. Markle was shattered... parents are always destroyed, and I guess it had only been a few years since she lost her husband to a heart attack, now this."

"If only Matt could have hung on... He was getting counseling, but when that girlfriend of his walked out on him, I guess he just couldn't see past it." Craig leaned forward in his chair and flipped open a photo album and showed Ron a picture of Cody and Matt with two girls dressed for prom. "It's hard to believe this was taken just a few years ago," he said showing Ron the picture. "Yeah, Cody's been going over to check on Matt's mom and sister pretty often. That's where he is today. Mrs. Markle asked him if he would come to dinner with her and Linda—that's Matt's sister—and Cody thinks it helps them to talk about the good times they had together."

"Yeah, I'm sure it does. Your son is good people, Mr. Reed."

"Stop that. I told you it's Craig... or Dad if you're comfortable with it."

Ron laughed and agreed to use *Craig*. *Dad* might come later, but didn't feel right just yet.

"Want to watch the game?" Craig asked grabbing the remote.

"Steelers? Absolutely!" It didn't take long for the two men to become absorbed, but a part of Ron's mind seized on a detail—probably unimportant, he thought—that made him think of the case he'd tried to put on hold.

The psychiatrist Matt Markle had been seeing, and who prescribed the pills he used to end his life, was Dr. Douglas Block.

The half-empty bottle of pills they'd found on Carol Burke and the empty one by David Sipe were also prescribed by Dr. Block.

And then there were Mia's drawings. Four images of the doctor. A picture of the body—Matt's body—by the lake. Somehow it all must mean something. Could it all be tied together?

But how? What does it mean?

Was the person who stole the doctor's prescription pad involved? Was Adam Grant—or whoever it was—writing these prescriptions? But if so, why? For money? *If so, these young people paid too high a price.*

Something else was tugging at the back of his mind... and then it hit him. He remembered something the doctor said the morning after the attack. He hadn't gone to the hospital to get checked, and he wasn't worried because his wife took such good care of him. Yet according to Mia, Mrs. Block was in bad shape—bone cancer—and needed round-the-clock care. They were even calling in hospice. *How could she be taking care of Dr. Block if she's dying?*

Chapter Forty-nine

Mia watched the transformation in her sister when Drake arrived about an hour after dinner. He had received a call earlier in the day and had to take care of one very sick Labrador retriever, but now that he was here, Julie warmed him up a plate and sat watching him eat and listening raptly while he told her all about it.

"Speaking of big dogs, how do you think Willie would get along with my Golden, Bailey?" he asked out of nowhere.

"Hmm, good question. Why?" Julie asked.

"Just wondered."

Mia overheard the question as she walked from the kitchen, through the dining room, to the family room with a tray full of brownies and ice cream. The lovebirds didn't even seem to see her, so she kept walking, but felt her lips curl into a smile thinking of her sister walking down the aisle to Drake one day, and thinking that day might come sooner than anyone expected.

When she finished enjoying her dessert, Mia went to get her phone off the console table where everyone usually left them during dinner. She saw right away that she had missed a call from Betsy, but there was also a voicemail.

"Ron, do you mind if we make a stop on the way back to my place? Betsy says she really needs to see me."

Ron agreed, but when Mia shot Betsy a quick text saying they'd stop by, she got an immediate reply that changed the plan.

"Oh, never mind, Ron. Betsy said she'd rather come to my place."

"Okay, but we're in the fourth quarter. Can we wait 'til the game's over?"

Mia let Betsy know she'd text her when they headed home, then settled in next to Ron to watch the end of the game. Everyone cheered as Big Ben secured the win with a great touchdown pass, then after the usual hugs, Mia and Ron headed back to Glen View Court. She was glad to finally have a little alone time with her guy.

"What are you thinking about?" she asked him. From his somewhat startled reaction, she knew he'd been somewhere far away.

"Oh, nothing."

"Seriously? Nothing?"

"Okay, not any one thing." Ron glanced her way then back at the road. "Mostly work stuff. Sorry."

"Does that work stuff have anything to do with Dr. Block... or Adam?"

"Yes, among other things. But enough about work." Ron reached over and took her hand in his. "What's on your mind?"

Mia didn't think she'd better say what was actually on her mind, looking at those beautiful blue eyes—it would be rated R at the least—so she chose to talk about the future instead. "I was thinking about Hawaii. We're definitely going to visit Pearl Harbor, right?"

"Absolutely, and the Dole plantation, and we'll tour the whole island."

"I can't wait! And when we fly over to Maui, what was that side trip you told me about? The one where we have to leave at like three o'clock in the morning?"

Ron laughed. "Trust me, it will be worth getting up early. It's the Haleakala sunrise. The travel agent said she did the trip once, and it was awesome."

"Yes, it sounds awesome, but you do realize three o'clock is the middle of the night, right?"

"And you do realize we'll be on our honeymoon? Maybe we won't even be asleep yet." Ron peeked over at her, winked, and grinned like a Cheshire cat.

Mia saw his wicked grin and felt the heat flooding her cheeks. A warmth traveled to other parts of her body as she thought about their honeymoon and finally being with the man she loved. Afraid

Ron could somehow read her mind, she had to think of something else, something less telling.

"So, I wonder what's going on with Betsy," she said.

Ron chuckled at that. "Oh, so we're changing the subject. Okay. I have no idea, sweetheart. She's your young friend. What do you think?"

"I'm not sure, but I hope it's not about my grandpa." Mia had put aside her anger with him, but the hurt was still fresh, and she feared Betsy could easily and unintentionally stir it up again. "I guess we'll find out soon enough," she said as Ron pulled into her driveway and turned off the engine.

He followed Mia inside but then asked if she wanted him to make himself scarce.

"No! I mean, I don't want you to go. Tell you what. I'll ask Betsy if she wants to talk privately, and if she does, I'll take her down to the studio." Mia moved into his arms. "That is, if you don't mind hanging around waiting."

"Hmm, let me think about that... nope, I guess you're worth waiting for." He proved he meant it with a kiss that made Mia wish they were already on that honeymoon.

It ended rather abruptly when the doorbell rang, and Betsy surprised Mia with something that had nothing at all to do with her biological father.

"The reason I said I'd rather meet you here," she said, "is because I'd like to look at those pictures you drew of the creepy doctor, if that's okay."

"Of course. They're downstairs... but why?"

"Let me take a look, then I'll explain."

"Mind if I tag along?" Ron asked. Mia had a pretty good idea why her detective boyfriend was suddenly interested, and since Betsy didn't object, they all three found themselves staring at the four images of Dr. Block.

Mia watched Betsy's face as she studied the pictures and saw the look of puzzlement gradually turn to one of conviction. "Yes, that's him," she said stepping back and turning to look into Mia's eyes. “I dreamed about him.” Those words and the look on her friend’s face gave Mia goosebumps. She knew about Betsy’s dreams.

She would never forget it was Betsy’s dream years ago—seeing Mia at that cabin in the woods when she’d been kidnapped—that helped the authorities to find her.

“Here, sit down.” Mia led Betsy to the big chair in the corner and sat on the ottoman facing her. “What exactly did you dream? Do you think it was because he looks so creepy to you?”

“No, I don’t think so. It felt more like one of those dreams that’s trying to tell me something.”

Mia glanced over her shoulder at Ron who was still standing in front of her drawings. She recognized the deep wrinkles across his forehead, but she couldn’t worry about that right now. She’d explain it all later.

She looked back at Betsy. “Tell me about it.”

“There’s not a lot to tell... and it probably doesn’t mean anything, but he was taking care of somebody—a woman—and then he was crying. It was so weird, though. He looked angry. Then he looked so sad. It was an awful look. And the woman was sleeping... and then he like... fell off the side of the bed.”

“Then what? Is that it?”

“Yeah, I mean he was just there on the floor, and that’s all I remember. But when I woke up, I had that feeling, you know? Like it was important. Like I should tell you.” Seeing the agonizing look on the young girl’s face was almost too much for Mia to bear. “Do you know what it means?”

“Thank you, Betsy. I’m glad you told me, but no, I’m not sure what it means unless...”

“Unless what?” It was the first time Ron had spoken since they looked at the drawings of Dr. Block.

Mia looked from Betsy to Ron then back to Betsy. “Dr. Block’s wife is very ill. She doesn’t have long to live, actually. And I don’t know, but maybe what you saw was her death.”

Chapter Fifty

Betsy's revelation about her dream hadn't added anything relevant to his case, yet Ron was intrigued and couldn't get it out of his mind. He had finally gotten used to the idea that Mia had a gift—one he couldn't truly understand but had come to accept—but now there's this young girl who has dreams and "sees" things. It all seemed a little too surreal to a detective who was used to dealing in cold, hard facts.

"About that other thing, how are you doing?" Mia asked Betsy as she was donning her winter coat and scarf.

"You mean the whole daddy thing?" Betsy snickered. "It's cool."

"Seriously? Are you sure?"

Ron, who was standing back out of the way, could see the look of doubt on Mia's face.

"Yes," Betsy said firmly. "Mom and I talked for hours. There were lots of tears, but then there were lots of hugs. And Dad, well he's still Dad. Period."

"And what about my grandpa? Is that going to be terribly awkward for you at the wedding and stuff?"

"Mia," Betsy said taking her friend's hands. "It's *your* wedding. That day will be all about you and Ron."

Ron appreciated the smile she sent his way.

"But to answer your question, Grandpa Andy and Grandma Val have always been special to me—almost like my own grandparents—and they still are. That other stuff is just biology. I'm glad I know... I certainly had a right to know, but nothing has really changed, okay?"

As she headed out the door, Betsy added, "Anyway, it was my mom who demanded it be kept secret—and that's who I was most angry with—but I understand why now..." She paused with one foot out the door. "It may take a while to rebuild the trust we had, but I love her... she's a good person, and besides, she's my mom."

Ron watched Mia standing at the door staring after her friend and heard Betsy call, "Love you!" then the sound of the car door slamming.

After waving, Mia closed the front door and leaned against it. Ron saw the tears slipping out of her eyes.

"Are you all right?" he asked hurrying to her side. He was relieved when she wiped the tears away and replaced them with the dimpled smile he loved.

"I'm good." Mia took a deep breath, blew the air out, then turned to face him. "And we are finally alone."

Wrapping her in his arms and pulling her close, Ron rested his chin on the top of her head. He was grateful to have some quiet time with his fiancée as he led her to the couch, but it didn't last long. Before they were even settled in, the sound of the garage door opening warned them they only had a few more seconds of solitude.

"Shall we make a quick getaway to the basement?" he asked jumping to his feet and pulling her up with him.

They were halfway down the steps, giggling like teenagers when they heard Julie call, "We heard you. Go ahead, hide! You're not the only ones who want to be alone."

Still laughing, Ron led Mia through her studio and into the small room that had been designed for just such a need. The laughter was soon forgotten as he took Mia in his arms, their lips met and that need took hold of him as they melted into each other.

It was only when he felt her gently pull back and heard himself groan that Ron realized how close he'd come to needing and taking more than she was ready to give.

"You're killing me," he said softly, aching to take her to his bed.

"I'm, I'm sorry," she whispered looking down at the floor.

He lifted her chin and looked in her eyes. "It's okay. I'll live... but I may need a little space right now."

"You know it's not easy for me either."

Hearing her say that was helpful, but Ron still needed time to temper his physical passion. "I think we need a little distance," he said moving back toward the studio.

"What? You're leaving?"

Looking back, he saw the confusion on Mia's face. "No, of course not. I'm just putting a little space between us. Good Lord, woman, I'm not made of stone... or ice. C'mon, come with me. Let's take another look at these four pictures of the good doctor."

"Well, if anything is going to cool the mood, that face ought to do it."

Ron agreed. This was not a mug that spoke of romance. As he stared at Block times four, if anything, he read a mix of pain and anger.

"What are you doing?"

Mia had grabbed her sketch pad and sat down, and was suddenly scribbling furiously.

"This will only take a minute," was all she said.

Ron waited... and watched.

He was amazed at the fluidity of the pencil as Mia's hand quickly created a fifth image, and when she finally dropped the pencil and fell back in the seat, Ron's jaw dropped. This picture wasn't as finished as the others as far as detail and shading, but it was clearly Dr. Block, and his expression was entirely different from the others.

"I don't think I've ever seen such wretchedness in a portrait." He looked from the drawing to the artist, then rushed to her side and took her in his arms again. "It's okay," he murmured trying to calm her trembling.

As he watched, he could see her chin begin to quiver. *What the hell? She's losing it.*

Ron took Mia's face in his hands and asked, "What's wrong, sweetheart? What is it?"

She looked back at him, and Ron saw almost as much sorrow on her face as he saw in the picture. “Ron,” she said with a catch in her throat, “I can feel his anguish.”

The reflection of misery he saw in Mia’s eyes filled him with foreboding.

Chapter Fifty-one

There was no sign of Julie or Drake when they went back upstairs, although Drake's coat was tossed across the back of the couch. When Ron looked at that, then glanced toward the steps leading to the second floor and shot her a roguish grin, Mia knew what he was thinking.

"Focus, Ron!" she said firmly while returning his mischievous smile. "What do you think we should do?"

Ron's smile faded as quickly as it had appeared. "I don't think there's anything we can do. The man is obviously overwhelmed, and we don't know, but maybe his wife is closer to death than we realized... or maybe she's already gone."

Mia couldn't shake the ominous feeling that had overtaken her when she completed her drawing, looked at it, and saw the doctor's pain.

Then she heard it.

"You have to help. Help him!"

She raised her head and looked at Ron wondering if she should tell him what she was thinking... and she wondered if they were *her* thoughts or a message, one that came from the same place as her drawing. Where did it come from?

"Go now!"

The voice was insistent. Mia pulled out her phone.

"What are you doing?"

"I'm calling Dr. Block."

"Why? What are you going to say?"

"I don't know, Ron. I just know I have to call. I have to *do something*."

The doctor's phone rang twice and went to voicemail.

Mia hadn't been prepared to say anything and stammered through her message. "Uh, hi... this is Mia. I, um... could you give me a call back?" Mia sat on the edge of the couch then popped back up and paced around the room.

"What are you going to say if he returns your call?" asked Ron who had taken a seat on the arm of the sofa next to where Mia perched moments before.

She shrugged and continued pacing. *"Help him!"* she heard again. "I can't just stand here waiting." Mia pulled her coat and Ron's from the closet.

"Where are we going?"

"I know where he lives. Mom pointed out his house a while back." Mia was already out the door and heading for Ron's car. She glanced back and saw Ron standing in the doorway, one arm in his coat sleeve fighting the December wind with his mouth hanging open. "Come on!"

Hurrying after her, Ron got in the driver's seat, and as he was fastening his seatbelt, Mia saw him shaking his head. "This is crazy. You know that, right?"

Mia heard Ron's words and understood where he was coming from, but none of that mattered. What mattered was that unshakeable feeling of foreboding, and those whispered words repeating themselves in her head. *"Help him!"*

Twenty minutes later they pulled into the long driveway of the doctor's house. In Mia's opinion, this place, which was even bigger than her parents' home, was absurdly large for two people.

"Now what?" Ron asked.

Dr. Block still hadn't returned her call, and there weren't many lights on in the house, but the garage was open and two cars were parked inside. Mia knew one was the doctor's and assumed the other belonged to Karen Block, but she saw no sign of a vehicle that might have belonged to the woman's nurse. "He's here."

"Yeah, it looks that way. And his wife is sick. So, are you sure you want to disturb them?"

"No, I don't *want* to. I *have* to." Mia was beyond grateful that, in spite of the look of doubt he threw her way, Ron didn't say she was crazy.

He followed her when she got out of the car and went to the front door.

There was no answer when she rang the bell nor when she banged on the door, so after what seemed entirely too long, Mia pushed back her windblown hair and headed into the attached garage.

"What are you doing?"

"People often don't lock the door from the garage into the house," she called over her shoulder.

Right on her heels, Ron said, "Slow down! You can't go barging into their house."

"I told you, I have to!" She banged on the door first, but after no more than fifteen seconds, she opened it and stepped inside. "Hello? Hello? Dr. Block... it's Mia Reed..." She moved through the mud room and laundry into a magnificent kitchen, then stood silently listening. Not a sound. No voices. No sound of music or a TV. Nothing.

"Maybe they're sleeping," Ron whispered.

"No... something's wrong." Mia continued moving through the dimly lit house until she came to the curved oak staircase. "Dr. Block, it's me... Mia Reed." Without hesitation or looking back to see if Ron was following, she hurried up the steps and dashed to the one room with light flowing from the doorway.

When she reached it, she froze. She was mesmerized by the scene... the very scene Betsy had described. Karen, lying perfectly still in the bed... Douglas Block beside the bed lying crumpled on the floor.

She felt Ron's hands taking her by the shoulders and moving her aside. He hurried to check the woman's pulse, shook his head. Next, he moved to the doctor, put two fingers on his neck to check his. Mia gathered he was alive when Ron pulled out his phone and called 9-1-1.

Chapter Fifty-two

"What are you doing? And where did you disappear to when they were working on Dr. Block?" Mia watched as Ron put on the gloves and pulled out an evidence bag. "Do you carry those bags around with you all the time?"

"Yeah, I always have them in my vehicle, and to answer your question, that's where I went. I needed to get this stuff out of the car."

"But why? Do you think this is some kind of crime scene?" Mia stood in the doorway. She hadn't come back into the bedroom since the EMTs had wheeled the doctor out. She could still hear the fading siren and hoped the patient would make it. But it was too late for Karen. Dr. Block's wife was gone before they arrived. Mia looked at the woman lying there as though she were sleeping and shuddered. Ron still hadn't answered, and Mia was confused by his sudden return to detective mode. "Ron, what is it?"

His head jerked up as though he'd forgotten Mia was even there. "Oh," He lifted his chin in the direction of the bedside table, and Mia scanned its contents. Besides the lamp, all she saw was a box of tissues, an empty glass and some pill bottles. After checking labels, Ron picked up the two empty ones with his gloved hand and dropped then into the plastic evidence bag.

"Ron, the woman had cancer. She was dying. It's certainly not surprising to find medication by her bed. What are you thinking?"

Before he could answer, a middle-aged man's voice startled Mia, and she jumped out of the way and into the room.

"Excuse me. Is she in here?" the man asked as he entered.

"Yes Doctor, and thanks for getting here so quickly." Ron gestured toward Mrs. Block's still, cold body.

"Sure thing. I only live a few miles down the road."

"Mia, this is Dr. Warner from the coroner's office. I called him when I went out to the car. Hey, are you all right?"

Mia felt the room tilt and fell back against the wall, holding on while the room righted itself. In two steps Ron was by her side, leading her out into the hall.

"I think it's exhaustion... and maybe hunger." Early afternoon Sunday dinner seemed like a distant memory. "But why did you call the coroner? Do you actually consider her death suspicious?"

"Just covering all my bases. Shall I check down in the kitchen? Maybe I can find you some crackers or something."

Mia shook her head and insisted she would be fine though she still felt lightheaded.

"All right, if you're sure. As soon as we're finished here, we'd better get you home."

"No. I want to go to the hospital and check on Dr. Block first. But I need to sit down."

Ron started to lead her back inside the big master bedroom where there was a sitting area with two comfortable looking chairs, but Mia resisted.

"I think I'll go downstairs and wait."

Although she swore she was fine, Ron insisted on walking her downstairs before going back to finish up with the coroner.

Though she hadn't hesitated to rush in earlier, Mia was now uncomfortable with the idea of roaming around in a house where she hadn't been invited. She settled for one of the upholstered chairs at the huge kitchen island, and eventually, with hunger getting the better of her, she went to the refrigerator. Finding nothing but bottled water and a few condiments, she looked around the kitchen for other possibilities.

She was impressed by the elegant opulence of the espresso cabinets and cream-colored quartz countertops and island. *Not what I would have imagined for The Block.* Mia had a twinge of guilt for thinking that way knowing the doctor could be dying, and his wife was lying dead upstairs.

That's when she saw it.

On the opposite side of the kitchen from the refrigerator was a desk, and propped up where it couldn't be missed, was an envelope with bold lettering on it. Curiosity got the better of her, so Mia moved closer. "ANDY" was all it said.

Mia didn't know if she dared pick it up and take it with her. *I should call Grandpa.* Mia knew he would want to know what was going on anyway.

Andy Reed appreciated Mia's call, and told her he'd meet her at the hospital and get the letter from her there if she didn't mind bringing it along. It was when she picked it up that she saw there was another envelope behind it addressed to "DET. BISHOP."

At the sound of approaching footsteps, Mia grabbed the second envelope.

"I'm sorry that took so long. Let's get out of here." Ron guided her back through the mud room into the garage. "We've got to get you something to eat... or did you find something in the kitchen while you were waiting?"

"No, but I found this." Mia handed him the envelope with his name on it as they exited the garage and the cold air slapped her in the face. "And there's one addressed to my grandfather, too," she said hurrying to the car.

After closing the passenger side door, Ron hopped in the driver's seat. "Do you want to stop for something to eat before we go check on the doctor?"

"No, I'd like to get to the hospital as soon as we can. I told Grandpa we'd meet him there."

"All right," Ron said reaching into the backseat for something. "But you'd better eat this until we can get you something more substantial."

Mia gratefully accepted the protein bar. "Thank you! Do you always keep snacks in your car?"

"Hey, I was a boy scout. I haven't forgotten our motto. Besides, when we're on a case, I'm never sure when I'll get chance to eat." He started the engine, but before putting the car in gear, he ripped open the envelope with his name on it. "I'll be damned... sorry. You're not going to believe this."

"What?"

"You were right. Apparently, Adam Grant is innocent. He didn't do anything to Block."

"Is that what the letter says? Does he say who did it? Ron... who assaulted him?"

Ron looked up from the page he'd been staring at. "Nobody."

Chapter Fifty-three

Standing at Adam Grant's door waiting for him to answer, Ron tried to anticipate the man's reaction. Relief... or anger? Ron was still reeling from the events of this evening himself and thought maybe he should have waited until morning to take care of this necessary but unpleasant task—it was rather late, after all—but on the other hand, he figured he owed it to Grant to let him know as soon as possible. So, at Mia's urging, he'd driven straight from the hospital to Adam's place.

"Are you serious?" Adam looked at the time and blocked the doorway. "Look, unless you're here to arrest me, you need to go."

"Wait," Ron said putting his hand up to keep the door from closing in his face. "You'll want to hear this."

Adam hesitated then stepped back and allowed Ron to enter. "All right, but I don't know what you could tell me that I'd want to hear... unless you finally figured out who really did it... Is that it?"

Ron saw the spark of hope in the other man's eyes.

"Did you catch the guy who did it?"

"Not exactly," Ron said stepping out of the wind and into Adam's now familiar living room. "But I'm here to tell you I know you didn't assault Dr. Block."

Adam dropped onto the nearest chair, and Ron could see relief wash over his face. "So how did you finally come to this startling revelation? And who did it?"

"Well, I can't get into that right now, but I can tell you this. Dr. Block cleared you. He said you did not assault him."

After a brief pause, Adam got to his feet. "Anything else, Detective?"

Ron understood there was still a great deal of animosity lurking just under Adam's effort at civility, and he couldn't really blame the man.

Ron turned to leave but paused at the door. "Just one more thing," he said. "I hope you understand, I was only following the evidence, and I'm glad I was wrong... but I guess I owe you an apology."

Adam smirked. "Yes, I guess you do."

"Okay, yeah. I'm sorry, Adam... and one other thing you ought to know. There's one person who never doubted your innocence for a minute, and that's Mia Reed."

For the first time since Adam had opened the door, the bitterness slipped away, and he nodded and showed a genuine smile. It faded when he looked back at Ron, and the detective knew he wasn't ready to join the Ron Bishop fan club, but that was okay.

Back in the car, Ron took Mia's hand. "I'm glad that's done."

"How's Adam?" she asked.

"Relieved. Still not loving me, but I'm sure he'll sleep easier tonight."

"Well, *I* love you, and I'm so glad you told him tonight... but I'm still dumbfounded. It's all so bizarre... and sad."

Ron couldn't believe it either. He'd read the doctor's letter three times before he could get it to sink in.

Det. Bishop,

You can stop looking for the person who attacked me because there is no such person. It was all a lie. I had my reasons. I had to do it. I'm sorry.

Douglas Block, M.D.

"Are you all right?" Mia's voice and her gentle touch on his arm brought him back to the present.

"Yeah, but let's get out of here. It's getting late, and you still haven't had a decent meal."

"That protein bar took the edge off, but you must be starving."

Ron could have gotten something out of the hospital vending machine, but he'd been too preoccupied to realized how hungry he was then. Now the rumbling and hollow feeling in his stomach demanded attention. "Yep," he said when Mia laughed at the loud growling. "Where to?"

"Home, if you're okay with sandwiches."

"After the meal your mother gave us, we don't need anything heavy. A sandwich sounds good to me."

On the short ride back to Mia's house, Ron thought about the second letter—the one addressed to Mia's grandfather, the owner of the Reed Mental Health Center. When Andy Reed had finished reading it, he'd shaken his head in disbelief and passed it to Ron.

Although it was hard to believe, everything began to make sense.

My dear friend,

Please forgive me for the actions I have taken. My beloved Karen was in so much pain. I couldn't bear to watch her suffer any longer. I had to do as she wished. Now she is no longer in agony.

You don't really need me in the practice any longer. Dr. Finney will do fine. And I have lived long enough and seen enough pain. I may be taking the coward's way out, but I am going to be with my sweet Karen.

Thank you for being my friend and supporting me, especially these last few months.

Doug

"What are you thinking about?" Mia asked, interrupting his memory.

"I was thinking about Block. Now that we know he's going to make it, I think he's going to be facing a pretty rough road. And I've got some questions to ask him when he's up to it. Some loose ends I need to tie up."

"Like what?"

"Like what, if anything, he had to do with three other deaths. If nobody took his prescription pads, then he's the only one who's been writing all these scrips for painkillers. I'm afraid Douglas Block may be responsible for a lot more than his wife's death."

Chapter Fifty-four

With Christmas only eight days away, Mia had discovered her clients delighted in showing their appreciation by showering her with little gifts. Besides the bath salts, candles, and some of the clients' very own drawings—which Mia found most endearing—there were more cookies and candy than the entire staff could possibly consume, so some went home with her to share with Ron, Julie, and Drake. However, that didn't stop Mia and Julie from joining their mom for their traditional cookie baking day. Unable to get away from her responsibilities in Pittsburgh the year before, Mia now reveled in old familiar family fun.

The Reed kitchen was filled with the aroma of Christmas as they baked chocolate chip, snickerdoodle, peanut butter, beautifully decorated sugar cookies, and gingerbread men. Tins were filled and lined up to gift various households of friends and service providers, and to take to each of their own homes.

Even Grandma Val joined the fun, though she was drinking more eggnog than baking. She said she was happy to supervise and look after the men this year. She carried a huge tray laden with an assortment of cookies and drinks to the family room where she was immediately besieged.

"Let me help you with that, Mom." Craig set the heavy tray on the coffee table.

"Grab a plate and your cookies of choice," Val said.

Cody and Drake each helped themselves to a beer off the tray, Craig and Ron took a glass of eggnog, and Andy took his glass of milk.

"You guys are crazy. There's nothing better than milk with cookies." Each of the other men took a handful of cookies, but

Andy looked at the tray and then questioningly at his wife. "I don't see my favorite on here."

"Here I come to save the day!" Mia said carrying another smaller tray, this one piled high with peanut butter cookies and gingerbread men. "I brought you your men, Grandpa."

Andy took a couple gingerbread cookies and kissed his granddaughter on the forehead. "That's my girl."

Happy that her relationship with her grandfather had been mended, Mia smiled and headed back to the kitchen, but remembering something, she stopped. "Grandpa, have you talked to Dr. Block in the last few days?"

"Not since Monday. It's as though he has decided he's said all he has to say. Doug is totally withdrawn now. I don't know whether it's grief or guilt... or a combination of the two, but I can't seem to reach him."

Ron shook his head. "It's a damn shame, but I'm glad I got some answers Monday morning before he clammed up."

"What kind of answers?" Cody asked. No one had filled him in on all the details of the doctor's involvement with the deaths of Carol Burke, David Sipe, and his own friend, Matt Markle.

Ron explained that after all those months of watching his wife suffer, Douglas Block said he got angry... angry with suffering—anybody's suffering—and he began issuing prescriptions to ease their pain as well as medicating himself. "He wasn't making a lot of sense, but from what I got, it seems he was getting worried about the number of narcotic prescriptions he was doling out... afraid someone could stop him before he finished what he was determined to do."

"What was that?" Drake asked.

Ron shook his head and sighed before answering. "End his wife's pain... and his own."

"I know it was wrong," Andy said, "but Doug actually believed he was doing a good thing, easing people's pain, and the way he loved Karen, well, all I can say is watching her suffer changed him. Destroyed him." Andy sighed.

"That may be, but the worse heartbreak," Ron broke in, "is the young people who died needlessly because of him. When I confronted him about that, seemed like the truth he needed to hear struck him hard... as it should."

"Yes, I think you're right," Andy said, "and adding guilt to his consuming grief may explain the total withdrawal."

Mia saw her grandfather's sadness for his friend and the irritation on Ron's face, but she had also been watching Cody, fearing his reaction. She'd watched her brother's eyes widen in disbelief.

Apparently unable to control whatever he was going through sitting down, he finally jumped to his feet. "So, that's the guy who's responsible for my best friend's death? Matt went to him for help. The doctor was supposed to help him... not kill him!" Cody's voice cracked and he stormed out of the room. Mia moved to follow him.

"I've got this," Craig said getting up to follow his son, and Mia recognized Cody needed his dad more than his sister right now, even if she was a therapist.

"Let me know if I can do anything to help," Andy called after him.

Sarah, who had come in from the kitchen in time to hear the end of the conversation said, "There may be three psychologists in the room, but for this kind of hurt, Cody doesn't need a therapist. He needs his dad."

There was no doubt in Mia's mind that Sarah was right, but she loved her brother and wished there was some way she could help. "I hope he's going to be okay," was all she could think to say.

Sarah gave her daughter a hug. "He will be. I'm sure of it. Losing his best friend, especially the way he did, has changed him, but strangely, I think something good will come of it."

"Seriously?" Mia asked incredulously. "What possible good can come from Matt's death?"

"Remember Romans 8:28... 'And we know that all things work together for good to them that love God.' Your brother has been spending a lot of time with Matt's mom and his sister, Linda. I think he and Linda are becoming more than friends." Sarah glanced in the direction Cody and Craig had gone before adding, "Right now they may be leaning on each other for support, but I honestly think there was a glimmer of something there before they lost Matt, and it may be developing into something more."

"Hey, what's going on in here?" Destiny who had been in the kitchen now stood in the doorway, arms akimbo. "Julie sent me in to find out why people keep disappearing out here and not coming back. We're not cleaning all this up by ourselves, you know!"

Mia and Sarah returned to the kitchen amidst laughter that chased away the somberness that had dampened the earlier festive mood.

"Are you coming, Grandma?"

Valerie Reed squeezed onto the couch between her husband and Drake. "I think I'll pass. You young people can handle the cleanup."

Ron slowly got to his feet as Mia waited. "Maybe I can help out."

"It appears my granddaughter is training you well." Andy laughed at his own joke and the rest of the men joined in while Val raised an eyebrow.

"You mean like I trained you?" she asked.

"Oh, she got you there, Grandpa," Cody said coming up from behind him and sitting on the arm of the sofa.

"You okay, kid?" Andy asked.

Cody said he would be, though it was a lot to take in, and then excused himself, making the rounds to say goodbye.

Worried how the news of Dr. Block's involvement in Matt's suicide affected him, Mia asked where he was going.

"Linda and her mom asked me to come over for supper. They know we have a big Sunday dinner, so Mrs. Markle said it would be something light."

"Wait, let me grab you a tin of cookies to take along. It's a good thing you didn't scarf down too many of them," Sarah said. "And maybe you could ask Linda to join us for dinner sometime."

"Subtle," Mia murmured.

"Yeah, thanks Mom. I might do that."

"What was that all about?" Julie asked.

Mia grinned at Ron, then her sister. "Mom thinks there may be a romance brewing so she's playing matchmaker."

Julie's jaw dropped. "Holy macaroni!"

Chapter Fifty-five

"Wow, you're back from your run already? You must have gotten an early start," Julie chuckled. "Running off wedding day jitters?"

"Something like that. I've been awake since five-thirty… too excited to get back to sleep." Unlacing her running shoes, Mia grinned up at her sister. "What's for breakfast? I'm starving."

"Bacon, a mushroom and cheese omelet, and toast."

"Mmm, sounds like an awful lot for a bride who's got to fit into her dress in a matter of hours."

Julie snickered and pulled bacon out of the refrigerator. "You'll be fine, and you'd better load up. You're gonna need lots of energy to get through the day… and tonight." She threw a look over her shoulder to see if Mia got her drift. Her rosy cheeks showed that she did. "You've got time if you want to get your shower before we eat."

Mia agreed, and returned to the kitchen twenty minutes later in a terrycloth robe and towel-turbaned hair. "Smells good!" She suddenly realized she was ravenous, and wolfed down every bit of her omelet before Julie was half finished.

"Whoa. Slow down, girl. Where's the fire?"

Mia checked the time and realized there was no need to rush, but she was restless and sitting still while her sister ate was challenging. She unconsciously drummed her fingers on the table.

Julie paused with her fork midair and smiled at her.

"What?"

"Nothing… but I don't think I've ever seen you so antsy. You know Mom won't be here for at least another hour, right?"

"Yes, I know. I should probably go dry my hair awhile though."

"Yes, go! By all means, go." Julie grinned and waved her away.

Mia dried her hair but her hands shook as she tried to put on makeup. She was really glad her mother would be styling her hair for the wedding. Sarah had been a hairdresser before putting herself through college to get her degree in psychology, so Mia knew she would do something wonderful.

Finding herself with time to spare, Mia went back over all the things she'd wanted to take care of before the big day and a two-week honeymoon. Her biggest concern had been her clients.

Samantha had finally adjusted to her medication and was practicing her relaxation with a little more regularity. Those two things coupled with the discovery that Sam's neighbor was actually a really kind widower who simply found her attractive had helped ease the paranoia. She and the neighbor had even had coffee together so things were looking up there.

Sweet little Jasmine was also making progress, and often smiled and chatted now. Mrs. Benson had even confided that she and her husband approached the child's caseworker about the possibility of adopting her someday. In the meantime, Mia had introduced Jasmine to Gabby, the therapist on staff who specialized in working with children, and had her join one of their sessions so the little one would be comfortable while Mia was on her honeymoon.

Other than forgetfulness, Edna was doing quite well since she and Aunt Bonnie had decided to become more than neighbors and were now living together. The arrangement eased the loneliness of both women, and Edna was now on an "I'll call you if I need you" plan for therapy. Mia was thrilled for them both.

Going through the checklist in her mind, Mia was satisfied that all of her clients would be fine until she returned. There was one who would be even better than fine. Adam and Melody's relationship was flourishing. For the first time since she'd met him as her very first client in Madison, Adam Grant appeared to be calm and at peace.

Mia's thoughts were interrupted by a sudden explosion of voices and laughter downstairs that indicated the arrival of at least some of her wedding party. She hurried down to find her mother, little sister Destiny, and Morgan greeting each other while juggling dress bags and totes filled with shoes, makeup, and whatever else they needed to get ready.

"Hey, there's the woman of the hour!" Sarah exclaimed when she saw her daughter coming down the steps. "You look beautiful already, but let's go put the finishing touches on with a gorgeous hairdo."

Glad she had let her hair grow longer than usual, Mia watched in the mirror as Sarah worked it into soft, natural-looking curls falling down her back, then gathered a few strands and magically wove them together with a delicate spray of tiny florals for a crown-like effect. When it was complete and Mia slipped into her wedding dress, she felt like a queen.

"You're beautiful," Sarah whispered.

By then Betsy had arrived, everyone had dressed and the beautiful bride stood admiring each of their red dress choices. Destiny looked lovely in her velvet long-sleeve V-neck, and Betsy looked totally grown-up in her chiffon double V-neck side slit dress with split sleeves. She had worried about wearing red with her red hair, but she looked beautiful. Mia's old roommate, Morgan, was striking with vintage red floral lace and her dark hair. But it was Julie who Mia thought was the most elegant in her flared long-sleeve floral lace mermaid dress.

"Look at you," she said to her sister. "Drake will be drooling."

"I hope so!" Julie laughed then added, "But I think everybody will be looking at you, Mia. You really are beautiful."

"Isn't she?" Sarah said.

"You look pretty spectacular yourself," Mia responded looking at Sarah's ivory-laced chiffon dress with a red skirt that flowed to the floor. Everyone agreed and continued complimenting each other until the maid of honor suggested they'd better head over to the church.

They piled into the limo giggling like schoolgirls.

On the way, Betsy asked, "Whatever happened with that creepy doctor? Did he go to jail, or what?"

Sarah was quick to answer. "No, Bets. At least not an actual jail, but he is in a different kind of facility—"

"Yeah, a mental facility because he lost his mind." Destiny's words carried bitterness. She had seen how much the doctor's actions hurt her brother when he lost his best friend. Mia understood her reaction as well as Cody's anger toward the man, but in spite of all he'd done, she couldn't help but pity Dr. Block. She knew his mind was imprisoned, and it was a jail he might never escape. And she had also seen that Cody and Linda's shared grief had drawn them closer together. They really did seem to be good for each other.

"Holy macaroni! My sister's about to be a married woman!" Julie's perfect timing quickly dismissed the somber mood. Then she looked over at her sister. "Well, are you ready to become Mrs. Ronald Bishop?"

Mia thought about how much her life was about to change. This time tomorrow she and her husband would be on a plane heading to Hawaii. "I'm ready."

Chapter Fifty-six

Sarah had been right about Cody and Linda, who were now standing side by side watching and smiling as Mia and Ron shared their first dance as husband and wife. When Mia glanced their way, she noticed Cody's arm draped around his girl's shoulders and saw the wink he sent her way. Then as she and Ron slowly turned to the music, she saw Julie and Drake standing next to them and thought her sister had never looked more beautiful. Whether it was the striking red gown Julie was wearing or the twinkle in her eyes reflecting the impressive diamond now on her left hand, Mia thought her sister looked gorgeous. Drake had popped the question just one week ago, and it seemed to Mia that Julie hadn't stopped smiling since. Love was definitely in the air.

At the sound of spoons and forks clinking on glasses, Mia smiled up at Ron who pulled her in even closer for another kiss, the third one since the first notes of Etta Jones's "At Last." The words being sung and the blue of her husband's eyes made her completely forget anyone else was in the room.

When her Grandma Val had first mentioned that song as a possibility for their first dance as man and wife, Mia hesitated, thinking they should choose something more modern, but when she and Ron listened to it together, they looked into each other's eyes and knew it was perfect. The song ended, and everyone clapped, but Ron still held her in his arms... until someone tapped on his shoulder.

"My turn," Craig said pulling the groom away from his daughter.

Ron bowed and backed away.

With the first notes of "I Loved Her First," Mia moved into her daddy's arms feeling like his little girl once more. When she saw the tears well up in his eyes, she too was overcome with the enormity of the moment. Listening to the words of the song, she knew they were true. He had always been her number one, and she had always been safe with him. She remembered how he had read to her and tucked her into bed after her mother died, even after Sarah became her stepmother.

They danced most of the song in silence, each fighting back tears that embodied a lifetime of memories. He had loved her first, and Mia knew he would always be there for her. “I love you, Daddy,” she murmured.

“And I love you, baby girl,” he whispered. “I hope you’ll always be as happy as you are today.”

Back in the arms of her groom, Mia was glad they had decided to have their reception in the Fellowship Hall of their church rather than her parents’ home. There was so much more room for dancing, and before long everyone was on their feet.

Mia noticed a lot of people had good moves, but there was one who stood out among the rest. The three-feet-tall, sandy haired little blue-eyed boy in a tux was feeling the music, and all the shyness he’d shown as ringbearer had vanished on the dance floor.

“Your nephew has got moves,” Mia said through her laughter.

“Yeah, I think Ronnie may have to give his uncle some lessons.” The little guy was doing a solo act while his parents stood nearby watching and holding hands.

“Look at Robin and Kevin. They look like they’re really having fun,” Mia said.

“I know. When you were dancing with your dad, I told her what we’d found out about that girl Buddy Jenkins was with when we arrested him. I swear I could see the relief on her face when I confirmed that the woman was with him by choice and there was no evidence he’d ever held another girl captive after her. The past finally seems to be in the past, and Robin is looking more and more like the sister I remember... Except...”

“Except what?”

"I don't know exactly. It's just a feeling. Like there's something she's not telling me."

Noticing the worry wrinkles that now lined Ron's forehead, Mia put her attention back on her new sister-in-law, but she saw nothing to be alarmed about. "Maybe you're imagining it," she said praying she was right.

"Yeah, maybe." He didn't sound convinced. "I think it's kind of a twin thing. We sort of have a connection you probably wouldn't understand. I'm worried she's still having flashbacks or something."

The music ended, and with a quick hug and kiss, Ron excused himself saying, "I'll be right back. I need to make sure she's okay."

And what if she's not? Mia's stomach flopped. Her thoughts were interrupted when Morgan swooped in for another congratulatory hug.

After their quick embrace, Mia excused herself and hurried toward where she saw Ron confronting his sister while Kevin looked on. *I have a right to know what's going on.* Her chest tightened with dread that they might not be on that plane tomorrow after all.

Swallowing her fear, Mia approached with a smile. "Is everything okay over here?" she asked trying to keep the dread out of her voice.

Kevin moved closer to Robin and put his arm around her. "I think you better just tell them, sweet cheeks."

Mia held her breath, but then was surprised to see Robin begin to smile.

"All right, we were going to wait until you got back from your honeymoon, but since you're such a worrier," Robin said grinning up at Ron, "I guess we'd better tell you... we're going to have another baby."

Mia let out her breath. *Thank you, Lord!*

After much relief, hugging and laughter, just beyond Robin and Kevin, another pair of dancers caught Mia's attention. She saw her grandpa and Betsy watching little Ronnie on the dance floor and laughing together just like old times. It was hard to believe the young girl's world had been turned upside down only months ago. She had forgiven them all... *She's so special.*

Three days earlier, Ron and Mia had begun to wonder if Valentine's Day had been a bad choice for when to have their wedding. February in Pennsylvania can bring some major snowstorms, and this year was no exception. With ten inches of snow on the ground, Mia had worried about people getting there—important people like her brother, Bobby, who had to drive out from Philadelphia, and her friend, Morgan, who had to come from Pittsburgh. But everyone made it, and the reception was everything Mia had hoped it would be. She almost hated to see it end, but at the appointed time, the bride and groom said their goodbyes and rushed to the car amid bubbles and laughter.

***

Mia thought she had never seen her brothers, Ron's partner, Jason, or his brother-in-law Kevin looking more elegant than they had standing at the front of the church when she'd walked down the aisle on her father's arm, but it had been Ron standing there, waiting for her, who made her catch her breath. And when she had reached him, and Craig put her hand in his, she'd looked into those eyes and could hardly believe the wait was over.

Now, standing alone together at last, she had that same feeling. There were flowers and champagne waiting in the airport hotel room where they would spend their wedding night before taking off for their honeymoon the next morning. Although it had been a long exhausting day, as she stood at the window waiting for Ron who was in the bathroom, she was no longer tired... but suddenly nervous.

She had waited for this moment, longed for it, for so long, but now she was scared. *What if...*

Then, without warning, she was encompassed in her husband's arms. "We are finally alone, Mrs. Bishop."

She turned slowly to face him. "Yes, we are," she said feeling surprisingly shy. When Ron lifted her chin and looked into her eyes, she wondered why.

"Are you all right, love?"

"I am now." Mia reached up, accepted his kiss, and let its warmth course through her body. This kiss was more, so much more, than all the earlier kisses of this or any other day. "Give me a moment to change into something a little more comfortable, okay?"

Grabbing what she needed from the open suitcase, she hurried into the bathroom, and after freshening up, brushing her teeth, and donning the luscious white peignoir Sarah had given her at her bridal shower, Mia opened the door to find Ron standing by the king-size bed. He was wearing a midnight blue silk robe loosely tied at the waist, and his jaw dropped when he looked at her.

"Wow," was all he said. It was enough.

Mia didn't remember crossing the room, but somehow, they were in each other's arms. Ron was gently kissing her lips, and when his lips moved to her neck, she felt her temperature rising and her whole body coming alive. She wanted more.

Moments later, her beautiful peignoir was on the floor next to the blue silk robe, and what they had both waited so long for was theirs.

Mia gasped when his hands reached where they'd never been allowed before, and the thrill of that touch was beyond anything she had imagined. She was on fire, and only he could satisfy her need. When he finally entered her and they became one, she fiercely clung to him, and when they were both satisfied, she lay content and complete.

Mia knew things that night she had never known before, and she understood exactly what the Bible meant when it said, "And the two shall become one flesh: so that they are no more two, but one flesh."

They didn't get a lot of sleep that night, but they would have plenty of time for that on the long flight to Hawaii. When Mia finally did doze off much later, she dreamed of the house they had found weeks earlier, and she woke to see her new husband lying next to her.

She couldn't resist the urge to touch his cheek, and when she did, a slow smile and those beautiful blue eyes appeared. He glanced at the time, then took her in his arms once more.

Mia reveled in his touch. *This is my life now. Thank you, Lord.*

About the Author

Gloria Bostic is a retired special education teacher from York, Pennsylvania. As a Masters level clinical psychologist, she also worked with women and children to help them overcome abuse. She lives in Dover, PA, with her husband, Lee, and enjoys spending time with her three sons and all her grandchildren.

Also by Gloria Bostic...

Deception Bridge (Book 1)

Valerie Reed is plagued by migraines, insomnia, and a growing anxiety that her happily-ever-after is about to come crumbling down. Tormented by the fear of losing her husband of nearly thirty years, she hangs onto the one thing she knows she can count on – her friendship with the women in her bridge group. They provide a safe-haven with warmth, laughter, and trust... until that trust is broken.

As Val searches for a way to save her marriage and learn to trust again, her life and her bridge group go through unanticipated transformations. Their lives will never be the same, and Val wonders if the power of prayer will be enough to save them all.

Broken Contracts (Book 2)

Through faith and forgiveness Valerie and Andy Reed's marriage has survived and grown stronger in spite of Andy's brief affair five years ago. However, the consequences of his tryst with Susan Walters, a former member of Val's bridge group, may now turn their world upside-down once again.

As Susan's marriage falls apart, all she wants is to be a good mother to the child she had always longed for... yet her life is becoming unmanageable as she continually succumbs to the need for her next drink.

When Valerie, Bonnie, Sarah, and Kathy gather around the bridge table, they share more than the game. Only time will tell what's in the cards.

Premonition Bridge (Book 3)

A threat... A former client warns that her husband is wildly angry that she left him and blames her therapist, Sarah Reed, for ruining his life. He vows to get even.

A disappearance... A member of the Reed family mysteriously disappears without a trace. The only clues to the victim's whereabouts may come from mystifying messages in drawings and dreams.

A reuniting... Family members separated, relationships lost, friendships dissolved... Will prayer and forgiveness be enough for the bridge club ladies to find resolution from the chaos that has invaded their lives?

Out of the Storm

Greta Friedman travels from victim to victory in this story of a young woman's search for the life she's been denied. A childhood filled with loss and abuse leaves her desperate to find love and normalcy, but as a young adult Greta is frustrated by unanswered prayers and a pattern of relationships that end badly... until she meets someone special. When Gabe Engel mysteriously comes into her life, Greta begins the journey that will give her the strength to escape impending danger and finally make her dreams a reality.

Watercolor Whispers (Book 1)

Art therapist Mia Reed has a calling to help her patients as well as a special gift... paintings that unlock mysteries and help solve crimes. However, Freddie Alessi—an assault victim whose wife has gone missing—leaves every session more disturbed than when he arrived... almost as disturbed as Mia feels about his charming and attractive older brother Anthony. Her brain says run, but his fervent kisses keep drawing her back.

Detective Ron Bishop is intrigued by Mia's gift as he struggles to solve missing persons and murder cases. But when Mia's hand is guided by an outside force, can the clues in her drawings lead to the killer and answer the questions in time?

Whispered Warnings (Book 2)

Mia Reed's artwork is a gift from a higher power and holds clues that help solve mysteries. Detective Ronald Bishop, the man she loves, is desperate to find his twin sister who disappeared fifteen years ago. But in the meantime he's lured to follow Mia to her hometown, where a clinical psychologist has jumped to her death. Or did she? When two more single women suffer the same fate, everyone realizes these are not suicides. A serial killer has invaded their peaceful small town! Will Mia's gift help them catch a murderer before he strikes too close to home?

The Greatest Aunt

It's a scary time for Flora when she learns her parents must go away. She will have to go live with her great-aunt, but can't understand why they call her great. Flora happily discovers why and agrees!